Tales of Ordinary Madness

TALES OF
ORDINARY MADNESS

by

Charles Bukowski

Edited by Gail Chiarrello

CITY LIGHTS BOOKS
San Francisco

Cover photograph of Charles Bukowski by Michael Montfort
Reproduced by courtesy of Michael Montfort

Some of these stories originally appeared in the following magazines: *Open City, Nola Express, Knight, Adam, Pix, The Berkeley Barb,* and *Evergreen Review.*

Library of Congress Cataloging-in-Publication Data

Bukowski, Charles
  Tales of ordinary madness

    Reprint of part 2 of Erections, ejaculations, exhibitions and general tales
of ordinary madness.
    I. Chiarrello, Gail. II. Bukowski, Charles. Erections, ejaculations,
exhibitions and general tales of ordinary madness. III. Title.
PS3552.U4T3   1983   813'.54   83-21031
ISBN: 0-87286-155-4
ISBN-13: 978-0-87286-155-8

Visit our website: www.citylights.com

CITY LIGHTS BOOKS are edited by Lawrence Ferlinghetti and Nancy J. Peters
and published at the City Lights Bookstore, 261 Columbus Avenue,
San Francisco, CA 94133.

CONTENTS

A .45 TO PAY THE RENT

Duke had this daughter, Lala, they named her, she was 4. it was his first child and he had always been careful not to have children, fearing that they would murder him somehow, but now he was insane and she delighted him, she knew everything that Duke was thinking, there was that line that ran from her to him, from him to her.

Duke was in the supermarket with Lala and they talked back and forth, saying things. they talked about everything and she told him everything she knew and she knew very much, instinctively, and Duke didn't know very much but he told her what he could, and it worked. they were happy together.

"what's that?" she asked.

"that's a coconut."

"what's inside?"

"milk and chewy stuff."

"why's it in there?"

"because it feels good in there, all that milk and chewy stuff, it feels good inside of that shell. it says to itself, 'oh my, I feel so good in here!' "

"why does it feel good in there?"

"because anything would. I would."

"no you wouldn't. you wouldn't be able to drive your car from inside of there, you wouldn't be able to see me from inside of there. you wouldn't be able to eat bacon and eggs from inside of there."

"bacon and eggs aren't everything."

"what *is* everything?"

"I dunno. maybe the inside of the sun, frozen solid."

"the INSIDE of the SUN . . .? FROZEN SOLID?"

"yep."

1

"what would the inside of the sun be like if it were frozen solid?"

"well, the sun's supposed to be this ball of fire. and I don't think the scientists would agree with me, but *I* think it would be like this."

Duke picked up an avocado.

"wow!"

"yeah, that's what an avocado is: frozen sun. we eat the sun and then we walk around feeling warm."

"is the sun in all that beer you drink?"

"yes, it is."

"is the sun inside of me?"

"more than anybody I have ever known."

"and I think you got a great BIG SUN inside of you!"

"thank you, my love."

they walked around and finished their shopping. Duke didn't select anything. Lala filled the basket with whatever she wished. some of it you couldn't eat: balloons, crayons, a toy gun. a space-man with a parachute that flipped out of his back when you shot him into the sky. hell of a spaceman.

Lala didn't like the woman cashier. she gave a most serious frown to the cashier. poor woman: her face had been scooped out and emptied — she was a horror show and didn't even know it.

"hello little sweetie!" the cashier said. Lala didn't answer. Duke didn't prompt her to. they paid their money and walked to the car.

"they take our money," said Lala.

"yes."

"and then you have to go to work at night and make more money. I don't like you going away at night. I want to play mama. I want to be mama and you be the baby."

"o.k., I'll be the baby right now. how's that, mama?"

"o.k., baby, can you drive the car?"

"I can try."

then they were in the car, driving. some son of a bitch hit his throttle and tried to ram them as they made a left turn.

"baby, why do people try to hit us with their cars?"

"well, mama, it's because they are unhappy and unhappy people like to hurt things."

2

"aren't there any happy people?"

"there are many people who pretend that they are happy."

"why?"

"because they are ashamed and frightened and don't have the guts to admit it."

"are you frightened?"

"I only have the guts to admit it to *you* – I'm so god damned scared, mama, that I think I'm going to die any minute."

"baby, do you want your bottle?"

"yes, mama, but let's wait until we get home."

they drove along, turned right on Normandie. it was harder for them to hit you when you were turning right.

"you are going to work tonight, baby?"

"yes."

"why do you work nights?"

"it's darker. people can't see me."

"why don't you want people to see you?"

"because if they do I might get caught and put in jail."

"what's jail?"

"everything's jail."

"I'M not jail!"

they parked and took the groceries inside.

"mama!" Lala said, "we got groceries! frozen suns, *spacemen,* everything!"

mama (they called her "Mag"), mama said, "that's fine."

then to Duke: "damn it, I wish you didn't have to go out tonight. I've got that feeling. don't do it, Duke."

"*you've* got that feeling? honey, *I* get that feeling everytime. it's part of the thing. I've got to do it. we're tapped out. the kid threw everything into that basket from canned ham to caviar."

"well, Christ, can't you control the kid?"

"I want her to be happy."

"she won't be happy with you in stir."

"look, Mag, in my profession you've just got to figure on doing a certain amount of time. you don't sweat it. that's all there is to it. I've done a bit of time. I've been luckier than most."

"how about some kind of honest job?"

"babe, it beats working a punch-press. and there aren't any

3

honest jobs. you die one way or the other. And I'm already along my little road — I'm some kind of dentist, say, pulling teeth out of society. it's all I know how to do. it's too late. and you know how they treat ex-cons. you know what they do to you, I've told you, I've . . ."

"I *know* what you've told me, but . . ."

"but but butt butttt!" said Duke, "god damn you, let me finish!"

"finish then."

"these industrial cocksuckers of slaves who live in Beverly Hills and Malibu. these guys specialize in 'rehabilitating' cons, ex-cons. it makes that shit parole smell like roses. it's a hype. slave labor. the parole boards know it, they know it, we know it. save money for the state, make money for somebody else. shit. all shit. everything. make you work triple the average man while they rob everybody within the law — sell them crap for ten or twenty times its actual value. but it's within the law, *their* law . . ."

"god damn, I've heard this so many times . . ."

"and god damn if you're not going to hear it AGAIN! you think I can't see or feel anything? you think I should keep quiet? even to my own wife? you are my wife, aren't you? don't we fuck? don't we live together, don't we?"

"*you're* the one who fucked up. now you're crying."

"fuck YOU! I made a mistake, a technical error! I was young; I didn't understand their chickenshit rules . . ."

"and now you're trying to justify your idiocy!"

"hey, that's *good!* I LIKE that. little wifey. you cunt. you cunt. you're nothing but a cunt on the whitehouse steps, wide open, and mentally siffed . . ."

"the kid's listening, Duke."

"good. and I'll finish. you cunt. REHABILITATE. that's the word, those Beverly Hills soul-cocksuckers. they're so god damned decent and HUMANE. their wives listen to Mahler at the Music Center and donate to charity, tax-free. and are elected the ten best women of the year by the *L.A. Times*. and you know what their HUSBANDS do to you? cuss you like a dog down at their crooked plant. cut your paycheck, pocket the difference, and no questions answered. everything's such shit, can't anybody see it? can't anybody SEE it?"

4

"I . . ."

"SHUT UP! Mahler, Beethoven, STRAVINSKY! make you work overtime for nothing. kick your whipped ass all hell's time. and ONE word out of you, they're on the phone to the parole officer: 'Sorry, Jensen, but I've got to tell you, your man stole 25 dollars from the till. we'd just gotten to like him too.' "

"so what kind of justice do you want? Jesus, Duke, I don't know what to do. you rant and you rant. you get drunk and tell me that Dillinger was the greatest man who ever lived. you rock back in your rocker, all drunk, and scream Dillinger. *I'm* alive too. listen to me . . ."

"fuck Dillinger! he's dead. justice? there ain't no justice in America. there's only *one* justice. ask the Kennedies, ask the dead, ask anybody!"

Duke got up out of the rocker, walked to the closet, dipped under the box of Christmas tree ornaments and got the heat. a .45.

"this, this. this is the only justice in America. this is the *only* thing anybody understands."

he waved the damn thing around.

Lala was playing with the spaceman. the parachute didn't open right. it figured: a con. another con. like the dead-eyed seagull. like the ballpoint pen. like Christ hollering for Papa with the lines cut.

"listen," said Mag, "put that crazy cannon away. *I'll* get a job. let me get a job."

"YOU'LL get a job! how long I been hearing that? only thing you're good for is fucking, for nothing, and laying around reading magazines and popping chocolates into your mouth."

"oh god, it's not for nothing — I LOVE you, Duke, I really do."

then he was tired. "all right, fine. then at least put the groceries away. and cook me something before I hit the streets."

Duke put the heat back in the closet. sat down and lit a cigarette.

"Duke," asked Lala, "you want me to call you Duke or call you Daddy?"

"either way, sweetie. just what you want."

"why is there hair on a coconut?"

"oh Christ, I dunno. why is there hair on my balls?"

Mag came out of the kitchen holding a can of peas in her hand. "I won't have you talking to my kid that way."

"*your* kid? see that money mouth on her? just like mine. see those eyes? see those insides? just like mine. your kid — just because she slid out of your crack and sucked your tits. she's nobody's kid. she's her own kid."

"I *insist*," said Mag, "that you don't talk around the child like that!"

"you insist . . . you insist . . ."

"yes, I do!" she held the can of peas in the air, balanced in the palm of her left hand. "I insist."

"I swear, if you don't get that can of peas out of my sight, so help me, God or no God, I'M GOING TO JAM THEM UP YOUR ASS ALL THE WAY FROM DENVER TO ALBUQUERQUE!"

Mag walked into the kitchen with the peas. she stayed in the kitchen.

Duke went to the closet for his coat and the heat. he kissed his little girl goodbye. she was sweeter than a December suntan and 6 white horses running over a low green hill. he thought of it like that; it began to hit him. he ducked out fast. but closed the door quietly.

Mag came out of the kitchen.

"Duke's gone," said the kid.

"yes, I know."

"I'm getting sleepy, mama. read to me from a book."

they both sat on the couch together.

"is Duke coming back, mama?"

"yeah, the son of a bitch, he'll be back."

"what's a son of a bitch?"

"Duke is. I love him."

"you love a son of a bitch?"

"yeah," laughed Mag. "yeah. come 'ere, lovely. on my lap."

she hugged the kid, "aw, you're so warm, like warm bacon, warm doughnuts!"

"I'm NOT bacon and DOUGHNUTS! YOU'RE bacon and doughnuts!"

"it's a full moon tonight. too light, too light. I'm scared, I'm scared. jesus, I love the man, oh jesus . . ."

Mag reached over into a cardboard carton and picked up a children's book.

6

"mama, why is there hair on a coconut?"

"hair on a coconut?"

"yes."

"listen, I put on some coffee. I hear the coffee boiling over. let me turn off the coffee."

"all right."

Mag went into the kitchen and Lala sat waiting on the couch.

while Duke stood outside a liquor store at Hollywood and Normandie, wondering: what the hell what the hell what the hell.

it didn't look right, didn't smell right. might be a prick in the back with a luger, staring through a hole. that's how they got Louie. blew him apart like a clay duck at the amusement park. legal murder. the whole fucking world swam in the shit of legal murder.

the place didn't look right. maybe a small bar tonight. a queer joint. something easy. enough money for a month's rent.

I'm losing my guts, thought Duke. next thing you know I'll be sitting around listening to Shostakovitch.

he got back into the black '61 Ford.

and began driving North. 3 blocks. 4 blocks. 6 blocks. 12 blocks into the freezing world. as Mag sat with the kid in her lap and began to read from a book, LIFE IN THE FOREST . . .

"the weasel and his cousins, the mink, the fisher, and the marten, are lithe, fast, savage creatures. They are meat eaters, and are in continuous, bloodthirsty competition for the . . ."

then the beautiful child was asleep and the moon was full.

DOING TIME WITH PUBLIC ENEMY NO. 1

I was listening to Brahms in Philadelphia, in 1942. I had a small record player. it was Brahms' 2nd movement. I was living alone at the time. I was slowly drinking a bottle of port and smoking a cheap cigar. it was a small clean room. as they say, — there was a knock on the door. I thought it was somebody come to give me the Nobel Prize or the Pulitzer. 2 big dumb peasant-looking men.

Bukowski?

yeah.

they showed me a badge: F.B.I.

come with us. better put on a coat. you'll be gone awhile.

I didn't know what I had done. I didn't ask. I figured everything was loss anyhow. one of them shut off Brahms. we went downstairs and out into the street. heads were out the windows as if everybody knew.

then the eternal woman's voice: oh, there goes that horrible man! they've got him!

I just don't make it with the ladies.

I kept trying to think of what I had done and the only thing I could think of was that I had murdered somebody while I was drunk. but I couldn't understand how the F.B.I. could get involved.

keep one hand on each knee and don't move your hands!

there were 2 men in the front seat and 2 in the back so I figured that I must have murdered somebody, somebody important.

we drove along and then I forgot and reached up to scratch my nose.

WATCH THAT HAND!!

when we got to the office one of the agents pointed to a row of photos around the 4 walls.

see those pictures? he asked sternly.

I looked around at the photos, they were nicely framed but none of the faces came through to me.

8

yes, I see the pictures, I told him.

those are men who have been killed in the service of the F.B.I.

I didn't know what he expected me to say so I didn't say anything.

they took me into another room. there was a man behind the desk.

WHERE'S YOUR UNCLE JOHN? he screamed at me.

what? I asked.

WHERE'S YOUR UNCLE JOHN?

I didn't know what he meant. for a minute I thought he meant I was carrying some kind of secret tool which I killed people with while I was drunk. I was nervous and nothing made any sense.

I mean — JOHN BUKOWSKI!

oh, he's dead.

shit, no WONDER we can't find him!

they took me down to an orange-yellow cell. it was a Saturday afternoon. from my cell window I could see the people walking along. how lucky they were! across the street there was a record shop. a microphone played music toward me. every thing seemed so free and easy out there. I stood there trying to figure what I had done. I felt like crying but nothing came out. it was just a sort of sad sickness, sick sad, when you can't feel any worse. I think you know it. I think everybody knows it now and then. but I think I have known it pretty often, too often.

Moyamensing Prison reminded me of an old castle. 2 large wooden gates swung open to let me in. I am surprised we didn't walk across a moat.

they stuck me in with a fat man who looked like a public accountant.

I'm Courtney Taylor, public enemy No. 1. he told me.

what are you in for? he asked.

(I knew then because I'd asked on the way in.)

draft dodging.

there's 2 things we can't stand here: draft dodgers and indecent exposure cases.

honor among thieves, eh? keep the country strong so you can rob it.

we still don't like draft dodgers.

9

I'm really innocent. I moved and forgot to leave a forwarding address with the draft board. I notified the post office. got a letter from St. Louis while I was in this town to report for a draft examination. I told them I couldn't make it to St. Louis, to have them examine me here. they put the make on me and hauled me in here. I don't understand it: if I were trying to dodge the draft I wouldn't have given them my address.

all you guys are innocent. sounds like bullshit to me.

I stretched out on the bunk.

a screw came by.

GET UP OFF YOUR DEAD ASS! he screamed at me.

I got off my dead draft dodging ass.

do you want to kill yourself? Taylor asked me.

yes, I said.

just pull down that overhead pipe that holds the cell light. fill that bucket with water and stick your foot in it. take out the lightbulb and stick your finger in the socket. then you're out of here.

I looked at the light a long time.

thank you, Taylor, you're very helpful.

at lights out I laid down and they started in. bedbugs.

what the shit's this? I screamed.

bedbugs said Taylor. we got bedbugs.

I'll bet I got more bedbugs than you've got, I said.

bet.

ten cents?

ten cents.

I began to catch and kill mine. I laid them on the little wooden table.

finally we called time. we took our bedbugs over to the cell door where there was light and we counted them. I had 13. he had 18. I gave him the dime. it wasn't until later that I found out he was breaking his in half and stretching them. he had been a swindler. a real pro. the son of a bitch.

I got hot with the dice in the exercise yard. I won day after day and was getting rich. jail-rich. I was picking up 15 or 20 bucks a day. dice were against the rules and they pointed their submachine guns at us from the towers and hollered BREAK IT UP! but we always managed to get a game going again. an indecent exposure case had sneaked the dice in. he was one indecent exposure case I didn't like. in fact, I didn't like any of them. they all had weak chins, watery eyes, small rumps, slimy ways. 1/10th men. not their fault, I suppose but I didn't like to gaze upon them. this one kept coming around after each game. you're hot, you're making it big, let me have a little. I'd drop some coins into that lily hand and he'd slink off, the snake swine prick, dreaming of showing his cock to 3 year old girls. it was all I could do to keep from belting him but they gave you solitary for belting anybody, and the hole was depressing but the bread and water were worse. I'd see them come out of there and it was a month before they looked the same again. but we were all freaks. I was a freak. I was a freak. I was too hard on him. when I wasn't looking at him I could rationalize.

I was rich. the cook came down after lights out with plates of food, good food and plenty of it, ice-cream, cake, pie, good coffee. Taylor said never to give him over 15 cents, that was tops. the cook would whisper his thanks and ask if he should come back the next night.

by all means, I'd tell him.

this was the food the warden ate and the warden evidently ate well. the prisoners were all starving and Taylor and I were walking around looking like 2 women 9 months pregnant.

he's a good cook, Taylor said. he's murdered 2 men. he killed one guy and then he got out and right away he killed another guy. he's here to stay now unless he can break out. he got hold of a sailor the other night and screwed him in the ass. he ripped that sailor wide open. that sailor couldn't walk for a week.

I like the cook, I said, I think he's a nice guy.

he is a nice guy, Taylor agreed.

we kept complaining about the bedbugs to the screw and the screw would holler at us:

WHATCHA THINK THIS IS? A HOTEL? YOU GUYS BROUGHT THEM THINGS IN WITH YOU!

which, of course, we considered an insult.

the screws were mean the screws were stupid and the screws were scared. I was sorry for them.

they finally put Taylor and I into different cells and fumigated the cell.

11

I met Taylor in the exercise yard.

I drew some kid, Taylor said, some raw kid, he's dumb, he don't know nothin'. it's awful.

I drew an old man who couldn't speak English and he sat on the pot all day and said, TARA BUBBA EAT, TARA BUBBA SHEET! over and over he'd say this. he had life figured: eat and shit. I think he was talking about some mythological figure of his homeland. ah, maybe Tarus Bulba? I don't know. the old man ripped up my bedsheet the first time I went to the exercise yard and made a clothesline out of it; he hung his socks and shorts on the thing and I came in and everything dripped on me. the old man never left the cell, even to shower. he had committed no crime, they said, just wanted to stay there and they let him. an act of kindness? I got mad at him because I don't like wool blankets rubbing on my skin. I've got a very tender skin.

You old fuck, I'd scream at him, I've killed one man already, and unless you straighten up I'll make it 2!

but he'd just sit on his pot and laugh at me and say TARA BUBBA EAT, BUBBA SHEET!

I had to give up. but anyhow, I never had to scrub the floor, his damn home was always wet and scrubbed. we had the cleanest cell in America. in the world. and he loved that extra meal at night. sure did.

the F.B.I. decided that I was innocent of deliberate draft dodging and they ran me down to the induction center, they ran a lot of us down there, and I passed the physical and then I went into see the psychiatrist.

do you believe in the war? he asked me.

no.

are you willing to go to war?

yes.

(I had some crazy idea of getting up out of a trench and walking forward into gunfire until I was killed.)

he didn't say anything for a long time and kept writing on a piece of paper. then he looked up.

by the way, next Wednesday night we're having a party of doctors and artists and writers. I want to invite you. will you come?

no.

all right, he said, you don't have to go.

go where?

to the war.

I just looked at him.

you didn't think we'd understand, did you?

no.

give this piece of paper to the man at the next desk.

it was a long walk. the paper was folded and stuck to my card with a paper clip. I lifted an edge and peeked: ". . . hides an extreme sensitivity under a poker face . . ." what a laugh, I thought, for christ's sake!: me: sensitive!!

and there went Moyamensing. and that was how I won the war.

SCENES FROM THE BIG TIME

They always put the new men to cleaning up the pigeon shit and while you were cleaning up the pigeon shit, the pigeons would come around and shit a little bit more in your hair and face and on your clothes. They didn't give you any soap — just water and a brush and the shit came off hard. Later they'd move you to the machine shop for your 3 cents an hour but as a new man you had to do the pigeon shit bit first.

I was with Blaine when Blaine got the idea. He saw one pigeon over in the corner and the bird couldn't fly. "Listen," said Blaine, "I know that these birds can talk to each other. Let's give this bird something to say to the others. We'll fix him and toss him on the roof up there and he'll tell those other birds what's happening."

"O.K.," I said.

Blaine walked over and picked up the bird. He had a small brown Gillette. He looked around. It was in the shady corner of the exercise yard. It was a hot day and quite a few of the prisoners were down there.

"Any of you gentlemen care to assist me with this operation?" Blaine asked.

There was no answer.

Blaine started cutting one leg off. Strong men turned away. I saw one or two rather touch their temples with the hand nearest the bird, blocking the sight.

"What the hell's the matter with you guys?" I screamed at them. "We're tired of pigeon shit in our hair and eyes! We're fixing this bird so when we throw him back on the roof, he's gonna tell those other birds, 'Those are some mean motherfuckers down there! Don't get near them!' That pigeon is going to tell those other pigeons to stop shitting on us!"

Blaine threw the bird up on the roof. I don't remember any-

14

more if the thing worked or not. But I remember while scrubbing, my brush came across these two pigeon legs. They looked very strange without a bird attached to them. I brushed them into the shit.

II

Most of the cells were overcrowded and there had been several race riots. But the guards were sadistic. They moved Blaine from my cell over to a cell full of blacks. When he walked in Blaine heard one black say: "There's my punk! Yes sir, I'm gonna make that man my punk! In fact, we *all* might as well have a piece! You gonna strip down, baby, or are we gonna hafta help ya?"

Blaine took off his clothes and stretched down flat on the floor.

He heard them moving around him.

"God! That's one UGLY-lookin' round-eye if I ever saw one!"

"I can't get a hard, Boyer, so help me I can't!"

"Jesus, it looks like a sick doughnut!"

They all walked away and Blaine got up and put his clothes back on. He told me in the exercise yard, "I was lucky. They would have torn me to pieces!"

"Thank your ugly asshole," I said.

III

Then there was Sears. They put Sears in a cell with a pack of blacks and Sears looked around and fought the biggest one. He was laying down. Sears leaped into the air and landed on the biggest one's chest with both knees. They fought. Sears whipped him. The others just watched.

Sears just didn't seem to care. Out in the exercise yard he crouched on his haunches doing a slow roll, smoking a butt. He looked at a black. Smiled. Exhaled.

"You know where I'm from?" he asked a black.

The black didn't answer.

"I'm from Two Rivers Mississippi," he inhaled, held it in, exhaled, smiled, rolling on his haunches, "You'd like it there."

Then he flipped his butt, rose, turned and walked across the yard . . .

IV

Sears was on the white guys too. Sears had this funny hair, it looked like it had been glued to his head and it stood straight up, a dirty red. He had a knife scar along one cheek and his eyes were round, very very round.

Ned Lincoln looked about 19 but he was 22 — open-mouthed, humped-backed with a white film half-covering his left eye. Sears sighted him in the yard on the kid's first day in.

"HEY, YOU!" he hollered at the kid.

The kid turned.

Sears pointed at him. "YOU! I'M GONNA WASTE YOU, MAN! BETTER GET READY, I'M GONNA GET YOU TOMORROW! I'M GONNA WASTE YOU, MAN!"

Ned Lincoln just stood there, not quite understanding. Sears got into a conversation with another inmate as if he had forgotten the whole thing. But we knew he hadn't. It was just his way. He had made his declaration, and that was it.

One of the kid's cellmates talked to him that night.

"You better get ready, kid, he means it. You better get yourself something."

"What?"

"Well, you can make yourself a little shiv by taking the handle off the waterfaucet and shaping it to a point by rubbing it along the cement. Or I can sell you a real good shiv for two bucks."

The kid bought the shiv but the next day he stayed in his cell, he didn't come out to the yard.

"The little shit's scared," said Sears.

"I'd be scared too," I said.

"You'd come out," he said.

"I'd stay in," I said.

"You'd come out," said Sears.

"O.k., I'd come out."

Sears cut the life out of him in the shower the next day. Nobody saw anything, just the raw red blood running down the drain with the soap and water.

V

Some men just can't be broken. Even the hole won't cure them. Joe Statz was one. He'd been down in the hole forever, it seemed. He was the warden's pet bad actor. If he could break Joe, then he'd have better control of the rest of the men.

One day the warden took 2 of his men and they pulled the lid off and the warden got down on his knees and hollered down to Joe:

"JOE! JOE, YOU HAD ENOUGH? YOU WANNA COME OUT, JOE? IF YOU DON'T WANNA COME OUT NOW JOE, I WON'T BE BACK FOR A LONG TIME!"

There wasn't any answer.

"JOE! JOE! YOU HEAR ME?"

"Yeah, I hear you."

"THEN WHAT'S YOUR ANSWER, JOE?"

Joe picked up his bucket of piss and shit and threw it in the warden's face. The warden's men put the lid back on. As far as I know, Joe's still down there, dead or alive. The word got out on what he did to the warden. We used to think about Joe, mostly after lights out.

VI

When I get out, I thought, I am going to wait a while and then I am going to come back to this place, I am going to look at it from the outside and know exactly what's going on in there, and I'm going to stare at those walls and I'm going to make up my mind never to get on the inside of them again.

But after I got out, I never came back again. I never looked at it from the outside. It's just like a bad woman. There's no use going back. You don't even want to look at her. But you can talk about her. That's easy. And that's what I did for a bit today. Luck to you, friend, in or out.

NUT WARD JUST EAST OF HOLLYWOOD

I thought I heard a knocking, looked at the clock — it was only one-thirty p.m., jesus christ, and I got into the old bathrobe (I always slept naked; pajamas seemed ridiculous to me) and opened one of the broken side-windows near the door.

"Yeah?" I asked. It was Mad Jimmy. "Were you asleep?" "Yes, were you?" "No, I was knocking." "Come on in." He'd ridden up on a bicycle. And had on a new Panama. "You like my new Panama? Don't you think I look handsome?" "No."

He sat down on my couch and looked up into the full-length mirror behind my chair, tugging at his hat, this way and that. He had two brown paper bags. One contained the usual bottle of port wine. The other he emptied out on the coffee table — knives, forks, spoons; little dolls — followed by a metal bird (light blue with broken beak and chipped paint job) and other various forms of junk. He peddled the shit — all of it stolen — at the various hippie shops and head shops along Sunset and Hollywood Boulevards — that is, the poor man's area of these boulevards where I lived, where we all lived. I mean we lived near there — in broken-down courts, attics, garages or slept on the floors of temporary friends.

Meanwhile Mad Jimmy thought he was a painter but I thought his paintings were very bad and I told him so. He also said that my paintings were very bad. It was possible that we both were right.

But I mean Mad Jimmy was really fucked-up. His eyes, ears and nose were essentially negative. Some wax in canals of left and right ears; mucous membrane of nose slightly inflamed. Mad Jimmy knew exactly what to steal to sell to these shops. He was an excellent and also a petty thief. But his respiratory system: upper borders of left and right lungs — some rales and congestion. When he wasn't smoking a cigarette he was rolling a joint or sucking at his wine bottle. He had a Systolic 112 and Diastolic 78 giving pulse pressure

18

of 34. He was good with the women but his hemoglobin was very low; being 73, no, 72 percent. Like the rest of us when he drank he didn't eat and he liked to drink.

Mad Jimmy just kept playing with the Panama in front of the mirror and making little awesome sounds. He smiled at himself. His teeth were essentially negative and the mucous membrane of his mouth and throat were inflamed.

Then he took a drink of wine from under that stupid Panama and that made me go get two beers for myself.

When I came back he said, "You changed my name from 'Crazy Jimmy' to 'Mad Jimmy.' I think you're right — 'Mad Jimmy' is much better."

"But you're really crazy, you know," I told him.

"How'd you get those two big holes in your right arm?" Mad Jimmy asked. "Looks like all the meat is burned away. I can almost see the bone."

"I was high and trying to read *Kangaroo* by D. H. Lawrence while I was in bed. My arm got tangled in the cord and brought the bed lamp down on my arm. Before I could rip the fucking thing off the light globe almost did me in. It was a hundred watt General Electric."

"Did you see your doctor?"

"My doctor's pissed at me. I just always sit there, diagnose myself, recommend treatment and then walk out and pay his nurse. He bugs me. He likes to stand there and tell me about his days in the Nazi army. The French captured him, you know, and they put the captured Nazis in a boxcar on the way to the prison camp and the civilians of the towns threw gasoline and stinkbombs and used rubbers full of ant poison at the poor innocent fellows and I get so damned tired of his stories. . . ."

"Look!" said Mad Jimmy, pointing to the coffee table. "Look at this silverware! Genuine antique!"

He handed me a spoon. "Now just *look* at that spoon!"

I just looked at the spoon.

"Look," he said, "do you have to let your robe fall open like that?"

I threw the spoon on the table. "Whatsamatta, never seen a man's cock before?"

"It's your *balls!* they're so big and hairy! Awful!"

I left the robe open. I don't like to take orders.

There he sat once again twisting that Panama. His stupid Panama and his palpitation over McBurney's point (appendix). Inferior border of liver also tender to palpation. Spleen negative. Everything negative and palpitation. Even goddamned gall bladder palpitation.

"Look, can I use your phone?" Mad Jimmy asked.

"Local?"

"Yes, it's local."

"Make *sure* it's local. I almost killed four guys the other night. Chased them all through town in my car. Finally, they pulled over. I parked behind them, cut the engine. I didn't realize they still had theirs running. When I got out, they pulled off. *Very* disappointing. By the time I got rolling, they were out of sight."

"They made a long distance call on your phone?"

"No; I didn't know them. It was another matter."

"This is a local call."

"Go ahead then, mother."

I finished my first beer and smashed the empty beerbottle into the big wooden box (coffin-sized) in the center of the room. Although the landlord gave me *two* garbage cans a week, the only way I could get everything to fit into the things was to break all the bottles. I was the only two garbage can man in the neighborhood, but then, they say, everybody's good at something.

Minor problem, though: I always liked to walk around barefoot and some of the glass from the broken bottles did flip out on the rug and I picked up chunks of stuff with my feet. This also pissed off my good doctor — slicing the stuff out every week while some dear old lady in the waiting room was dying of cancer — so I learned to incision the larger pieces out by myself and left the small ones in to do whatever they wanted to do. And of course, if you are not too stoned you feel the things going in and get them *then*. That's the nicest way. You pluck the thing out right *then* and the blood squirts out like jism and you feel just a little bit heroic — that is, *I* do.

Mad Jimmy looked oddly at the telephone in his hand. "She doesn't answer."

"Hang up then, asshole!"

"The phone just keeps ringing."

"And I'm going to tell you one last time to hang up!"

He hung up. "— A woman sat on my face last night. Twelve hours. I finally peeked out from under her cheeks and the sun was coming up. Man, I feel like my tongue is split in half, I feel like I got a forked tongue."

"That would be a real break."

"Yeah. I could do two pussies at once."

"Sure. And Casanova would shit in his grave."

He played with his Panama. Rectally, he showed some indication of hemorrhoid tissue. Rectal sphincter very tight. The Panama Kid. Prostate somewhat enlarged and tender on palpation.

Then the poor fuck jumped up and dialed the same number over again.

He played with his Panama. "It just keeps ringing," he said.

There he sat, listening to the ringing, musculoskeletal system fucked-up — I mean, shitty posture (kyphosis). At 5L (lower spine) shows possible anomaly.

He played with his Panama. "It just keeps ringing."

"Of course," I said, "she's fucking somebody."

"Of course. And it just keeps ringing."

I walked over and hung the phone up.

Then I screamed out, "Oh shit!"

"Whatzamatta, man?"

"Glass! There's glass all over this fucking floor!"

I stood on one foot and picked the glass out of the other. It was a nice. one. It beat squeezing boils. The blood popped right out.

I walked over to my chair and took an old paint rag I used to wipe my brushes with and wrapped it around my bloody heel.

"That rag's dirty," said Mad Jimmy.

"Your mind's dirty," I told him.

"*Please* close your robe!"

"There," I said, "You *see?*"

"I know I see. That's why I ask you to close it."

"All right. Shit."

I very reluctantly threw the robe over my genitals. Anybody can expose their genitals at night. At two p.m. in the afternoon it took some balls.

"Listen," said Mad Jimmy, "you know the other night you pissed on a police car in Westwood Village?"

"Where were they?"

"About fifty yards off, settling something or other."

"Probably jerking each other off."

"Maybe. But that wasn't enough for you. You had to go back and piss on the car a second time."

Poor Jimmy. Really fucked-up. 1, 5 and 6C (neck) luxated.

There was also a weakness of the right inguinal ring.

And there he was complaining because I pissed on a police car.

"All right, Jimmy, you think you're hot shit, huh? With your little stolen bag of trinkets. Well, I'm gonna tell *you* something!"

"What?" he asked, looking into the mirror and twisting the Panama again. Then he sucked at his wine bottle.

"*You're* wanted in court! You don't remember but you busted Mary's rib and then came back a couple of days later and hit her in the face."

"I'm wanted in COURT? In COURT? Oh no, man, you don't really *mean* I'm wanted in COURT?"

I smashed my second beerbottle into the huge wooden box in the center of the room. "Yes, my boy, you are crazy as hell, you need help. And Mary has an assault-and-battery out against you . . ."

"What's 'battery' mean?"

I trotted off for two more beers (for myself), came back.

"Listen, asshole, you know what 'battery' means! You haven't driven a bicycle *all* your life!"

I looked at him. His skin was somewhat dry with loss of natural elasticity. I also knew that he had a small growth on his left buttocks (center).

"But I don't *understand* this COURT thing! What the hell does it mean? Sure, we had a little argument. So I went to George's place in the desert. We drank port wine for thirty days. When I came back she SCREAMED at me! You should have *seen* her! I didn't mean any harm. All I did was kick her big ass and tits . . ."

"She's frightened of you, Jimmy. You're a sick man. I've made a very close study of you. You know when I'm not jacking-off or stoned I'm reading books, all kinds of books. You are demented, my friend."

22

"But we were all such good friends. She even wanted to fuck you but she wouldn't fuck you because she loved me. That's what she told me."

"But, Jimmy, that was *then*. You have no idea how things change. Mary's a very fine person. She . . ."

"God oh *mighty!* Close your robe! PLEASE!"

"Ooooops! Sorry."

Poor Jimmy. His genital system — left vas deferens and somewhat on the right there appears to be some scar or adhesion tissue. Probably caused by some pathology in the past.

"I'll phone Anna," he said, "Anna is Mary's best friend. She'll know. Why would Mary want to take me to court?"

"Phone then, mother."

Jimmy adjusted his Panama in the mirror, then dialed.

"Anna. Jimmy. What? No, it can't be! Hank just told me. Listen, I don't play these games. What? No, I didn't bust her rib! I just kicked her big ass and titties. You mean she's *really* going to court? Well, I'm not going. I'm going to Jerome, Arizona. Got a place. Two hundred and twenty-five a month. I just made twelve thousand dollars on a big land deal . . . Oh shut up, goddamn you, about that COURT thing! You know what I'm going to do right *now?* I'm going over to Mary's right NOW! I'll kiss her and chew her lips off! I'll eat every cunthair off her snatch! What do I care about court? I'll jam it up her ass, under armpits, between the tits, in her mouth, in her . . ."

Jimmy looked at me. "She hung up."

"Jimmy," I said, "you should flush your ear canals. You show indications of symptoms of emphysema. Exercise and discontinue smoking. You need spinal therapy. For your weak inguinal ring there should be care in heavy lifting, straining at the stool . . ."

"What is all this bullshit?"

"The growth on your buttocks appears to be verracae."

"What's verracae?"

"A wart, mother."

"You're a wart, mother."

"Yeah," I said. "Where'd you get the bicycle?"

"It belongs to Arthur. Arthur's holding a lot of shit. Let's go over to Arthur's and smoke some shit."

23

"I don't like Arthur. He's such a delicate little snit. Some delicate little snits I like. Arthur's the other kind."

"He's going to Mexico for six months next week."

"Many of those delicate little snits are always going somewhere. What is it? A grant?"

"Yes, a grant. But he can't paint."

"I know that. But it's his statues," I said.

"I don't like his statues," said the Panama Kid.

"Listen, Jimmy, I may not like Arthur but I have been very close to his statues."

"But it's the same old stuff — the Greek shit — gals with big tits and asses in flowing robes. Guys wrestling, grabbing at each other's cocks and beards. What the hell is it?"

So, reader, let's forget Mad Jimmy for a minute and get into Arthur — which is no big problem — what I mean is also the way I write: I can jump around and you can come right along and it won't matter a bit, you'll see.

Well, the *secret* of Arthur was that he built them oversize. Very very impressive. All that fucking cement. His *smallest*-sized man or woman loomed over eight feet tall in sunlight or in moonlight or smog, depending upon when you arrived.

I tried to get into his place in the back there one night and here were all these cement people, all these big cement people just standing around outside there. Some of them were as high as twelve or fourteen feet. Huge breasts, pussies, cocks, balls, all about the place. I had just finished listening to *The Elixir of Love* by Donizetti. It didn't help. I still felt like some kind of pygmy in hell. I'm out there screaming, "Arthur, Arthur, help me!" But he was on the hash or something, or maybe I was. Anyhow, the god-damned fear builds.

Well, I am six foot and 232 pounds, so I just threw a bodyblock on the biggest sonofabitch there.

I got him from the back when he wasn't looking. And he fell face-forward, and I mean — he FELL! You could hear it all over town.

Then, out of curiosity, I rolled him over, and sure enough I'd broken off his cock, one ball, and another ball neatly sliced in half; part of the nose gone too, and about half the beard.

I felt like a killer.

Then Arthur stepped out and said, "Hank, good to see you!"

And I said, "Sorry about the noise, Art, but I stumbled into one of your little pets out there and the fucking thing tripped-up and fell apart."

And he said, "That's all right."

So I went in and we smoked shit all night. And the next thing I knew the sun was up and I was in my car driving along — around nine a.m. — and I drove through all the stoplights and red lights. No trouble at all. I even managed to park the car a block and a half from where I lived.

But when I got to my door I found I had this cement cock in my pocket. The damn thing must have been at least two feet long. I walked down and stuck the thing into my landlady's mailbox, but there was plenty left over that stuck out, bending and immortal, and topped by that huge head, left to the mailman's discretion.

Okay. Back to Mad Jimmy.

"But I mean," said Mad Jimmy, "do they *really* want me in COURT? In COURT?"

"Listen, Jimmy, you really need help. I'll drive you to Patton or Camarillo."

"Ah, I'm tired of those fucking shock-treatments. . . . Burrrrrrr!!!! Burrrrrrr!!!!"

Mad Jimmy rattled his body all about the chair taking the treatments again.

Then he adjusted his new Panama in the mirror, smiled, got up and walked to the phone again.

He dialed his number, looked at me and said, "It just keeps ringing."

He just hung up and dialed again.

They all come to see me. Even my doctor phones me. "Christ was the greatest head-shrinker and ego of them all — claiming he was the Son of God. Throwing those money-changers out of the temple. Naturally, that was His mistake. They got His ass. Even asked Him to fold his feet so they could save one nail. What shit."

They all come to see me. There's one guy with a last name like Ranch or Rain, something of the sort, and he's always coming by with his sleeping bags and a sad story. He hits between Berkeley and

New Orleans. Back and forth. Once every two months. And he writes bad, old-fashioned rondos. And it's a fiver and/or a couple of bucks each time he hits (or as they like to say, "crashes"), plus whatever he eats and drinks. That's all right, I've given away more money than I have cock, but these people have got to realize that I *also* have some trouble staying alive.

So there's Mad Jimmy and so there's me.

Or there's Maxie. Maxie is going to shut off all the sewers in Los Angeles to help the Cause of the People. Well, it's a damn nice gesture, you've got to admit that. But Maxie, buddy, I say, let me know when you are going to shut off all the sewers. I'm for the People. We've been friends a long time. I'll leave town a weak early.

What Maxie doesn't realize is that Causes and Shit are different things. Starve me, but don't cut off my shit and/or shit-disposal unit. I remember once my landlord left town on a nice two week vacation to Hawaii. Okay.

The day after he left town, my toilet stopped. I had my own personal plunger, being very frightened of shit, but I plunged and plunged and it didn't work. You know what that left me.

So I called up my own personal friends, and I'm the type who doesn't have too many personal friends, or if I have them, they don't have toilets let alone telephones ... more often, they don't have anything.

So, I called the one or two who had toilets. They were very nice.

"Sure, Hank, you can shit at my place anytime!"

I didn't take up their invitations. Maybe it was the way they said it. So here was my landlord in Hawaii watching the hula girls, and those fucking turds just lay on top of the water and whirled around and looked at me.

So each night I had to shit and then pluck the turds out of water, place them in wax paper and then into a brown paper bag and get into my car and drive around town looking for some place to toss them.

So mostly, double-parked with the motor running, I'd just toss the god-damned turds over some wall, any wall. I tried to be non-prejudiced, but this one Home for the Aged seemed a particularly quiet place and I think I gave them my little brown bag of turds at least three times.

Or sometimes I'd just be driving along and roll up the window and rather flick the turds out as one would, say, cigarette ashes or a couple of dozen burnt-out cigars.

And speaking of shit, constipation has always been a greater fear to me than cancer. (We'll get back to Mad Jimmy. Listen, I told you I write this way.) If I miss one day without shitting, I can't go anywhere, do anything — I get so desperate when that happens that oftentimes I try to suck my own cock to unclog my system, to get things going again. And if you've ever tried to suck your own cock then you only know the terrible strain on the backbone, neckbone, every muscle, everything. You stroke the thing up as long as it will get then you *really* double up like some creature on a torture rack, legs way over your head and locked around the bedrungs, your asshole twitching like a dying sparrow in the frost, everything bent together around your great beer belly, all your muscle sheathes ripped to shit, and what *hurts* is that you don't miss by a foot or two — you miss by an eighth of an inch — the end of your tongue and the tip of your cock that close, but it might as well be an eternity or forty miles. God, or whoever the hell, knew just what He was doing when He put us together.

But back to the insane.

Jimmy just dialed the same number over and over from one-thirty p.m. until six p.m. when I gave way. No, it was six-thirty p.m. when I gave way. What does it matter? So, after the 749th phone call, I allowed my robe to flop open, walked over to Mad Jimmy, took the phone out of his hand and said, "No more."

I was listening to Hayden's Symphony #102. I had enough beer to last the rest of the night. And Mad Jimmy was boring me. He was a boor. A sandfly. A crocodile's tail. Dogshit on the heel.

He looked at me. "Court? You mean she's going to take me to court? Oh no, I don't believe in these games people play . . ."

Platitudes. And wax in his ears.

So I yawned and phoned Izzy Steiner, his best friend who had dropped him on me. Izzy Steiner claimed to be a writer. I said he couldn't write. He said I couldn't write. It was possible that one of us was right, or wrong. You know.

Izzy was a young huge Jewish lad around 5-5 tipping in at 200 pounds — thick-armed, thick-wristed, bull neck with head-tick; small little eyes and a very unsympathetic mouth – just a small hole in his head that whistled out the glory of Izzy Steiner and ate continually: chickenwings, turkeylegs, loaves of Frenchbread, spider-dung – anything, anything that held still long enough for him to letch upon it.

"Steiner?"

"Uh?"

He was studying to be a Rabbi but he didn't want to be a Rabbi. All he wanted to do was eat and grow larger and larger. You could go in for a one minute piss and when you came out your refrigerator would be empty, or he'd be standing there with that greedy, ashamed look, chunking the last of it down. The only thing that saved you from complete ambush when Izzy came around is that he wouldn't eat raw meat – he likes it rare, very, but not raw.

"Steiner?"

"Glub. . . ."

"Look, finish your mouthful. I have something to say to you."

I listened to him chewing. It sounded like twelve rabbits fucking in the straw.

"Listen, man. Mad Jimmy's here. He's your boy. He rode up on a bicycle. I'm about to vomit. Come right over. Hurry. I warn you. You're his friend. You're his only friend. You better hurry over here. Take him away from me, take him away from my eyes. I can't be responsible for myself much longer."

I hung up.

"Did you call Izzy?" asked Jimmy.

"Yeah. He's your only friend."

"Oh, jesus christ," said Mad Jimmy, and then he started dumping all his spoons and stuff and wooden dolls into a sack and he ran out to his bicycle and hid them in the paper-rack.

Poor Izzy was on the way. The tank. Little air-hole mouth sucking in the sky. He was fucked-up mainly on Hemingway, Faulkner and a minor admixture of Mailer and Mahler.

Then suddenly, there was Izzy. He never walked. He just seemed to swing through a door. I mean, he ran along on little balls of air – hungry and damned near invincible.

Then he saw Mad Jimmy and his wine bottle.

"I need money, Jimmy! Stand up!"

Izzy ripped Jimmy's pockets inside out and found nothing.

"Watcha doin', man?" asked Mad Jimmy.

"The last time we got in a fight, Jimmy, your ripped my shirt, man. You ripped my pants. You owe me $5 for the pants and $3 for the shirt."

"Fuck man, I didn't rip your fucking shirt."

"Shut up, Jimmy, I'm warning you!"

Izzy ran out to the bicycle and began going through the papersack which hung over the back rack. He came in with the brown bag. Dumped it on the coffee table.

Spoons, knives, forks, rubber dolls ... carved wooden images. . . .

"This stuff ain't worth shit!"

Izzy ran back to the bicycle and searched the paper bags some more.

Mad Jimmy came up and began dumping his shit back into the brown paper bag. "This silver alone is worth twenty bucks! You see what an asshole he is?"

"Yeah."

Izzy ran back on it. "Jimmy, you ain't got shit on that bike! You owe me eight bucks, Jimmy. Listen, the last time I beat you up, you tore my clothes!"

"Fuck you, mother!"

Jimmy adjusted his new Panama once again in the mirror.

"Look at me! Look how handsome I look!"

"Yeah, I see," said Izzy, and then he walked over and took the Panama and ripped a long hole in the outer brim. Then he ripped a slit on the other and put the Panama back on Jimmy's head. Jimmy didn't look so handsome anymore.

"Get me some scotch tape," said Jimmy, "I gotta fix my hat."

Izzy walked over, found some scotch tape, jammed tassles of it into the hole, then he ran a whole hunk of it over the rip, but missed most of it, and a big strip of tape ran over the brim and down into Jimmy's face, dangling right over the nose.

"Why do they want me in court? I don't play games! What the hell is this?"

"All right, Jimmy," said Izzy, "I'm driving you to Patton. You're a sick man! You need help! You owe me $8, you busted Mary's rib, you hit her in the face ... you're sick, sick, sick!"

29

"Fuck you, mother!" Mad Jimmy got up and swung at Izzy, missed, then fell to the floor. Izzy picked him up and began to give him the airplane spin.

"Don't, Izzy," I said, "you'll slash him to ribbons. There's too much glass on the floor."

Izzy tossed him on the couch. Mad Jimmy ran out with his brown paper bag, stuffed it into the paperholder and then began cussing.

"Izzy, you stole my bottle of wine! I had another bottle of wine in that papersack! You stole it, bastard! Come on now, that bottle cost me 54 cents. When I bought it, I had 60 cents. Now I only have six cents."

"Look, Jimmy, would Izzy take your bottle of wine? What's that next to you there? On the couch?"

Jimmy picked it up. He looked down into the eye of the bottle.

"No, this isn't the one. There's another one, Izzy took it."

"Look, Jimmy, your friend doesn't drink wine. He doesn't want your bottle. Why don't you get off your imaginary kick and ride your bike the hell out of here?"

"I'm sick of you too, Jimmy," said Izzy, "now peddle off. You've had it."

Jimmy stood in front of the mirror adjusting what was left of the Panama. Then he walked out, got on Arthur's bicycle and rode off under the moon. He'd been at my place for hours. Now it was night.

"Poor crazy bastard," I said, watching him peddle off, "I'm sorry for him."

"Me too," said Izzy.

Then he reached under a bush and got the wine bottle. We walked inside.

"I'll get a couple of glasses," I said.

I came back and we sat there, drinking the wine.

"Have you ever tried sucking your own dick?" I asked Izzy.

"I'll try it when I get home."

"I don't think it can be done," I said.

"I'll let you know."

"I fall about an eighth of an inch short. It's frustrating."

We finished the wine and then walked down to Shakey's and drank the deep brown beer by the pitcherful and watched the old-time fights — we saw Louis get dumped by the Dutchman; the third Zale-Rocky G. fight; Braddock-Baer; Dempsey-Firpo, all of them, and then they put on some old Laurel and Hardy flicks . . . there was one where the bastards were fighting for covers in the sleeper of a Pullman. I was the only one who laughed. People stared at me. I just cracked peanuts and kept on laughing. Then Izzy began laughing. Then everybody started laughing at them fighting for the covers in the Pullman. I forgot all about Mad Jimmy and felt like a human being for the first time in hours. Living was easy — all you had to do was let go. And have a little money. Let the other men fight the wars, let the other men go to jail.

We closed the place up and then Izzy went to his place and I went to mine.

I stripped, worked up a lather, hooked my toes in the bed rungs and doubled into a circle. It was the same — an eighth of an inch short. Well, you couldn't have it all. I reached over, opened it in the middle, and began reading Tolstoy's *War and Peace.* Nothing had changed. It was still a lousy book.

WOULD YOU SUGGEST WRITING AS A CAREER?

The bar. Sure. It overlooked the takeoff ramp. We sat at the bar but the bartender ignored us. Bartenders in airport bars are snobs, I decided, just like porters on trains used to be snobs. I suggested to Garson that rather than scream at the man, which is what he (the bartender) wanted, that we take a table. We took a table.

Well-dressed thieves all about, looking comfortable and dull, sipping at drinks, talking quietly and waiting on their flight. Garson and I sat and looked at the barmaids.

"Shit," said Garson, "look — their dresses are cut so that you can see their panties."

"Ummm hum," I said.

Then we made comments about them. That one had no ass. The other one's legs were too thin. And they both looked stupid and thought they were hot shit. The one without the ass walked over. I told Garson to name his and then I ordered a scotch and water. She went off for the drinks, then came back. The drinks weren't higher than at an ordinary bar but then I had to tip her well for seeing her panties — up close like that too.

"You scared?" asked Garson.

"Yes," I said, "but what about?"

"Flying for the first time."

"I thought I might be. But now, looking at these—" I waved about the bar "— it doesn't matter . . ."

"How about the readings?"

"The readings I don't like. They're stupid. Like digging a ditch. It's survival."

"At least you're doing what you like to do."

"No," I said, "I'm doing what you like to do."

"All right, then, at least people will appreciate what you're doing."

"I hope so. I'd hate to get lynched for reading a sonnet."

I reached into my travel bag, put the bag between my legs and refilled my drink. I had that, then I ordered Garson and myself one more.

The one without the ass in ruffled panties: I wondered if she wore other panties *under* those ruffled panties? We finished our drinks. I gave Garson a 5 or a ten for the ride in and we went upstairs for my seat on the plane. I no sooner sat down in the last seat, last row, when the plane began to roll. Close.

It seemed to take a long time to get off the ground. An old grandma had the window seat next to me. She looked calm, almost bored. Probably took 4 or 5 flights a week, ran a string of whorehouses. I couldn't get the safety belt quite right but since nobody else was complaining, I let mine dangle rather loosely. It would be less embarrassing to get thrown out of my seat than to ask the stewardess how to fasten the belt.

We were in the air and I hadn't screamed. It was calmer than a trainride. No motion. Boring. We seemed to be doing 30 miles an hour; the mountains and clouds didn't hurry by at all. 2 stewardesses walked up and down, smiling smiling smiling. One of them didn't look too bad but she had these huge cords of veins running up and down her neck. Too bad. The other stewardess didn't have any ass.

We ate and then the drinks came around. One dollar. Not everybody wanted a drink. Strange turds. Then I began hoping the plane would lose a wing and then I'd really get to see what the faces of the stewardesses looked like. I knew the one with the cords would scream very loudly. The one without the ass — well, who knew? I'd grab the one with the cords and rape her on the way down to our death. A quickie. Clutching, finally, in mutual ejaculation just before we hit the ground.

We didn't crash. I had my second allowable drink, then sneaked an extra one right in front of grandma. She didn't flinch. I did. A full glass. Straight down. No water.

Then we were there. Seattle . . .

I let them all get off first. I had to. Now I couldn't get *out* of my seatbelt.

I called to the one with the big veins in her neck.

"Stewardess! Stewardess!"

She walked back.

"Look I'm sorry ... but how do you ... open this damn thing?"

She wouldn't touch the belt or get close to me.

"Turn it over, sir."

"Yes?"

"Just pull on that little clip on the back ..."

She walked away. I pulled at the little clip. Nothing. I pulled and I pulled. Oh, Christ! ... then, it gave.

I grabbed my flightbag and tried to act normal.

She smiled at me at the gangplank door.

"Good afternoon and come again, sir!"

I walked down the runway. A young boy with long blonde hair was standing there.

"Mr. Chinaski?" he asked.

"Yes, is that you, Belford?"

"I kept watching the faces ..." he said.

"That's all right," I said, "let's get out of here."

"We still have a few spare hours before the reading."

"Great," I said.

They were tearing up the airport. You had to take a bus to get to the parking lot. They let you wait. There was a big crowd waiting for the bus. Belford started to walk toward them.

"Wait! Wait!" I said. "I just can't *stand* there among all those damned people!"

"They don't know who you are, Mr. Chinaski."

"How well I know. But I know who they are. Let's stand here. When the bus comes we'll dash up. Meanwhile how about a little drink?"

"No thanks, Mr. Chinaski."

"Look, Belford, call me Henry."

"I'm Henry too," he answered.

"Oh yes, I forgot." ...

We stood and I drank.

"Here comes the bus, Henry!"

"O.k., Henry!"

We ran for the bus ...

After that, we decided that I was "Hank" and he was "Henry."

He had an address in his hand. A friend's cabin. We could lay up there together until the reading. His friend was gone. The reading wasn't until 9 p.m. Somehow Henry couldn't find the cabin. It was nice country. Sure, it was nice country. Pines and pines and lakes and pines. Fresh air. No traffic. It bored me. There wasn't any beauty in me. I thought, I'm not a very nice fellow. Here's life the way it should be and I feel as if I were in jail.

"Nice country," I said, "but I suppose some day they'll get to it."

"They will," said Henry. "You ought to see it when the snow comes down."

Thank god, I thought, I'm spared that . . .

Belford stopped outside a bar. We went in. I hated bars. I'd written too many stories and poems about bars. Belford thought he was doing me a favor.

You can get just so much out of bars and they won't go down anymore. They come up. People in bars were like people in 5 and dime stores: they were killing time and everything else.

I followed him in. He knew some people at a table. Lo, here was a professor of something. And there was a professor of something. And there was this and there was that. A tableful of them. Some women. Somehow the women looked like margarine. Everybody sat there drinking this green poison beer in big mugs.

A green beer arrived in front of me. I lifted it, held my breath and took a pull.

"I've always liked your work," said one of the profs, "You remind me of . . ."

"Pardon me," I said, "I'll be right back . . ."

I hustled toward the crapper. Naturally it stank. A nice quaint place.

Bar . . . coming up!

I didn't have time to get a toilet door open. It had to go into the urinal. Further down the urinal from me was the bar clown. The town "mayor." In his red cap. Funny guy. Shit.

I let it go, gave him the dirtiest look I could, then he walked out.

Then I walked out and sat in front of my green beer.

"You're reading tonight at ....?" one of them asked me.
I didn't answer.

"We'll all be there."

"I'll probably be there too," I said.

I had to be. I'd already cashed and spent their check. The other place, the next day, maybe I could get out of that.

All I wanted to do was get back to my room in L.A., all the shades down while drinking COLD TURKEY and eating hard-boiled eggs with paprika, and hoping for some Mahler on the radio . . .

9 p.m. . . . Belford guided me in. There were little round tables with people sitting at them. There was a stage.

"You want me to introduce you?" Belford asked.

"No," I said.

I found the steps that led up to the stage. There was a chair, a table. I put my traveling bag up on the table and started taking things out.

"I'm Chinaski," I told them, "and this is a pair of shorts and here are some stockings and here is a shirt and here is a pint of scotch and here are some books of poetry."

I left the scotch and the books on the table. I peeled the cellophane from the scotch and had a drink. "Any questions."

They were quiet.

"Well, we might as well begin then."

I gaeve them some of the old stuff first. Each time I took another drink the next poem sounded better — to me. College students were all right anyhow. They only asked one thing — that you didn't purposely lie to them. I thought that was fair.

I got through the first 30 minutes, asked for a ten minute break, got down off the stage with my bottle and sat at a table with Belford and 4 or 5 other students. A young girl came up with one of my books. God o mighty, baby, I thought, I'll autograph anything you've got!

"Mr. Chinaski?"

"Sure," I said with a wave of my genius hand. I asked her name. Then wrote something. Drew a picture of a naked guy chasing a naked woman. Dated it.

"Thanks very much, Mr. Chinaski!"

So this was how it worked? Just a bunch of bullshit.

I took my bottle out of some guy's mouth. "Look mother, that's the 2nd hit you've taken. I've got to sweat another thirty minutes up there. Don't touch that bottle again."

I sat in the middle of the table. Then I took a pull, sat it back down.

"Would you suggest writing as a career?" one of the young students asked me.

"Are you trying to be funny?" I asked him.

"No, no, I'm serious. Would you advise writing as a career?"

"Writing chooses you, you don't choose it."

That got him off me. I had another drink, then climbed back on stage. I always saved what I preferred for last. It was my first college reading but I'd had a drunken two night stand at an L.A. bookstore for a warmup. Save the best for last. That's what you did when you were a kid. I read it on out, then closed the books.

The applause surprised me. It was heavy and it kept on. It was embarrassing. The poems weren't that good. They were applauding for something else. The fact that I'd made it through, I suppose . . .

There was a party at this professor's house. This professor looked just like Hemingway. Of course, Hemingway was dead. The professor was rather dead too. He kept on talking about literature and writing – of all the disgusting fucking subjects. No matter where I went he trailed me. He followed me everywhere but to the bathroom. Everytime I turned around, there he was –

"Ah, Hemingway! I thought you were dead!"

"Did you know that Faulkner was a drunkard too?"

"Yeh."

"What do you think of James Jones?"

The old boy was sick: he never got off it.

I found Belford. "Listen, kid, the refrigerator is dry. Hemingway doesn't stock much shit . . ."

I gave him a 20. "Look, you know anybody who can go out and get some more beer, at least?"

"Yes, I know somebody."

"Fine, then. And a couple of cigars."

"What kind?"

"Any kind. Cheap. Ten or 15 cents. And thanks."

There were 20 or 30 people there and I had already stocked the refrigerator once. So this is the way this bullshit works?

I picked out the finest looking woman in the house and decided to make her hate me. I found her in the breakfastnook sitting at a table alone.

"Baby," I said, "that damned Hemingway is a sick man."

"I know it," she said.

"I know he wants to be nice but he can't let go of Literature. Christ, what a disgusting subject! You know, I never met a writer I liked? They're all little figs, the worst of human crap . . ."

"I know," she said, "I know . . ."

I pulled her head around and kissed her. She didn't resist. Hemingway saw us and walked into the other room. Hey! The old boy had some *kool!* Remarkable!

Belford got back with the stuff and I piled a bunch of beer in front of us and I talked, and kissed and fondled with her for hours. It wasn't until the next day that I found out she was Hemingway's wife . . .

I awakened in bed, alone, on a second floor somewhere. I was probably still in Hemingway's house. I was more seriously hungover than usual. I turned my face away from the sunlight and closed my eyes.

Somebody shook me.

"Hank! Hank! Wake up!"

"Shit. Go away."

"We've got to leave now. You're reading at noon. It's a long drive. We'll barely make it."

"Let's not make it."

"We've got to make it. You signed a contract. They're waiting. They're going to put you on t.v."

"T.v.?"

"Yes."

"Oh my god, I might vomit in front of the camera . . ."

"Hank, we've got to make it."

"All right, all right."

I got out of bed and looked at him. "You're all right, Belford, to look after me and take all my shit. Why don't you get angry and cuss me or something?"

"You're my favorite living poet," he said.

I laughed. "God, I could probably take my pecker out and piss all over you . . ."

"No," he said, "it's your words not your piss that I'm interested in."

There, he had properly put me down and I felt good for him. I finally got on what I had to and Belford helped me down the stairway. There was Hemingway and his wife.

"God, you look awful!" said Hemingway.

"I'm sorry about last night, Ernie. I didn't know it was your wife until . . ."

"Forget it," he said, "how about a bit of coffee?"

"Fine," I said, "I need something."

"How about something to eat?"

"Thanks. I don't eat."

We all sat around quietly drinking our coffees. Then Hemingway said something. I don't know what it was about. James Joyce, I think.

"Oh god damn it!" said his wife, "can't you *ever* shut up?"

"Listen, Hank," said Belford, "we better be leaving. It's a long drive."

"O.k.," I said.

We stood up and walked toward the car. I shook Hemingway's hand.

"I'll walk you to the car," he said.

Belford and H. walked toward the door. I turned to her.

"Goodbye," I said.

"Goodbye," she said, and then she kissed me. I'd never been kissed like that. She just gave over, gave everything up. I'd never been *screwed* like that.

Then I walked outside. Hemingway and I shook hands again. Then we drove off and he walked back into his house to his wife . . .

"He teaches Literature," said Belford.

"Yeah," I said.

I was really sick. "I don't know if I can make it. It's senseless to give a reading at high noon."

"That's when most of the students can get to see you."

We drove along and that's when I knew there was never any escape. There was always something that *had* to be done or they blotted you out. It was a hard fact but I noted it down and wondered if there would ever be any way to escape it.

"You don't look like you're going to make it," said Belford.

"Make a stop somewhere. We'll get a bottle of scotch."

He pulled into one of those strange-looking Washington stores. I bought a half pint of vodka to try to get straight on and a pint of scotch for the reading. Belford said that they were fairly conservative at the next place and that I'd better get a thermos to drink the scotch out of. So I bought a thermos.

We stopped for breakfast somewhere. Nice place but the girls didn't show their panties.

Christ, there were women everywhere and over ½ of them looked good enough to fuck, and there was nothing you could do — just look at them. Who'd ever devised such an awful trick? Yet they all looked pretty much alike — overlooking a roll of fat here, no ass there — just so many poppies in a field. Which one did you pick? Which one picked you? It didn't matter, and it was all so sad. And when the picks were made, it never worked, it never worked for anybody, no matter what they said.

Belford ordered hotcakes for both of us, side order of eggs. Over easy.

A waitress. I looked at her breasts and hips and lips and eyes. Poor thing. Poor thing, hell. There probably wasn't a thought on her mind except raping some poor son of a bitch out of every dime he had . . .

I managed to get down most of the hotcakes, then we were back in the car.

Belford was intent upon the reading. A dedicated young man.

"That guy who drank out of your bottle twice at intermission . . ."

"Yeah. He was looking for trouble."

"Everybody's afraid of him. He's flunked-off campus but he still hangs around. He's always on lsd. He's crazy."

"I don't give a damn about that, Henry. You can steal my women but don't play with my whiskey."

We stopped for gas, then drove on. I'd poured the scotch into the thermos and was trying to get the vodka down.

"We're getting close," said Belford, "you can see the campus towers now. Look!"

I looked.

"Lord have Mercy!" I said.

As soon as I saw the campus towers I had to stick my head out the side of the car and I began vomiting. Smears of vomit slid and stuck along the side of Belford's red car. He drove on, dedicated. Somehow he felt as if I could make it, as if I were vomiting as some kind of joke. It kept coming.

"Sorry," I managed to say.

"It's all right," he said. "It's almost noon. We have about 5 minutes. I'm glad we made it," he said.

We parked. I grabbed my travel bag, got out, vomited in the parking lot.

Belford tromped ahead.

"Just a minute," I said.

I held to a post and vomited again. Some students walking by looked at me: that old man, what's he doing?

I followed Belford this way and that ... up this path, down that. The American University — a lot of shrubbery and paths and bullshit. I saw my name on a sign — HENRY CHINASKI, READING POETRY AT ...

' That's me, I thought. I almost laughed. I was pushed into this room. There were people everywhere. Little white faces. Little white pancakes.

They sat me in a chair.

"Sir," said the guy behind the tv camera, "when I hold up my hand, you begin."

I'm going to vomit, I thought. I tried to find some poetry books. I played around. Then Belford started telling them who I was ... what a grand time we had together in the great Pacific Northwest ...

The guy held up his hand.

I began. "My name's Chinaski. First poem is called ..."

After 3 or 4 poems I began to hit the thermos. People were laughing. I didn't care at what. I hit the thermos some more, began to relax. No intermission, this one. I looked up into a side-view tv, saw that I had been reading for 30 minutes with one long hair hanging straight down the center of my forehead and folded over my nose. That amused *me* anyhow; then I brushed it aside and got to work. I seemed to have gotten away with it. The applause was good though not as good as the other place. Who cared? Just get me out alive. Some had my books, came down for signatures.

Uh huh, a huh, I thought, this is the way this bullshit works.

Not much more. I signed a paper for my hundred bucks, was introduced to the head of the Literature dept. All sex, she was. I thought, I'll rape her. She said she might come over to this cabin in the hills later — Belford's place — but, of course, after hearing my poems she never did. It was over. I was returning to my musty court and madness but my kind of madness. Belford and a friend drove me to the airport and we sat in the bar. I bought the drinks.

"That's funny," I said, "I must be going crazy. I keep hearing my name."

I was right. When we reached the ramp my plane was rolling off, just rising into the air. I had to go back and enter a special room where I was interviewed. I felt like a schoolboy.

"All right," he said, "we'll put you on our next flight. But be *sure* to make this one."

"Thank you, sir," I said. He said something into a telephone and I walked back to the bar and ordered some more drinks.

"It's o.k.," I said, "I'm on the next flight."

Then it occurred to me that I could miss that next flight *forever.* And going back and seeing that same man. Each time a little worse: he more angry; I more apologetic. It *could* happen. Belford and his friend would disappear. Others would arrive. A little fund would be taken up for me . . .

"Mommy, what ever happened to daddy?"

"He died at a bar table in Seattle airport while trying to get on a flight for Los Angeles."

You may not believe it, but I just *did* make that 2nd flight. I no sooner sat down and the plane was moving. I couldn't understand it. Why was it so difficult? Anyway, I was on board. I uncapped the bottle. The stewardess caught me. Against the rules. "You know, you can be put off, sir." The captain had just announced that we were at 50,000 feet.

"Mommy, what ever happened to daddy?"

"He was a poet."

"What's a poet, mommy?"

"He said he didn't know. Now come on, wash your hands, we're having dinner."

"He didn't know?"

"That's right, he didn't know. Now come on, I said wash your *hands* . . ."

THE GREAT ZEN WEDDING

I was in the rear, stuck in with the Rumanian bread, liverwurst, beer, soft drinks; wearing a green necktie, first necktie since the death of my father a decade ago. Now I was to be best man at a Zen wedding, Hollis driving 85 m.p.h., Roy's four-foot beard flowing into my face. It was my '62 Comet, only I couldn't drive — no insurance, two drunk-driving raps, and already getting drunk. Hollis and Roy had lived unmarried for three years, Hollis supporting Roy. I sat in the back and sucked at my beer. Roy was explaining Hollis' family to me one by one. Roy was better with the intellectual shit. Or the tongue. The walls of their place were covered with these many photos of guys bending into the muff and chewing.

Also a snap of Roy reaching climax while jacking off. Roy had done it alone. I mean, tripped the camera. Himself. String. Wire. Some arrangement. Roy claimed he had to jackoff six times in order to get the perfect snap. A whole day's work: there it was: this milky glob: a work of art. Hollis turned off the freeway. It wasn't too far. Some of the rich have driveways a mile long. This one wasn't too bad: a quarter of a mile. We got out. Tropical gardens. Four or five dogs. Big black woolly stupid slobbering-at-the-mouth beasts. We never reached the door — there *he* was, the rich one, standing on the veranda, looking down, drink in hand. And Roy yelled, "Oh, Harvey, you bastard, so good to see you!"

Harvey smiled the little smile: "Good to see you too, Roy."

One of the big black woollies was gobbling at my left leg. "Call your dog off, Harvey, bastard, good to see you!" I screamed.

"Aristotle, now STOP that!"

Aristotle left off, just in time.

And.

We went up and down the steps with the salami, the Hungarian pickled catfish, the shrimp. Lobstertails. Bagels. Minced dove assholes.

Then we had it all in there. I sat down and grabbed a beer. I was the only one with a necktie. I was also the only one who had bought a wedding gift. I hid it between the wall and the Aristotle-chewed leg.

"Charles Bukowski . . ."

I stood up.

"Oh, Charles Bukowski!"

"Uh huh."

Then:

"This is Marty."

"Hello, Marty."

"And this is Elsie."

"Hello, Elsie."

"Do you *really,* she asked, "break up furniture and windows, slash your hands, all that, when you're drunk?"

"Uh huh."

"You're a little old for that."

"Now listen, Elsie, don't give me any shit . . ."

"And this is Tina."

"Hello, Tina."

I sat down.

Names! I had been married to my first wife for two-and-one-half years. One night some people came in. I had told my wife: "This is Louie the half-ass and this is Marie, Queen of the Quick Suck, and this is Nick, the half-hobble." Then I had turned to them and said, "This is my wife . . . this is my wife . . . this is . . ." I finally had to look at her and ask: "WHAT THE HELL *IS* YOUR NAME ANYHOW?"

"Barbara."

"This is Barbara," I had told them . . .

The Zen master hadn't arrived. I sat and sucked at my beer.

Then here came *more* people. On and on up the steps. All Hollis' family. Roy didn't seem to have a family. Poor Roy. Never worked a day in his life. I got another beer.

They kept coming up the steps: ex-cons, sharpies, cripples, dealers in various subterfuges. Family and friends. Dozens of them. No wedding presents. No neckties.

I pushed further back into my corner.

One guy was pretty badly fucked-up. It took him 25 minutes to get up the stairway. He had especially-made crutches, very powerful looking things with round bands for the arms. Special grips here and there. Aluminum and rubber. No wood for that baby. I figured it: watered-down stuff or a bad payoff. He had taken the slugs in the old barber chair with the hot and wet shaving towel over his face. Only they'd missed a few vital spots.

There were others. Somebody taught class at UCLA. Somebody else ran in shit through Chinese fishermen's boats via San Pedro Harbor.

I was introduced to the greatest killers and dealers of the century.

Me, I was between jobs.

Then Harvey walked up.

"Bukowski, care for a bit of scotch and water?"

"Sure, Harvey, sure."

We walked toward the kitchen.

"What's the necktie for?"

"The top of the zipper on my pants is broken. And my shorts are too tight. End of necktie covers stinkhairs just above my cock."

"I think that you are the modern living master of the short story. Nobody touches you."

"Sure, Harvey. Where's the scotch?"

Harvey showed me the bottle of scotch.

"I always drink this kind since you always mention it in your short stories."

"But I've switched brands now, Harv. I found some better stuff."

"What's the name of it?"

"Damned if I can remember."

I found a tall water glass, poured in half scotch, half water.

"For the nerves," I told him. "You know?"

"Sure, Bukowski."

I drank it straight down.

"How about a refill?"

"Sure."

I took the refill and walked to the front room, sat in my corner. Meanwhile there was a new excitement: The Zen master had ARRIVED!

46

The Zen master had on this very fancy outfit and kept his eyes very narrow. Or maybe that's the way they were.

The Zen master needed tables. Roy ran around looking for tables.

Meanwhile, the Zen master was very calm, very gracious. I downed my drink, went in for a refill. Came back.

A golden-haired kid ran in. About eleven years old.

"Bukowski, I've read some of your stories. *I* think that you are the greatest writer I have ever read!"

Long blond curls. Glasses. Slim body.

"Okay, baby. You get old enough. We'll get married. Live off of your money. I'm getting tired. You can just parade me around in a kind of glass cage with little airholes in it. I'll let the young boys have you. I'll even watch."

"Bukowski! Just *because* I have long hair, you think I'm a girl! My name is Paul! We were introduced! Don't you *remember?*"

Paul's father, Harvey, was looking at me. I saw his eyes. Then I knew that he had decided that I was not such a good writer after all. Maybe even a bad writer. Well, no man can hide forever.

But the little boy was all right: "That's okay, Bukowski! You are still the greatest writer I have ever read! Daddy has let me read *some* of your stories. . . ."

Then all the lights went out. That's what the kid deserved for his big mouth . . .

But there were candles everywhere. Everybody was finding candles, walking around finding candles and lighting them.

"Shit, it's just a fuse. Replace the fuse," I said.

Somebody said it wasn't the fuse, it was something else, so I gave up and while all the candle-lighting went on I walked into the kitchen for more scotch. Shit, there was Harvey standing there.

"Ya got a beautiful son, Harvey. Your boy, Peter . . ."

"Paul."

"Sorry. The Biblical."

"I understand."

(The rich understand; they just don't do anything about it.)

Harvey uncorked a new fifth. We talked about Kafka. Dos. Turgenev, Gogol. All that dull shit. Then there were candles everywhere. The Zen master wanted to get on with it. Roy had given me the two rings. I felt. They were still there. Everybody was waiting on us. I was waiting for Harvey to drop to the floor from drinking all that scotch. It wasn't any good. He had matched me one drink for two and was still standing. That isn't done too often. We had knocked off half a fifth in the ten minutes of candle-lighting. We went out to the crowd. I dumped the rings on Roy. Roy had communicated, days earlier, to the Zen master that I was a drunk — unreliable — either faint-hearted or vicious — therefore, during the ceremony, don't ask Bukowski for the rings because Bukowski might not be there. Or he might lose the rings, or vomit, or lose Bukowski.

So here it was, finally. The Zen master began playing with his little black book. It didn't look too thick. Around 150 pages, I'd say.

"I ask," said the Zen, "no drinking or smoking during the ceremony."

I drained my drink. I stood to Roy's right. Drinks were being drained all over the place.

Then the Zen master gave a little chickenshit smile.

I knew the Christian wedding ceremonies by the sad rote of experience. And the Zen ceremony actually resembled the Christian, with a small amount of horseshit thrown in. Somewhere along the way, three small sticks were lit. Zen had a whole box of the things — two or three hundred. After the lighting, one stick was placed in the center of a jar of sand. That was the Zen stick. Then Roy was asked to place his burning stick upon one side of the Zen stick, Hollis asked to place hers on the other.

But the sticks weren't quite right. The Zen master, smiling a bit, had to reach forward and adjust the sticks to new depths and elevations.

Then the Zen master dug out a circle of brown beads.

He handed the circle of beads to Roy.

"Now?" asked Roy.

Damn, I thought, Roy always read up on everything else. Why not his own wedding?

Zen reached forward, placed Hollis' right hand within Roy's left. And the beads encircled both hands that way.

"Do you . . ."

48

"I do . . ."

(This was Zen? I thought.)

"And do you, Hollis . . ."

"I do . . ."

Meanwhile, in the candlelight, there was some asshole taking hundreds of photos of the ceremony. It made me nervous. It could have been the F.B.I.

"*Plick! Plick! Plick!*"

Of course, we were all clean. But it was irritating because it was careless.

Then I noticed the Zen master's ears in the candlelight. The candlelight shone through them as if they were made of the thinnest of toilet paper.

The Zen master had the thinnest ears of any man I had ever seen. *That* was what made him holy! I *had* to have those ears! For my wallet or my tomcat or my memory. Or for under the pillow.

Of course, I knew that it was all the scotch and water and all the beer talking to me, and then, in another way, I didn't know that at all.

I kept staring at the Zen master's ears.

And there were more words.

". . . and you Roy, promise not to take any drugs while in your relationship with Hollis?"

There seemed to be an embarrassing pause. Then, their hands locked together in the brown beads: "I promise," said Roy, "not to . . ."

Soon it was over. Or seemed over. The Zen master stood straight up, smiling just a touch of a smile.

I touched Roy upon a shoulder: "Congratulations."

Then I leaned over. Took hold of Hollis' head, kissed her beautiful lips.

Still everybody sat there. A nation of subnormals.

Nobody moved. The candles glowed like subnormal candles.

I walked over to the Zen master. Shook his hand: "Thank you. You did the ceremony quite well."

He seemed really pleased, which made me feel a little better. But the rest of those gangsters — old Tammany Hall and the Mafia: they were too proud and stupid to shake hands with an Oriental.

Only one other kissed Hollis. Only one other shook the hand of the Zen master. It could have been a shotgun wedding. All that *family!* Well, I'd be the last to know or the last to be told.

Now that the wedding was over, it seemed very cold in there. They just sat and stared at each other. I could never comprehend the human race, but *somebody* had to play clown. I ripped off my green necktie, flipped it into the air:

"HEY! YOU COCKSUCKERS! ISN'T ANYBODY HUNGRY?"

I walked over and started grabbing at cheese, pickled-pigs' feet and chicken cunt. A few stiffly warmed up, walked over and grabbed at the food, not knowing what else to do.

I got them to nibbling. Then I left and hit for the scotch and water.

As I was in the kitchen, refilling, I heard the Zen master say, "I must leave now."

"Oooh, don't leave . . ." I heard an old, squeaky and female voice from among the greatest gangland gathering in three years. And even she didn't sound as if she meant it. What was I doing in with these? Or the UCLA prof? No, the UCLA prof belonged there.

There must be a repentance. Or something. Some action to humanize the proceedings.

As soon as I heard the Zen master close the front door, I drained my waterglass full of scotch. Then I ran out through the candlelit room of jabbering bastards, found the door (that was a job, for a moment), and I opened the door, closed it, and there I was . . . about 15 steps behind Mr. Zen. We still had 45 or 50 steps to go to get down to the parking lot.

I gained upon him, lurching, two steps to his one.

I screamed: "Hey, Masta!"

Zen turned. "Yes, old man?"

Old man?

We both stopped and looked at each other on that winding stairway there in the moonlit tropical garden. It seemed like a time for a closer relationship.

Then I told him: "I either want both your motherfucking ears or your motherfucking outfit — that neon-lighted bathrobe you're wearing!"

"Old man, you are crazy!"

"I thought Zen had more moxie than to make unmitigated and offhand statements. You disappoint me, Masta!"

Zen placed his palms together and looked upward.

I told him, "I either want your motherfucking outfit or your motherfucking ears!"

He kept his palms together, while looking upward.

I plunged down the steps, missing a few but still flying forward, which kept me from cracking my head open, and as I fell downward toward him, I tried to swing, but I was all momentum, like something cut loose without direction. Zen caught me and straightened me.

"My son, my son . . ."

We were in close. I swung. Caught a good part of him. I heard him hiss. He stepped one step back. I swung again. Missed. Went way wide left. Fell into some imported plants from hell. I got up. Moved toward him again. And in the moonlight, I saw the front of my own pants — splattered with blood, candle-drippings and puke.

"You've met your master, bastard!" I notified him as I moved toward him. He waited. The years of working as a factotum had not left muscles entirely lax. I gave him one deeply into the gut, all 230 pounds of my body behind it.

Zen let out a short gasp, once again supplicated the sky, said something in the Oriental, gave me a short karate chop, kindly, and left me wrapped within a series of senseless Mexican cacti and what appeared to be, from my eye, man-eating plants from the inner Brazilian jungles. I relaxed in the moonlight until this purple flower seemed to gather toward my nose and began to delicately pinch out my breathing.

Shit, it took at least 150 years to break into the Harvard Classics. There wasn't any choice: I broke loose from the thing and started crawling up the stairway again. Near the top, I mounted to my feet, opened the door and entered. Nobody noticed me. They were still talking shit. I flopped into my corner. The karate shot had opened a cut over my left eyebrow. I found my handkerchief.

"Shit! I need a drink!" I hollered.

Harvey came up with one. All scotch. I drained it. Why was it that the buzz of human beings talking could be so senseless? I noticed the woman who had been introduced to me as the bride's mother was now showing plenty of leg, and it didn't look bad, all that long nylon with the expensive stiletto heels, plus the little jewel tips down near the toes. It could give an idiot the hots, and I was only half-idiot.

I got up, walked over to the bride's mother, ripped her skirt back to her thighs, kissed her quickly upon her pretty knees and began to kiss my way upward.

The candlelight helped. Everything.

"Hey!" she awakened suddenly, "whatcha think you're *doing?*"

"I'm going to fuck the shit out of you, I am going to fuck you until the shit falls outa your ass! Whatcha thinka that?"

She pushed and I fell backwards upon the rug. Then I was flat upon my back, thrashing, trying to get up.

"Damned Amazon!" I screamed at her.

Finally, three or four minutes later I managed to get to my feet. Somebody laughed. Then, finding my feet flat upon the floor again, I made for the kitchen. Poured a drink, drained it. Then poured a refill and walked out.

There they were: all the goddamned relatives.

"Roy or Hollis?" I asked. "Why don't you open your wedding gift?"

"Sure," said Roy, "why not?"

The gift was wrapped in 45 yards of tinfoil. Roy just kept unrolling the foil. Finally, he got it all undone.

"Happy marriage!" I shouted.

They all saw it. The room was very quiet.

It was a little handcrafted coffin done by the best artisans in Spain. It even had this pinkish-red felt bottom. It was the exact replica of a larger coffin, except perhaps it was done with more love.

Roy gave me his killer's look, ripped off the tag of instructions on how to keep the wood polished, threw it inside the coffin and closed the lid.

It was very quiet. The only gift hadn't gone over. But they soon gathered themselves and began talking shit again.

I became silent. I had really been proud of my little casket. I had looked for hours for a gift. I had almost gone crazy. Then I had seen it on the shelf, all alone. Touched the outsides, turned it up-side-down, then looked inside. The price was high but I was paying for the perfect craftsmanship. The wood. The little hinges. All. At the same time, I needed some ant-killer spray. I found some Black Flag in the back of the store. The ants had built a nest under my front door. I took the stuff to the counter. There was a young girl there, I set the stuff in front of her. I pointed to the casket.

"You know what that is?"

"What?"

"That's a casket!"

I opened it up and showed it to her.

"These ants are driving me crazy. Ya know what I'm going to do?"

"What?"

"I'm going to kill *all* those ants and put them in this casket and bury them!"

She laughed. "You've saved my whole day!"

You can't put it past the young ones anymore; they are an entirely superior breed. I paid and got out of there . . . .

But now, at the wedding, nobody laughed. A pressure cooker done up with a red ribbon would have left them happy. Or would it have?

Harvey, the rich one, finally, was kindest of all. Maybe because he could afford to be kind? Then I remembered something out of my readings, something from the ancient Chinese:

"Would you rather be rich or an artist?"

"I'd rather be rich, for it seems that the artist is always sitting on the doorsteps of the rich."

I sucked at the fifth and didn't care anymore. Somehow, the next thing I knew, it was over. I was in the back seat of my own car, Hollis driving again, the beard of Roy flowing into my face again. I sucked at my fifth.

"Look, did you guys throw my little casket away? I love you both, you know that! Why did you throw my little casket away?"

"Look, Bukowski! Here's your casket!"

Roy held it up to me, showed it to me.

"Ah, fine!"

"You want it back?"

"No! No! My gift to you! Your *only* gift! Keep it! Please!"

"All right."

The remainder of the drive was fairly quiet. I lived in a front court near Hollywood (of course). Parking was mean. Then they found a space about a half a block from where I lived. They parked my car, handed me the keys. Then I saw them walk across the street toward their own car. I watched them, turned to walk toward my place, and while still watching them and holding to the remainder of Harvey's fifth, I tripped one shoe into a pantscuff and went down. As I fell backwards, my first instinct was to protect the remainder of that good fifth from smashing against the cement (mother with baby), and as I fell backwards I tried to hit with my shoulders, holding both head and bottle up. I saved the bottle but the head flipped back into the sidewalk, BASH!

They both stood and watched me fall. I was stunned almost into insensibility but managed to scream across the street at them: "Roy! Hollis! Help me to my front door, please I'm hurt!"

They stood a moment, looking at me. Then they got into their car, started the engine, leaned back and neatly drove off.

I was being repaid for something. The casket? Whatever it had been — the use of my car, or me as clown and/or best man . . . my use had been outworn. The human race had always disgusted me. Essentially, what made them disgusting was the family-relationship illness, which included marriage, exchange of power and aid, which like a sore, a leprosy, became then: your next door neighbor, your neighborhood, your district, your city, your county, your state, your nation . . . everybody grabbing each other's assholes in the honeycomb of survival out of a fear-animalistic stupidity.

I got it all there, I understood it as they left me there, pleading.

Five more minutes, I thought. If I can lay here five more minutes without being bothered I'll get up and make it toward my place, get inside. I was the last of the outlaws. Billy the Kid had nothing on me. Five more minutes. Just let me get to my cave. I'll mend. Next time I'm asked to one of *their* functions, I'll tell them where to put it. Five minutes. That's all I need.

Two women walked by. They turned and looked at me.

"Oh, look at him. What's wrong?"

"He's drunk."

"He's not sick, is he?"

"No, look how he holds to that bottle. Like a little baby."

Oh shit. I screamed up at them:

"I'LL SUCK BOTH YOUR SNATCHES! I'LL SUCK BOTH YOUR SNATCHES DRY, YOU CUNTS!"

"Ooooooh!"

They both ran into the high-rise glass apartment. Through the glass door. And I was outside unable to get up, best man to something. All I had to do was make it to my place – 30 yards away, as close as three million light years. Thirty yards from a rented front door. Two more minutes and I could get up. Each time I tried it, I got stronger. An old drunk would always make it, given enough time. One minute. One minute more. I could have made it.

Then there they were. Part of the insane family structure of the World. Madmen, really, hardly questioning what made them do what they did. They left their double-red light burning as they parked. Then got out. One had a flashlight.

"Bukowski," said the one with the flashlight, "you just can't seem to keep out of trouble, can you?"

He knew my name from somewhere, other times.

"Look," I said, "I just stumbled. Hit my head. I never lose my sense or my coherence. I'm not dangerous. Why don't you guys help me to my doorway? It's 30 yards away. Just let me fall upon my bed and sleep it off. Don't you think, really, that would be the really decent thing to do?"

"Sir, two ladies reported you as trying to rape them."

"Gentlemen, I would *never* attempt to rape two ladies at the same time."

The one cop kept flashing his stupid flashlight into my face. It gave him a great feeling of superiority.

"Just 30 yards to Freedom! Can't you guys understand that?"

"You're the funniest show in town, Bukowski. Give us a better alibi than that."

"Well, let's see – this thing you see sprawled here on the pavement is the end-product of a wedding, a Zen wedding."

"You mean some woman really tried to *marry* you?"

55

"Not *me,* you asshole . . ."

The cop with the flashlight brought it down across my nose.

"We ask respect toward officers of the law."

"Sorry. For a moment I forgot."

The blood ran down along my throat and then toward and upon my shirt. I was very tired — of everything.

"Bukowski," asked the one who had just used the flashlight, "why can't you stay out of trouble?"

"Just forget the horseshit," I said, "let's go off to jail."

They put on the cuffs and threw me into the back seat. Same sad old scene.

They drove along slowly, speaking of various possible and insane things — like, about having the front porch widened, or a pool, or an extra room in the back for Granny. And when it came to sports — these were *real* men — the Dodgers still had a chance, even with the two or three other teams right in there with them. Back to the family — if the Dodgers won, they won. If a man landed on the moon, *they* landed on the moon. But let a starving man ask them for a dime — no identification, fuck you, shithead. I mean, when they were in civvies. There hasn't been a starving man yet who ever asked a *cop* for a dime. Our record is clear.

Then I was pushed through the gristmill. After being 30 yards from my door. After being the only human in a house full of 59 people.

There I was, once again, in this type of long line of the somehow guilty. The young guys didn't know what was coming. They were mixed up with this thing called THE CONSTITUTION and their RIGHTS. The young cops, both in the city tank and the county tank, got their training on the drunks. They had to show they had it. While I was watching they took one guy in an elevator and rode him up and down, up and down, and when he got out, you hardly knew who he was, or what he had been — a black screaming about Human Rights. Then they got a white guy, screaming something about CONSTITUTIONAL RIGHTS; four or five of them got him, and they rushed him off his feet so fast he couldn't walk, and when they brought him back they leaned him against a wall, and he just stood there trembling, these red welts all over his body, he stood there trembling and shivering.

I got my photo taken all over again. Fingerprinted all over again.

They took me down to the drunk tank, opened that door. After that, it was just a matter of looking for floorspace among the 150 men in the room. One shitpot. Vomit and piss everywhere. I found a spot among my fellow men. I was Charles Bukowski, featured in the literary archives of the University of California at Santa Barbara. Somebody there thought I was a genius. I stretched out on the boards. Heard a young voice. A boy's voice.

"Mista, I'll suck your dick for a quarter!"

They were supposed to take all your change, bills, ident, keys, knives, so forth, plus cigarettes, and then you had the property slip. Which you either lost or sold or had stolen from you. But there was always still money and cigarettes about.

"Sorry, lad," I told him, "they took my last penny."

Four hours later I managed to sleep.

There.

Best man at a Zen wedding, and I'd bet they, the bride and groom, hadn't even fucked that night. But somebody had been.

REUNION

I got off the bus at Rampart, then walked one block back to Coronado, went up the little hill, went up the steps to the walk, walked along the walk to the doorway of my upper court. I stood in front of that door quite a while, feeling the sun on my arms. Then I found the key, opened the door and began climbing the stairway.

"Hello?" I heard Madge.

I didn't answer. I walked slowly up. I was very white and somewhat weak.

"Hello? Who is it?"

"Don't get jumpy, Madge, it's just me."

I stood at the top of the stairway. She was sitting on the couch in an old green silk dress. She had a glass of port in her hand, port with ice cubes, the way she liked it.

"Baby!" she jumped up. She seemed glad, kissing me.

"Oh Harry, are you really back?"

"Maybe. If I last. Anybody in the bedroom?"

"Don't be silly! Want a drink?"

"They say I can't. Have to eat boiled chicken, soft boiled eggs. They gave me a list."

"Oh, the bastards. Sit down. You want a bath? Something to eat?"

"No, just let me sit down."

I walked over and sat in the rocker.

"How much money is left?" I asked her.

"Fifteen dollars."

"You spent it fast."

"Well —"

"How much time we got on the rent?"

"Two weeks. I couldn't find a job."

"I know. Look, where's the car? I didn't see it out there."

58

"Oh God, bad news. I loaned it to somebody. They crashed in the front. I was hoping to get it fixed for you before you got back. It's down at the corner garage."

"Does the car still run?"

"Yeah but I wanted to get the front fixed for you."

"You drive a car like that with a banged-up front. It doesn't matter as long as the radiator is okay, and you have headlights."

"Well, Jesus! I was just trying to do the right thing!"

"I'll be right back," I told her.

"Harry, where ya going?"

"To check on the car."

"Why don't you wait until tomorrow, Harry? You don't look good. Stay with me. Let's talk."

"I'll be back. You know me. I don't like unfinished business."

"Oh shit, Harry!"

I began to walk down the stairway. Then I walked back up.

"Give me the fifteen dollars."

"Oh shit, Harry!"

"Look, somebody's got to keep this boat from sinking. You're not going to do it, we know that."

"Honesta Christ, Harry, I got off my can. I got out of the sack every morning while you were gone. I couldn't find a damn thing."

"Give me the fifteen dollars."

Madge picked up her purse, looked into it.

"Look, Harry, leave me enough money for a bottle of wine tonight, this one's about gone. I wanta celebrate your being back."

"I know you do, Madge."

She reached into the purse and gave me a ten and four ones. I grabbed the purse and turned it upside-down on the couch. All her shit came out. Plus change, a small bottle of port, a dollar bill and a five dollar bill. She reached for the five but I got there first, straightened up and slapped her across the face.

"You bastard! You're still a mean son of a bitch, aren't you?"

"Yeah, that's why I didn't die."

"You hit me again and I'm pulling out!"

"You know I don't like to hit you, baby."

"Yeah, you'd hit me but you wouldn't hit a man, would you?"

"What the hell's that got to do with it?"

I took the five, walked down the stairway again.

The garage was around the corner. As I walked onto the lot this Japanese guy was putting silver paint on a newly installed grille. I stood there.

"Jesus, you're making a Rembrandt out of it," I told him.

"This your car, mister?"

"Yeah. What do I owe you?"

"Seventy-five dollars."

"What?"

"Seventy-five dollars. A lady brought it in here."

"A whore brought it in here. Now look, that whole car wasn't worth seventy-five dollars. It still isn't. You bought that grille for five bucks at the junkyard."

"Look, mister, the lady said —"

"Who?"

"Well, that woman said —"

"I'm not responsible for her, man. I just got out of the hospital. Now I'll pay you what I can when I can, but I don't have a job and I need that car to get a job. I'm going to need it now. If I get a job I can pay you. If I don't, I can't. Now, if you don't trust me you'll just have to keep the car. I'll give you the pink slip. You know where I live. I'll walk up there and get it if you say so."

"How much money can you give me now?"

"Five bucks."

"That's not much."

"I told you, I just got out of the hospital. After I get a job I can pay you off. Either that, or you keep the car."

"All right," he said, "I trust you. Give me the five."

"You don't know how hard I worked for that five."

"What do you mean?"

"Forget it."

He took the five and I took the car. It started. The tank was even half-full. I didn't worry about the oil and water. I drove it around the block a couple of times just to see how it felt to drive a car again. It felt good. Then I drove it up outside the liquor store.

"Harry!" said the old guy in the dirty white apron.

"Oh, Harry!" said his wife.

"Where you been?" asked the old guy in the dirty white apron.

"Arizona. Working on a land deal."

"See, Sol," said the old gal, "I always told you he was a smart man. He looks like brains."

"All right," I said, "I want two six-packs of Miller's in the bottle, on the tab."

"Now wait a minute," said the old guy.

"What's wrong? Haven't I always paid my tab? What's this shit?"

"Oh, you've been fine, Harry. It's her. She's run up a tab for . . . let me see here . . . it's thirteen-seventy-five."

"Thirteen-seventy-five, that's nothing. I've had that thing up to twenty-eight bucks and cleaned it up, haven't I?"

"Yes, Harry but —"

"But what? You want me to take it somewhere else? You want me to leave the tab? You won't trust me for two lousy six-packs after all these years?"

"All right, Harry," said the old guy.

"Okay, throw it in the bag. And a pack of Pall Malls and two Dutch Masters."

"Okay, Harry, okay . . ."

Then I was going up the steps again. I reached the top.

"Oh, Harry, you got beer! Don't drink it, Harry. I don't want you to die, baby!"

"I know you don't, Madge. But the medics never know shit. Now open me a beer. I'm tired. I've been doing too much. I've only been out of that place two hours."

Madge came out with the beer and a glass of wine for herself. She'd put on her high heels and she crossed her legs high. She still had it. As far as body went.

"Did you get the car?"

"Yeah."

"That little Jap is a nice guy, isn't he?"

"He had to be."

"What do you mean? Didn't he fix the car?"

"Yeah. He's a nice guy. He been up here?"

"Harry, don't start shit now! I don't fuck them Japs!"

She stood up. Her belly was still flat. Her haunches, hips, ass, just right. What a whore. I drained a half a bottle of beer, walked up to her.

"You know I'm crazy about you, Madge, babe, I'd kill for you, you know that don't you?"

I was up real close to her. She gave me a little smile. I tossed my beer bottle off, then took the wine glass out of her hand and drained it. I was feeling like a decent human being for the first time in weeks. We got real close. She pursed those red wild lips. Then I pushed against her, hard, with both hands. She fell back on the couch.

"You whore! You ran up a tab at Goldbarth's for thirteen-seventy-five, didn't you?"

"I dunno."

Her dress was pulled back high over her legs.

"You whore!"

"Don't call me a whore!"

"Thirteen-seventy-five!"

"I dunno whatcher talkin' about!"

I climbed up on her, got her head back and started kissing her, feeling her breasts, her legs, her hips. She was crying.

"Don't ... call me ... a ... whore ... don't, don't ... You know I love you, Harry!"

Then I leaped back and stood in the center of the rug.

"I'm going to lay the works into you, baby!"

Madge just laughed.

Then I walked up and picked her up and carried her into the bedroom and dumped her on the bed.

"Harry, you just got outa the hospital!"

"Which means you got a couple weeks' worth of sperm coming!"

"Don't talk filthy!"

"Fuck you!"

I leaped into bed, my clothing already ripped off.

I worked her dress up, kissing and fondling her. She was a lot of meat-woman.

I got the pants down. Then, like old times, I was in.

I sliced it eight or ten good slow ones, easy. Then she said, "You don't think I'd fuck a dirty Jap, do you?"

"I think you'd fuck a dirty anything."

She pulled her box back and dropped me out.

"What the shit?" I screamed.

"I love you, Harry, you know I love you; it hurts me when you talk like that!"

"Okay, baby, I know you wouldn't fuck a dirty Jap. I was just kidding."

Madge's legs opened up and I dropped back in.

"Oh, daddy, it's been a long time!"

"Has it?"

"Whatcha mean? You're starting some shit again!"

"No I'm not, baby! I love you, baby!"

I pulled my head up and kissed her, riding.

"Harry," she said.

"Madge," I said.

She was right.

It had been a long time.

I owed the liquor store thirteen-seventy-five plus two six-packs plus cigars and cigarettes and I owed the L.A. County General Hospital $225, and I owed the dirty Jap $70 and there were some minor utility bills, and we clutched each other and the walls closed in.

We made it.

CUNT AND KANT AND A HAPPY HOME

Jack Hendley took the escalator up into the clubhouse. he didn't really take it into the clubhouse — he just rode up on the damn thing.

53rd. racing program. night. got the program from old grey — 40 cents, flipped to the first page — mile and one eighth pace, 25 hundred dollar claimer — you could get a horse cheaper than a new car.

Jack-stepped off the escalator and heaved into the trashcan nearby. god damn whiskey nights were killing him. should have got the reds from Eddie before Eddie left town. but it had been a good week anyhow, a $600 week, which was a long way from that 17 bucks a week he once worked for in New Orleans, 1940.

but his whole afternoon had been mutilated by a door-tapper and Jack had gotten out of bed and let the guy in — a snippet — and the snippet sat on his couch for 2 hours — talking about LIFE. only thing was, the snippet didn't know anything about LIFE. the punk just talked about it, didn't bother to live it.

the snippet did manage to drink Jack's beer, smoke Jack's smokes, and keep him from getting at the Form, from getting his pre-race work done.

the next guy who bothers me, so help me, the very next guy who bothers me, I am going to lay it into him. otherwise they will eat you up, one by one, one after the other, until you are done, he thought. I'm not the cruel type, but they are, and that's the secret.

he hit for a coffee. there were the old men hanging about, staring and joking with the coffee girls. what miserable and lonely dead meat they were.

Jack lit a smoke, gagged, tossed it off. found a spot in the stands, down front, nobody around. with luck and nobody bothering him, he might be able to line up the card. But — there were always the dead dogs — guys with nothing but TIME, nothing to do — no knowledge, no program (the form at the harness was enclosed in the program); they had nothing to do but creep about, looking and sniffing. they came hours early, vacant, all vacant, and simply stood.

the coffee was good, hot. clear clean cold air. not even any fog. Jack was beginning to feel better. he got out his pen and began to mark up the first race. he might get out yet. that son of a bitch talking away his afternoon from his couch, that son of a bitch had put him on the cross. it was going to be close, very close — he had just an hour to first post to figure the whole card. it couldn't be done between races — the crowd was too much there and you had to watch the lay-ins on the tote.

he got to inking up the first race. so far — fine.

then he heard it. a dead dog. Jack had seen him staring out over the parking lot as he came down the steps to his seat. now the dead dog was tired of playing "look-at-automobiles." he was coming toward Jack, a step at a time, middle-aged guy in overcoat. no eyes, no vibration. dead meat. a dead dog in an overcoat.

the dead dog moved slowly toward him. one human being to another, yes. brotherhood, yes. Jack heard him. he'd reach a step, then stop. then take another step down.

Jack turned and looked at the bastard. the dead dog just stood there in his overcoat. there wasn't another person within a hundred yards but the dog just had to come sniffing at him.

Jack put his pen back in his pocket. then the dog stepped right up behind him and looked over his shoulder at his program. Jack cursed, folded the program, got up and took a seat 30 yards to the left, over by the next aisle.

he opened the program and began again, at the same time thinking of the racetrack crowd — an immense and stupid animal, it was, greedy, lonely, vicious, impolite, dull, hostile, egotistical and hooked. unfortunately, the world was molested with billions of people who had nothing to do with their time except murder it and murder you.

he was halfway through the first race, inking it in, when he heard it again. the slow steps down toward him. he looked around. he couldn't believe it. it was the same dog!

Jack folded the program, stood up.

"what do you want with me, Mr.?" he asked the dog.

"whatcha mean?"

"I mean, why do you come around poking over my shoulder? there are a couple of miles of space around here and you keep ending up next to me. now what the hell do you want?"

"it's a free country, I . . ."

"it's not a free country — everything is bought and sold and owned."

"I mean, I can walk around anywhere I want to. I paid to get in here just like you. I can walk anywhere I want."

"sure you can as long as you don't fuck with my privacy. you're being rude and stupid. like they say, man, you're BUGGING me."

"I paid to get in here. you can't tell me what to do."

"all right, it's up to you. I'm moving my seat again. I'm doing all I can to control myself. but if you come up on me a THIRD TIME, I promise you this — I'm going to belt you out!"

Jack moved his seat again and he saw the dog move off in search of another victim. but the bastard was still laying across his mind and Jack had to move up to the bar and get a scotch and water.

when he got back the horses were already on the track warming up for the first race. he tried to line up the first race but the crowd was there now. some guy with a megaphone voice, drunk, telling people he hadn't missed a Saturday at the races since 1945. a complete subnormal idiot. a good guy. wait until the fog came in some night and they sent him back to his lonely closet for a hand-job.

well, thought Jack, I'm on the cross. be kind and they put you on the cross. that son of a bitch on his couch talking about Mahler and Kant and cunt and revolution, not really knowing about any of them.

he'd have to play the first race cold. 2 minutes to post. one minute. he pushed through the daily double mob. zero. "here they come!" came the call. a guy walked over both his feet. he was bayoneted by an elbow, a pickpocket bounced off his left haunch.

rat-dog crowd. he went for Windale Ladybird. shit, the morning line favorite. standard play. he was losing his head early.

Kant and cunt. dogs.

Jack moved on out toward the far end of the stands. the car had the rolling starting gate and the horses were just about up to the beginning of the mile and one eighth.

he hadn't made his seat when here came another dog. in trance-like state. head staring up at something in the rafters. body moving directly at him. there was no way out. a crash. as they ran together Jack pushed his elbow out, dug it deep into the soft gut. the guy bounced off and groaned.

when he got to his seat, Windale Ladybird had opened up 4 lengths on the turn for home. Bobby Williams was going to try to steal a mile and an eighth. but the horse didn't look live to Jack. after 15 years at the races he could instinctively tell by the stride whether a horse was running easy or hard. the Ladybird was straining — 4 lengths but she was praying.

3 at the top of the stretch. then Hobby's Record moved out. that horse was stepping briskly and high. Jack was dead. at the top of the stretch with 3 lengths, he was dead. 15 yards from the wire Hobby's Record rolled past by what looked like a length and one half. a good 7/2 second choice.

Jack tore up 4 five dollar win tickets. Kant and cunt, I should go home now. save the roll. this is one of those nights.

the 2nd race, a one mile pace, happened to be simple. you didn't need a time-class breakdown. the crowd was buying Ambro Indigo, because of an inside post, early foot and Joe O'Brien in the bike. the other contender, Gold Wave was stuck on the outside, post 9, with the unheralded Don McIlmurray. if they were all that easy he would have been in Beverly Hills ten years ago. but still, because the first race had gone bad, because of Kant and cunt, Jack went 5 win.

then Good Candy got the late action on the total money-earned gimmick and all the boys came running to get on Good Candy. Candy had dropped from a morning line of 20 down to 9. now it read 8. the boys went insane. Jack smelled the fish and just tried to get out of the way. then a GIANT came rushing at him — the son of a bitch must have been 8 feet tall — where'd he come from? Jack had never seen him before.

the GIANT wanted CANDY and all he could see was the window, and the car was rolling the gate toward the beginning line. the guy was young, tall, wide, stupid, pounding the floor toward Jack. Jack tried to duck. too late. the giant gave him an elbow across the temple, knocked him 15 feet. red, blue, yellow, blue shots of light spun the air.

"hey, you son of a bitch!" Jack yelled at the giant. but the giant was leaning into the win window buying losing tickets. Jack got back to his seat.

Gold Wave came around the curve with 3 lengths at the top of the stretch. and stepping easy. it was a walkaway at 4 to one. but Jack only had 5 win, which put him $6.50 up. well, it beat sweeping shit.

he lost the 3rd., 4th. and 5th. races, hooked Lady Be Fast, 6 to one in the 6th., went to Beautiful Handover, 8/5 in the 7th., got away with it and was riding a mere $30 high, merely on instinct, then put 20 win on Propensity in the 8th., 3 to one, and Propensity broke at the start and there went that.

one more scotch and water. this whole thing, no pre-race set-up, it was like trying to screw a beachball in a dark closet. go home — dying was a little easier with a breather now and then at Acapulco.

Jack looked over at the girls showing it from the chairs against the wall. that clubhouse stuff was nice and clean, good to look at. but it was there to take the money away from the winners. he allowed himself to enjoy the girls' legs for a few moments. then turned to the tote. he felt a hip and leg up against him. a touch of breast, the faintest of perfume.

"say, mista, pardon me."

"sure."

she put her flank against him good. all he had to do was say the magic words and he had a 50 dollar piece of ass, but he'd never seen a piece of ass worth 50 dollars.

"yeh." he asked.

"who's the 3 horse?"

"May Western."

"you think she'll win?"

"not against these. maybe next time in a little better spot."

"I just need a horse in the money. who do you think will be in the money?"

"you will," Jack said and then slid away from her flank.

cunt and Kant and a happy home.

they were still buying May Western and Brisk Risk was dropping.

ONE MILE PACE, FILLIES AND MARES, NON-WINNERS OF $10,000 IN 1968. horses made more than most men did, only they couldn't spend it.

a stretcher on rollers slid by with an old grey-haired woman under the blankets.

the tote whirled around. Brisk Risk dropped again. May Western flicked up a notch.

"hey, mista!"

it was a man's voice behind him.

Jack was concentrating on the tote.

"yeah?"

"lemme have a quarter."

Jack didn't turn around. he reached into his pocket and got the quarter. he put it into the palm of his hand and put the hand around behind his back. he felt the fingers dip into his hand, get the quarter.

he never saw the guy. the board read zero.

"here they come!"

oh, shit.

he hit the ten dollar window, got one win ticket on PIXIE DEW, 20 to one and two tickets on CECELIA, 7/2. he didn't know what he was doing. there was a certain way of doing things, of fighting bulls of making love of frying eggs of drinking water and wine, and if you didn't do them right you choked on them, they could kill you.

Cecelia took the lead and took them down the backstretch. Jack checked the stride of the horse. a chance. it wasn't straining yet and the driver had a light hold. a fair shot. so far. but the horse behind looked better. Jack checked the program. Kimpam, 12 on the line, off at 25, the crowd hadn't wanted it. the horse had Joe O'Brien in the bike but Joe had failed on the same horse at 9 to one, two races back. the perfect blind. Lighthill let out all the string on Cecelia, Cecelia was open, throttle down, Lighthill had to steal it or chuck it. there was a chance. he had 4 lengths at the head of the stretch. O'Brien let Lighthill take the 4. then he leaned forward and let Kimpam go. shit, no, not at 25 to one, thought Jack. high-rein that mare, Lighthill. we got 4. let's go. 20 win at 7/2 can be 98 bucks. we can save the night.

he checked Cecelia. the legs were not lifting high at the knees. cunt and Kant and Kimpam. Cecelia shortened stride, almost stopped at midstretch. O'Brien sailed by with his 25 to one, rocking in the bike, flipping the reins, talking to the horse.

then Pixie Dew came running on out from the outside, Ackerman giving the 20 to one shot all the string it needed and going to the whip — 20 times ten, 200 bucks plus change. Ackerman closed down to a length and a few Chinese tokens to O'Brien, and that's the way they came down — O'Brien holding that space open, clucking to his horse, sailing by, smiling just a bit, as he does, and it was over. Kimpam, chestnut mare 4, by Irish-Meadow Wick. Irish? and O'Brien? shit, it was too much. the insane hat-pin ladies from the madhouses of hell had finally got themselves one.

the two dollar win and two dollar show windows were filled with little old ladies on pension checks with half pints of gin in their purses.

Jack took the stairway down. the escalators were jammed. he switched his wallet to left front pocket to get the pickpockets off. they hit his left rear pocket 5 or 6 times a night, but all he ever gave them was a broken-toothed comb and an old handkerchief.

he got to his car, got out with the jam, managed not to get a fender ripped off, the fog was coming down good now. but he made it up North without trouble, except getting near his place he saw something good in the fog, young, short dress, hitch-hiking, oh mother, he tapped his brake, good legs but by the time he slowed he was 50 yards from her with other cars behind him. well, let her get raped by some idiot. he wasn't going to circle back.

he checked for lights in his place, nobody there, good. he made it in, sat down, split the next day's Form with his thumb, opened the half pint, a can of beer and got to work. he'd been there 5 minutes when the phone began to ring. he looked up, gave the phone the finger, bent down over the Form again. the old pro was back in business.

in two hours a tall six pack was gone and a half pint of whiskey and he was in bed, asleep, the next day's card completely worked out, and a small smile of surety on his face. there were dozens of ways a man could go mad.

GOODBYE WATSON

it's after a bad day at the track that you realize that you will never make it, coming in stinking at the socks, a few wrinkled dollars in your wallet, you know that the miracle will never arrive, and worse, thinking about the really bad bet you made on the last race on the eleven horse, knowing it couldn't win, the biggest sucker bet on the board at 9/2, all the knowledge of your years ignored, you going up to the ten buck window and saying, "eleven twice!" and the old grey-haired boy at the window, asking again: "eleven?" he always asks again when I pick a real bad one. he may not know the actual winner but he knows the sucker bets, and he gives me the saddest of looks and takes the twenty. then to go out and watch that dog run last all the way, not even working at it, just loafing as your brain starts saying, "what the fuck, I gotta be crazy."

I've discussed this thing with a friend of mine who has many years at the track. he's often done the same thing and he calls it the "death-wish," which is old stuff. we yawn at the term now, but strangely, there's still some basis in it yet. a man does get tired as the races progress and there IS this tendency to throw the whole game overboard. the feeling can come upon one whether he is winning or losing and then the bad bets begin. But, I feel, a more real problem is that you ACTUALLY want to be somewhere else — sitting in a chair reading Faulkner or making drawings with your child's crayons. the racetrack is just another JOB, finally, and a hard one too. when I sense this and I am at my best, I simply leave the track; when I sense this and I am not at my best I go on making bad bets. another thing that one should realize is that it is HARD to win at anything; losing is easy. it's grand to be The Great American Loser — anybody can do it; almost everybody does.

a man who can beat the horses can do almost anything he makes up his mind to do. he doesn't belong at the racetrack. he should be on the Left Bank with his mother easel or in the East Village writing an avant-garde symphony. or making some woman happy. or living in a cave in the hills.

but to go the racetrack helps you realize yourself and the mob too. there's a lot of murky downgrading of Hemingway now by critics who can't write, and old ratbeard wrote some bad things from the middle to the end, but his head was becoming unscrewed, and even then he made the others look like schoolboys raising their hands for permission to make a little literary peepee. I know why Ernie went to the bull-fights — it was simple: it helped his writing. Ernie was a mechanic: he liked to fix things on paper. the bullfights were a drawingboard of everything: Hannibal slapping elephant ass over mountain or some wino slugging his woman in a cheap hotel room. and when Hem got in to the typer he wrote standing up. he used it like a gun. a weapon. the bullfights were everything attached to anything. it was all in his head like a fat butter sun: he wrote it down.

with me, the racetrack tells me quickly where I am weak and where I am strong, and it tells me how I feel that day and it tells me how much we keep changing, changing ALL the time, and how little we know of this.

and the stripping of the mob is the horror movie of the century. ALL of them lose. look at them. if you are able. one day at a racetrack can teach you more than four years at any university. if I ever taught a class in creative writing, one of my prerequisites would be that each student must attend a racetrack once a week and place at least a 2 dollar win wager on each race. no show betting. people who bet to show REALLY want to stay home but don't know how.

my students would automatically become better writers, although most of them would begin to dress badly and might have to walk to school.

I can see myself teaching Creative Writing now.

"well, how did you do Miss Thompson?"

"I lost $18."

"who did you bet in the feature race?"

"One-Eyed Jack."

"sucker bet. the horse was dropping 5 pounds which draws the crowd in but also means a step-up in class within allowance conditions. the only time a class-jump wins is when he looks bad on paper. One-Eyed Jack showed the highest speed-rating, another crowd draw, but the speed rating was for 6 furlongs and 6 furlong speed ratings are always higher, on a comparative basis, than speed ratings for route races. furthermore, the horse closed at 6 so the crowd figured he would be there at a mile and a sixteenth. One-Eyed Jack has now shown a race around in 2 curves in 2 years. this is no accident. the horse is a sprinter and only a sprinter. that he came in last at 3 to one should not have been a surprise."

"how did you do?"

"I lost one hundred and forty dollars."

"who did you bet in the feature race?"

"One-Eyed Jack. class dismissed." —

before the racetrack and before the sterilized unreal existence of the t.v. brain-suck, I was working as a packer in a huge factory that turned out thousands of overhead lighting fixtures to blind the world, and knowing the libraries useless and the poets carefully complaining fakes, I did my studying at the bars and boxing matches.

those were the nights, the old days at the Olympic. they had a bald little Irishman making the announcements (was his name Dan Tobey?), and he had *style,* he'd seen things happen, maybe even on the riverboats when he was a kid, and if he wasn't *that* old, maybe Dempsey-Firpo anyhow. I can still see him reaching up for that cord and pulling the mike down slowly, and most of us were drunk before the first fight, but we were easy drunk, smoking cigars, feeling the light of life, waiting for them to put 2 boys in there, cruel but that was the way it worked, that is what they did to us and we were still alive, and, yes, most of with a dyed redhead or blonde. even me. her name was Jane and we had many a good ten-rounder between us, one of them ending in a k.o. of me. and I was proud when she'd come back from the lady's room and the whole gallery would begin to pound and whistle and howl as she wiggled that big magic marvelous ass in that tight skirt — and it *was* a magic ass: she could lay a man stone cold and gasping, screaming love-words to a cement sky. then she'd come down and sit beside me and I'd lift that pint like a coronet, pass it to her, she'd take her nip, hand it back, and I'd say about the boys in the galley: "those screaming jackoff bastards, I'll kill them."

and she'd look at her program and say, "who do you want in the first?"

74

I picked them good – about 90 percent – but I had to see them first. I always chose the guy who moved around the least, who looked like he didn't want to fight, and if one guy gave the Sign of the Cross before the bell and the other guy didn't you had a winner – you took the guy who didn't. but it usually worked together. the guy who did all the shadow boxing and dancing around usually was the one who gave the Sign of the Cross and got his ass whipped.

there weren't many bad fights in those days and if there were it was the same as now – mostly between the heavyweights. but we let them know about it in those days – we tore the ring down or set the place on fire, busted up the seats. they just couldn't afford to give us too many bad ones. the Hollywood Legion ran the bad ones and we stayed away from the Legion. even the Hollywood boys knew the action was at the Olympic. Raft came, and the others, and all the starlets, hugging those front row seats. the gallery boys went ape and the fighters fought like fighters and the place was blue with cigar smoke, and how we screamed, baby baby, and threw money and drank our whiskey, and when it was over, there was the drive in, the old lovebed with our dyed and vicious women. you slammed it home, then slept like a drunk angel. who needed the public library? who needed Ezra? T.S.? E.E.? D.H.? H.D.? any of the Eliots? any of the Sitwells?

I'll never forget the first night I saw young Enrique Balanos. at the time. I had me a good colored boy. he used to bring a little white lamb into the ring with him before the fight and hug it, and that's corny but he was tough and good and a tough and good man is allowed certain leeways, right?

anyway, he was my hero, and his name might have been something like Watson Jones. Watson had good class and the flair – swift, quick quick quick, and the PUNCH, and he *enjoyed* his work. but then, one night, unannounced, somebody slipped this young Balanos in against him, and Balanos had it, took his time, slowly worked Watson down and took him over, busted him up good near the end. my hero. I couldn't believe it. if I remember, Watson was kayoed which made it a very bitter night, indeed. me with my pint screaming for mercy, screaming for a victory that simply would *not* happen. Balanos certainly had it – the fucker had a couple of snakes for arms, and he didn't *move* – he slid, slipped, jerked like some type of

75

evil spider, always getting there, doing the thing. I knew that night that it would take a very excellent man to beat him and that Watson might as well take his little lamb and go home.

it wasn't until much later that night, the whiskey pouring into me like the sea, fighting with my woman, cursing her sitting there showing me all that fine leg, that I admitted that the better man had won.

"Balanos. good legs. he doesn't think. just reacts. better not to think. tonight the body beat the soul. it usually does. goodbye Watson, goodbye Central Avenue, it's all over."

I smashed the glass against the wall and went over and grabbed me some woman. I was wounded. she was beautiful. we went to bed. I remember a light rain came through the window. we let it rain on us. it was good. it was so good we made love twice and when we went to sleep we slept with our faces toward the window and it rained all over us and in the morning the sheets were all wet and we both got up sneezing and laughing, "jesus christ! jesus christ!" it was funny and poor Watson laying somewhere, his face slugged and pulpy, facing the Eternal Truth, facing the 6 rounders, the 4 rounders, then back to the factory with me, murdering 8 or ten hours a day for pennies, getting nowhere, waiting on Papa Death, getting your mind kicked to hell and your spirit kicked to hell, we sneezed, "jesus christ!" it was funny and she said, "you're blue all over, you've turned all BLUE! jesus, look at yourself in the mirror!" and I was freezing and dying and I stood in front of the mirror and I was all BLUE! ridiculous! a skull and shit of bones! I began to laugh, I laughed so hard I fell down on the rug and she fell down on top of me and we both laughed laughed laughed, jesus christ we laughed until I thought we were crazy, and then I had to get up, get dressed, comb my hair, brush my teeth, too sick to eat, heaved when I brushed my teeth, I went outside and walked toward the overhead lighting factory, just the sun feeling good but you had to take what you could get.

GREAT POETS DIE IN STEAMING POTS OF SHIT

let me tell you about him. with sick hangover I crawled out from under the sheets the other day to try to get to the store, buy some food, place food inside of me and make the job I hate. all right. I was in this grocery store, and this little shit of a man (he must have been as old as I) but perhaps more comfortable and stupid and idiotic, a chipmunk full of beatlenuts and BOW WOW and no regard for anything except the way *he* felt or thought or expressed . . . he was a hyena-chipmunk, a piece of sloth. a slug. he kept staring at me. then he said:

HEY!!!

he walked on up and stood there staring. HEY! he said HEY! he had very round eyes and he stood there staring up at me from out of those very round eyes. the eyes had bottoms like the dirty bottoms of swimmingpools — no reflection. I didn't have but a few minutes, had to rush. I had missed the job the day before and had already been counciled — god knows how many times — for excessive absenteeism. I really wanted to walk away from him but I was too sick to gather myself. he looked like the manager of an apartment house I had once lived in a few years back. one of those who was always standing in the hall at 3 a.m. when you entered with a strange woman.

he kept staring so I said, I CAN'T REMEMBER YOU. I'M SORRY, I JUST CAN'T REMEMBER YOU. I'M JUST NOT VERY GOOD AT THAT SORT OF THING. meanwhile, thinking, why don't you go away? why do you have to *be* here? I don't *like* you.

I WAS AT YOUR PLACE, he said. OVER THERE, he pointed. he turned around and pointed south and east, where I had never lived.worked, but never lived. good, I thought, he's a nut. I don't know him. never knew him. I'm free. I can shove him off.

SORRY, I said, BUT YOU'RE MISTAKEN — I DON'T KNOW YOU. NEVER LIVED OVER THERE. SORRY, MAN.

I started to push my basket off.

WELL, MAYBE NOT THERE. BUT I KNOW YOU. IT WAS A PLACE IN THE BACK, YOU LIVED IN A PLACE IN THE BACK, ON THE SECOND FLOOR. IT WAS ABOUT A YEAR AGO.

SORRY, I told him, BUT I DRINK TOO MUCH. I FORGET PEOPLE. I DID LIVE IN A PLACE IN BACK, SECOND FLOOR, BUT THAT WAS 5 YEARS AGO.

LISTEN, I'M AFRAID YOU'RE MIXED UP. I'M IN A HURRY, REALLY. I HAVE TO GO, I'M REALLY DOWN TO THE MINUTE NOW.

I rolled on off toward the meat dept.

He ran along beside me.

YOU'RE BUKOWSKI, AREN'T YOU?

YES, I AM.

I WAS THERE. YOU JUST DON'T REMEMBER. YOU WERE DRINKING.

WHO THE HELL BROUGHT YOU OVER?

NOBODY. I CAME ON MY OWN. I WROTE A POEM ABOUT YOU. YOU DON'T REMEMBER. BUT YOU DIDN'T LIKE IT.

UMM, I said.

I ONCE WROTE A POEM TO THAT GUY WHO WROTE 'THE MAN WITH THE GOLDEN ARM.' WHAT'S HIS NAME?

ALGREN. NELSON ALGREN, I said.

YEAH, he said. I WROTE A POEM ABOUT HIM. SENT IT TO THIS MAGAZINE. THE EDITOR SUGGESTED THAT I SEND THE POEM TO HIM. ALGREN WROTE BACK, HE WROTE ME BACK A NOTE ON A RACING FORM. 'THIS IS MY LIFE,' HE WROTE ME.

FINE, I said, SO WHAT'S YOUR NAME?

IT DOESN'T MATTER. MY NAME IS 'LEGION.'

VERY FUNNY, I smiled. we trotted along, then stopped. I reached over and got a package of hamburger. then I decided to give him the brushoff. I took the hamburger and stuck it in his hand and shook his hand with it, saying, WELL, OK, GOOD TO SEE YOU, BUT MAN, REALLY, I'VE GOT TO GO.

then I shifted into high and pushed my basket out of there. toward the bread dept. he wouldn't shake.

ARE YOU STILL IN THE POST OFFICE? he asked, trotting along.

I'M AFRAID SO.

YOU OUGHT TO GET OUT OF THERE. IT'S A HORRIBLE PLACE. IT'S THE WORST PLACE YOU CAN BE.

I THINK IT IS. BUT YOU SEE, I CAN'T DO ANYTHING, I DON'T HAVE ANY SPECIAL TRAINING.

YOU'RE A GREAT POET, MAN.

GREAT POETS DIE IN STEAMING POTS OF SHIT.

BUT YOU'VE GOT ALL THAT RECOGNITION FROM THE LEFT-WING PEOPLE. CAN'T ANYBODY DO ANYTHING FOR YOU?

left-wing people? this guy *was* crazy. we trotted along.

I HAVE RECOGNITION. FROM MY BUDDIES AT THE POST OFFICE. I'M RECOGNIZED AS A LUSH AND A HORSE-PLAYER.

CAN'T YOU GET A GRANT OR SOMETHING?

I TRIED LAST YEAR. THE HUMANITIES. ALL I GOT BACK WAS A FORM-LETTER OF REJECTION.

BUT EVERY ASS IN THE COUNTRY IS LIVING ON A GRANT.

YOU FINALLY SAID SOMETHING.

DON'T YOU READ AT THE UNIVERSITIES?

I'D RATHER NOT. I CONSIDER IT PROSTITUTION. ALL THEY WANT TO DO IS . . .

he didn't let me finish. GINSBERG, he said, GINSBERG READS AT THE UNIVERSITIES. AND CREELEY AND OLSON AND DUNCAN AND . . .

I KNOW.

I reached over and got my bread.

THERE ARE ALL FORMS OF PROSTITUTION, he said.

now he was getting profound. jesus. I ran toward the vegetable dept.

LISTEN, COULD I SEE YOU AGAIN, SOMETIME?

MY TIME'S SHORT. REALLY TIGHT.

he found a matchbook. HERE, PUT YOUR ADDRESS DOWN IN HERE.

oh christ, I thought, how do you get out without hurting a man's feelings? I wrote the address down.

HOW ABOUT A PHONE NUMBER? he asked. SO YOU'LL
KNOW WHEN I'M COMING OVER.

NO, NO PHONE NUMBER. I handed the book back.

WHEN'S THE BEST TIME?

IF YOU'VE GOT TO COME, MAKE IT SOME FRIDAY
NIGHT AFTER 10.

I'LL BRING A SIX-PACK. AND I'LL HAVE TO BRING MY
WIFE. I'VE BEEN MARRIED 27 YEARS.

TOO BAD, I said.

OH NO. IT'S THE ONLY WAY.

HOW DO YOU KNOW? YOU DON'T KNOW ANY OTHER
WAY.

IT ELIMINATES JEALOUSY AND STRIFE. YOU OUGHT
TO TRY IT.

IT DOESN'T ELIMINATE, IT ADDS. AND I'VE TRIED IT.

OH YEAH, I REMEMBER READING IT IN ONE OF YOUR
POEMS. A RICH WOMAN.

we hit the vegetables. the frozen ones.

I WAS IN THE VILLAGE IN THE 30's. I KNEW BODEN-
HEIM. TERRIBLE. HE GOT MURDERED. LAYING AROUND IN
ALLEYS LIKE THAT. MURDERED OVER SOME TRASHY
WOMAN. I WAS IN THE VILLAGE THEN. I WAS A BOHEMIAN.
I'M NO BEAT. AND I'M NO HIPPY. DO YOU READ THE 'FREE
PRESS'?

SOMETIMES.

TERRIBLE.

he meant that he thought the hippies were terrible. he was
being profoundly sloppy.

I PAINT TOO. I SOLD A PAINTING TO MY PSYCHIA-
TRIST. $320. ALL PSYCHIATRISTS ARE SICK, VERY SICK
PEOPLE.

more 1933 profundity.

YOU REMEMBER THAT POEM YOU WROTE ABOUT GO-
ING DOWN TO THE BEACH AND CLIMBING DOWN THE CLIFF
TO THE SAND AND SEEING ALL THOSE LOVERS DOWN
THERE AND YOU WERE ALONE AND WANTED TO GET OUT
FAST, YOU GOT OUT SO FAST YOU LEFT YOUR SHOES
DOWN THERE WITH THEM. IT WAS A GREAT POEM ABOUT
LONELINESS.

it was a poem about how HARD it was to EVER GET alone, but I didn't tell him that.

I picked up a package of frozen potatoes and made for the check stand. he trotted along beside me.

I WORK AS A DISPLAYMAN. IN THE MARKETS. $154 A WEEK. I ONLY HIT THE OFFICE ONCE A WEEK. I WORK FROM ELEVEN A.M. TO FOUR P.M.

ARE YOU WORKING NOW?

OH YEAH, I'M WORKING ON DISPLAYS IN HERE NOW. WISH I HAD SOME INFLUENCE. I'D GET YOU ON.

the boy at the checkstand began tabbing the groceries.

HEY! my friend yelled, DON'T MAKE HIM PAY FOR THOSE GROCERIES! HE'S A POET!

the boy at the checkstand was all right. he didn't say anything. just went on tabbing it up.

my friend screamed again: HEY! HE'S A GREAT POET! DON'T MAKE HIM PAY FOR HIS GROCERIES.

HE LIKES TO TALK, I said to the checkstand boy.

the checkstand boy was all right. I paid and took my bag.

LISTEN, I'VE GOT TO GO, I said to my friend.

somehow, he could not leave the store. some fear. he wanted to keep his good job. wonderful. it felt very good to see him standing in there by the checkstand. not trotting along beside me.

I'LL BE SEEING YOU, he said.

I waved him away from under the bag.

outside were the parked cars, and the people walking around. none of them read poetry, talked poetry, wrote poetry. for once the masses looked very reasonable to me. I got to my car, threw the stuff in and sat there a moment. a woman got out of the car next to me and I watched as her skirt fell back and showed me flashes of white leg above the stockings. one of the world's greatest works of Art: a woman with fine legs climbing out of her car. she stood up and the skirt fell back down. for a moment she smiled at me, then she turned and moved it all, wobbling, balancing, shivering toward the grocery store. I started the car and backed out. I had almost forgotten my friend. but he wouldn't forget me. tonight he would say:

DEAR, GUESS WHO I SAW IN THE GROCERY TODAY? HE LOOKED ABOUT THE SAME, MAYBE NOT AS BLOATED. AND HE HAS THIS LITTLE THING ON HIS CHIN.

WHO WAS IT?

CHARLES BUKOWSKI.

WHO'S THAT?

A POET. HE'S SLIPPED. HE CAN'T WRITE AS WELL AS HE USED TO. BUT HE USED TO WRITE SOME GREAT STUFF. POEMS OF LONELINESS. HE'S REALLY A VERY LONELY FELLOW BUT HE DOESN'T KNOW IT. WE'RE GOING TO SEE HIM THIS FRIDAY NIGHT.

BUT I DON'T HAVE ANYTHING TO WEAR.

HE WON'T CARE. HE DOESN'T LIKE WOMEN.

HE DOESN'T LIKE WOMEN?

YEAH. HE TOLD ME.

LISTEN, GUSTAV, THE LAST POET WE WENT TO SEE WAS A TERRIBLE PERSON. WE HADN'T BEEN THERE MUCH MORE THAN AN HOUR AND HE GOT DRUNK AND STARTED THROWING BOTTLES ACROSS THE ROOM AND CUSSING.

THAT WAS BUKOWSKI. ONLY HE DOESN'T REMEMBER US.

NO WONDER.

BUT HE'S VERY LONELY. WE SHOULD GO SEE HIM.

ALL RIGHT, IF YOU SAY SO, GUSTAV.

THANK YOU, SWEETIE.

don't you wish you were Charles Bukowski? I can paint too. lift weights. and my little girl thinks that I am God.

then other times, it's not so good.

MY STAY IN THE POET'S COTTAGE

for those of you interested in madness, yours or mine, I can tell you a little about mine. I stayed at the poet's cottage at the University of Arizona, not because I am established but because nobody but a damn fool or a poor man ever visits or stays in Tucson in the summer months. it averaged around 106 degrees during my whole stay. nothing to do but drink beer. I am a poet who has made it known that I do not give readings. I am also a person who becomes quite a jackass when drunk. and when sober I don't have anything to say, so there weren't many knocks at the poet's cottage. and I didn't mind. except I had heard that there was a young colored maid, vury vury nicely built who came around once in a while, so I quietly laid plans to rape her, but she had evidently heard of me too and stayed away. so I scrubbed out my own bathtub; dumped out my own bottles into a large trashcan with painting on the top in black: UNIV. OF ARIZ. I usually heaved right into the top of the can after dumping my bottles around 11 a.m. each morning. then it was mostly a matter of going back to bed after my morning beer and trying to cool off and get well. poet-in-residence, indeed, drunk-in-residence would have been better. I drank around 4 or 5 six-packs a day and night.

well, the cooling system was not bad and with my balls just beginning to unlimber and my stomach getting straight, and my stick still thinking of the colored maid, and my soul still retching from the Creeley's etc. who had shit in the same shitter, slept in the same bed — about this time the phone would ring. it would be the great editor —

Bukowski?
yeh. yeh. I think so.
would you like some breakfast?
some *what?*

breakfast.

yeh. that's what I thought ya said.

my wife and I are kind of around the corner. how about meeting us at the campus cafeteria?

the campus cafeteria?

yes, we'll be there. all you have to do is to keep walking the opposite way of Speedway and just keep asking everybody you meet, WHERE IS THE CAMPUS CAFETERIA? just keep asking everybody you meet, WHERE IS THE CAMPUS CAFETERIA?

oooooooh, jesus . . .

what's wrong? all you have to do is to keep asking everybody you meet, WHERE IS THE CAMPUS CAFETERIA? we'll have breakfast together.

listen, let's put it off. not this morning.

well, o.k., buk, I only thought since we were out this way —

sure, thanks.

around after 3 or 4 beers and a bath and trying to read some of the books of poesy around there, and naturally finding them not well-written, they put me to sleep: Pound, Olson, Creeley, Shapiro. there were hundreds of books, old magazines. none of my books were there, not in that cottage, so it was a very dead place. when I awakened, it was another beer and a walk in the 100 plus heat 8 or 10 blocks to the great editor's place. I'd usually stop somewhere and pick up a couple of six-packs. they weren't drinking. they were getting old and having all sorts of physical troubles. it was sad. for them and for me. but her 81-year-old father almost matched me beer for beer. we liked each other.

I was out there to cut a record but when the Ariz. prof in charge of that sort of thing heard I was coming to town he ended up at St. Mary's hospital with an ulcer. on the day he was due to be discharged I phoned him personally while I was half drunk and they kept him in there 2 more days. so nothing to do but drink with an 81-year-old man and wait for something to happen: maids, fire, the end of the world. I got into an argument with the great editor and went to the back bedroom and sat there with Pops and watched some kind of T.V. program where all the women danced and wore miniskirts. I sat there with a big hard-on. anyway, with a hard-on. I don't know about Pops.

but one night I found myself on the other side of town. big tall guy with beard all over his face. Archer, or Archnip, or something, he was called. we drank and drank and drank and smoked — Chesterfields. we kept talking out of the skulltops of our underwear. and then the big guy with the hairyface, Archnip, he folded across the top of the table and I began feeling his wife's legs. she let me. she let me. she had the finest white hairs on these legs — wait! she was around 25! — I only mean they looked kind of white under the electric light on those g.d. big legs. and she kept saying, I really don't want you but if you can get something ready you can have me. well, that's more than most of them say. and I kept feeling her legs and trying to get something ready but the Chesterfields and the beer had got me beyond it, so all I could ask her was to run away to Los Angeles with me and that she could get a job as a waitress and support me. she didn't seem interested, for some reason. and after all that talk with her husband, wherein I had dissected Law, History, Sex, Poetry, the Novel, Medicine . . . I had even set the husband up by taking him to a bar and having 3 quick scotch and waters after and on top of the other. all she told me was that she *was* interested in Los Angeles. I told her to go take a piss and forget it. I should have stayed in the bar. some girl had come out of the wall and danced on the bar; she had kept shaking these red satin panties in my face. but probably only a communist conspiracy, so what the hell.

the next day I got a ride back with a shorter guy with a shorter beard. he gave me a Chesterfield. whatch do, swaddler, I asked him, you got all that hair on your face, whatcha do?

I paint, he said.

so when we got back to the cottage I broke out the beers and straightened him out on painting. I paint too. I told him my secret formula on how to tell whether a new painting was any good or not. I also told him the difference between painting and writing, and what painting could do for you that writing could not. he didn't say much. after a few beers he decided to leave.

thanks for the ride, I told him.

it's all right.

when the great editor phoned to ask me to breakfast I had to tell him no once more but I told him about the guy who drove me home.

nice guy, I said, nice kid.

what did you say his name was?

I stated the name.

oh, he said, that was professor – –, he teaches painting at Arizona U.

oh, I said.

there weren't any symphony programs on the little A.M. radio so I listened to the other music, crashed the beer down and listened to the other music, crazy: if you come to San Francisco, wear a flower in your hair; hey hey, live for today; and so forth and so on. on one station they had a contest or some damn thing – they asked you to name the month of your birth. August, I told them. were you born in November? the lady sang back. I'm sorry, sir, you just missed, the announcer told me. yeh? I said. yeh? the announcer hung up. you had to first match the month of your birth with the record they spun. then if you hit that, you tried for the day of your birth, that is the 7th., 19th., so on. then if you tied them together you won A FREE TRIP TO LOS ANGELES WHERE YOU GOT TO STAY IN SOME MOTEL, EXPENSES PAID. phony sons of bitches. the whole thing's rigged, I said to myself. I went to the refrigerator. it is now 109 degrees, the announcer said.

my last day in town the colored maid still hadn't shown so I began packing. the great editor told me the bus schedule. all I had to do was walk 3 blocks north, then catch the bus going east on Park ave. to Elm.

if you get to the bus stop too early don't just stand there. go into the drugstore and wait. get a coke or something.

well, I got packed and walked up to the bus stop in the 105 degree heat. the damn bus was nowhere in sight. shit, I said. I began walking east, fast. the booze came out of me like the Niagara falls. I switched hands on the suitcase. I could have taken a taxi from my place to the train depot but the great editor had wanted to give me some books, something called CRUCIFIX IN A DEATHHAND, that I had to pack into the suitcase. nobody had a car. I just got to the place and broke out a beer when here came the prof out of the hospital, driving up in his car, making sure, I guess, that I left town. he came in.

I was just over at the cottage, he said.

you just missed buk, said the editor. buk always builds his own cage. he won't eat breakfast in the campus cafeteria. then I told him to WAIT IN THE DRUGSTORE IF THE BUS WAS LATE. you know what he did? he walked all the way over here in this heat with that suitcase.

god damn it, can't you see? I told the editor, I don't like drugstores! I don't like to be in drug stores, waiting. they have this marble fountain. you sit there and stare at this marble fountain, this soda fountain circle thing. an ant shakes by or some kind of bug lays dying in front of you, one wing whirling and the other still. you are a stranger. 2 or 3 dull and cool people stare at you. then the waitress finally comes up. she wouldn't let you smell the stink of a pair of her dirty panties, yet she's ugly as hell and doesn't even know it. with great reluctance she takes your order. a coke. it comes to you in a warm, bent paper cup. you don't want it. you drink it. the bug is still not dead. the bus is still not there. the marble in the fountain is covered in slimy dust. everything's a farce, can't you see? if you go to the counter and try to buy a pack of smokes it will be 5 minutes before somebody arrives. you feel raped-over 9 times before you get out of there.

there's nothing wrong with drugstores, buk, the editor says.

and I know another guy who says 'there's nothing wrong with war.' but jesus christ, I've got to go with my neuroses and prejudices because that's all I've got to go by. I don't like drugstores, I don't like campus cafeterias, I don't like Shetland ponies and I don't like Disneyland and I don't like motorcycle policemen and I don't like yogurt and I don't like the Beatles and Charley Chaplin and I don't like windowshades and that big blob of manic-depressive hair that falls over Bobby Kennedy's forehead.... jesus, jesus, I turned to the prof. — this guy's been printing me for ten years, hundreds of poems, and HE DOESN'T EVEN KNOW WHO I AM!

the prof laughed, which was something.

the train was 2 hours late, so the prof drove us up to his place in the hills. it began to rain. a big glass window looked over the lousy town. just like in the movies. I got revenge on the great editor. the prof's wife sat down at the piano and wailed out a bit of Verdi. I knew, at last, that the editor was suffering. I HAD HIM IN MY DRUGSTORE. I applauded and egged her on into another one. she wasn't bad really, plenty of power but she disengaged it carelessly — too much power continually without the tonality of variation. I tried to send her into another one but since I was the only one who insisted, she, like a lady, desisted.

they got me down to the train station in the rain with little bottles in all my pockets — peach brandy, all that kind of stuff. I checked my suitcase in and let them all stand there bunched waiting for the train. I walked down to the end of the baggage platform and sat on a truck in the rain and began working on the peach brandy. it was a hot rain that dried as soon as it hit you; it was almost like sweat. I sat and waited for my train to Los Angeles, the only city in the world. I mean, yes it was more full of shits than any other city and that's what made it funny. it was my town. it was my peach brandy. I almost loved it. here it came toward me, at last. I finished the peach brandy and walked on in toward it, looking for the coach number, number 110. but there wasn't any 110. turned out one-ten was 42. I got on with the Indians, Mexicans, madmen and hustlers. there was a girl in a blue dress whose ass looked like the bottom of heaven. she was crazy. she talked to a little doll like it was her baby. she sat across from me talking to the little doll. you could have her, old man, if you tried, I told myself. but you'd only make her un- happy. to hell with it. better to be a peep-freak. so I turned on my side and looked at those delicious legs through the moonlit train windows. L.A. came toward me. the Mexicans and Indians snored. I stared at the moonlit legs and listened to her talk to her doll. what would the great editor expect of me now? what would Hem have done? Dos Passos? Tom Wolfe? Creeley? Ezra? the moonlit legs be- gan to lose meaning. I turned on my other side and faced the purple mountains. maybe a cunt in there too. and Los Angeles moving toward me, full of cunts. and in that poet's cottage now, with Bukowski gone, I could see her now, that colored maid, bending, lifting, bending, sweating, listening to the radio — if you go to San Francisco be sure to wear a flower in your hair — that colored maid popping with love and nobody around, and I reached into my pock- et and opened another little bottle. something something, and I sucked at it sucked at it, and here came L.A., to hell with it.

THE STUPID CHRISTS

three men had to lift the mass of rubber and place it into the machine and the machine chopped it up into the various things it was meant to be; heated it and chopped it and shitted it out: bicycle pedals, bathing caps, hot water bottles . . . you had to be careful how you put the thing into the machine or you'd get an arm sheared off, and when you had a hangover you were always particularly worried about getting an arm sheared off. it had happened to two men in the last three years: Durbin and Peterson. they put Durbin in Payroll — you could see him sitting in there with one sleeve hanging. they gave Peterson a broom and a mop and he cleaned out the crappers, emptied the wastebaskets, hung the toiletpaper, so forth. everybody said it was amazing how well Peterson did all these things with one arm.

now the eight hours were about up. Dan Skorski helped lift in the last mass of rubber. he'd worked the eight hours with one of the worst hangovers of his career. as he worked, the minutes had been hours, the seconds had been minutes. and whenever you looked up there were these 5 guys sitting on the rotunda. whenever you looked up there were these ten EYES looking at you.

Dan turned to go to the timecard rack when a thin thin man built like a cigar walked in. when the cigar walked his feet didn't even touch the floor. the cigar's name was Mr. Blackstone.

"where the hell do you think you're going?" he asked Dan.

"out of here, that's where I'm going."

"OVERTIME," said Mr. Blackstone.

"what?"

"I said: OVERTIME. look around. we've got to get this stuff out of here."

Dan looked around. as far as you could see there were these stacks and stacks of rubber for the machines. and the worst thing with overtime was that you could never tell when it would end. it could be from 2 to 5 hours. you never knew. just time to get back to bed, lay down, then get up again and begin feeding that rubber into the machines. and it never ended. there was always *more* rubber, *more* backorders, *more* machines. the whole building was exploding, *coming*, pewking with rubber, mounds of rubber rubber rubber and the 5 guys on the rotunda got richer and richer and richer.

"get back to WORK!" said the cigar.

"no, I can't do it," said Dan. "I can't lift one more piece of rubber."

"how are we going to get this stuff out?" asked the cigar. "we've got to make floor space for the incoming shipment tomorrow."

"get another building, hire more people. you're working the same people to death, you're beating their brains out. they don't even know where they are, LOOK at them! look at those poor jerks!"

and it was true. the workers were hardly human. their eyes were glazed, stricken, insane. they laughed at anything and mocked each other continually. their insides were stamped out. they had been murdered.

"those are good men," said the cigar.

"sure they are. half their salaries go to state and federal taxes; the other half goes to new cars, color t.v., stupid wives and 4 or 5 different types of insurance."

"either you work the overtime as the others do or you're out of a job, Skorski."

"then I'm out of a job, Blackstone."

"I've got a good mind not to pay you."

"State Labor Board."

"we'll mail you your check."

"fine. and do it promptly.

leaving that building he had the same free and wonderful feeling he got every time he was fired or when he quit a job. leaving that building, leaving them in there — "you've found a home, Skorski. you never had it so good!" no matter how shitty the job was, the workers always told him that.

Skorski stopped at the liquor store, got a pint of Grandad and drove on in. it was an easy evening and he finished the pint and went to bed and slept in an easy grace he hadn't felt in years. no 6:30 a.m. alarm clock to startle him into a false and beastly humanity.

he slept until noon, got up, took 2 alka seltzers and went out to the mailbox. there was one letter.

Dear Mr. Skorski:

We have long been an admirer of your short stories and poems, and also appreciated your recent exhibit of paintings at the University of N. We have an opening in the editorial department here at WorldWay Books, Inc. I'm sure that you have heard of us. Our publications are distributed in Europe, Africa, Australia, and yes, even the Orient. We have been watching your work for some years and noted that you were once editor of the little magazine LAME-BIRD, years 1962-63 and very much liked your choice of poetry and prose. We believe that you are the man for us, here, in our editorial department. I feel we could work something out. The position begins at $200 a week and we would be much honored to have you with us. Should you feel so inclined, please phone us collect at – – – – –, and we will telegraph you plane fare and, we feel, a generous sum for incidental expenses.

> *yours must humbly,*
> *D. R. Signo,*
> *editor-in-chief*
> *WorldWay Books, Inc."*

Dan had a beer, put a couple of eggs on to boil, and phoned Signo. Signo sounded as if he were talking through a piece of rolled-up steel. But Signo had printed some of the world's greatest writers. and Signo seemed very off-hand, not at all like his letter.

"do you really want me out there?" Dan asked him.

"surely," said Signo, "just as we have indicated."

"all right, telegraph me the funds and I'll be on the way."

"the money is on the way," said Signo. "we look forward."

he hung up. Signo did, that is. Dan turned off the eggs. went to bed and slept two more hours . . .

on the plane toward New York, it could have been better. whether it was because he had never flown before or the strange sound of Signo speaking through rolled-up steel, Dan didn't know. from rubber to steel. well, maybe Signo was very busy. that could be

it. some men were very busy. always. anyhow, when Skorski board-
ed the plane he was quite well along the way, and also had a bit of
Grandad with him. however that ran out about half way across and
he began getting on the stewardess for drinks. he had no idea what
the stewardess was serving him — it was purplish sweet and didn't
seem to sit too well upon the Grandad. soon he was talking to all the
passengers and telling them that he was Rocky Graziano, ex-fighter.
they laughed at first, then became quiet as he kept insisting upon his
point:

"I'm the Rock, yes, I'm the Rock and how I could belt them
out! guts and a punch! how I had the mob *howling!*"

then he got sick and just made it to the crapper. when he
heaved some of it somehow got into his shoes and stockings and he
took off his shoes and stockings and washed his stockings and then
came out barefooted. he put his stockings somewhere to dry and
then he put his shoes somewhere and then he forgot where he put
either of them.

he walked up and down the aisle. barefooted.

"Mr. Skorski," the stewardess told him, "please stay in your
seat."

"Graziano. the Rock. and who the hell stole my shoes and
socks? I'll bust 'em in half."

he vomited there in the aisle and an old woman actually hissed
at him like a snake.

"Mr. Skorski," the stewardess said, "I insist that you go to
your seat!"

Dan grabbed her by the wrist.

"I like you. I think I'll rape you right here in the aisle. think of
it! rape in the sky! you'll LOVE it! ex-boxer, Rocky Graziano rapes
stewardess while passing over Illinois! come 'ere!"

Dan grabbed her about the waist. her face was atrociously
blank and stupid; young, egotistical and ugly. she had the IQ of a
tit-mouse and no tits. but she was strong. she broke away and ran to
the pilot's compartment. Dan vomited just a bit, went over and sat
down.

the co-pilot came out. a man with huge buttocks and a large
jaw and a 3 story house with 4 children and an insane wife.

"hey, buddy," said the co-pilot.

92

"yeah, mother?"

"shape up. I hear you been raising a ruckus."

"a ruckus? what's that? are you some kind of queer, flyboy?"

"I'm tellin' you to shape up!"

"jam it, mother! I'm a paying passenger!"

Huge buttocks took the safety belt and fastened him to his seat with an easy disdain and a great show and threat of strength like an elephant pulling a mango tree out of the ground with his trunk.

"now STAY there!"

"I'm Rocky Graziano," he told the co-pilot. the co-pilot was already up in his front compartment. when the stewardess came by and saw Skorski all strapped in his seat, she tittered.

"I'll show you TWELVE INCHES!" he screamed at her.

the old woman hissed at him again like a snake . . .

at the airport, barefooted, he caught a taxi to the new Village. he found a room without any trouble, and also, a bar around the corner. he drank in the bar until early morning and nobody even said anything about his bare feet. nobody even noticed him or spoke to him. he was in New York all right.

even when he bought shoes and socks the next morning, walking into the store barefooted, nobody said anything. the city was centuries old and sophisticated beyond meaning and/or feeling.

a couple of days later he phoned Signo.

"did you have a nice trip, Mr. Skorski?"

"oh yeah."

"well, I'm having lunch at Griffo's. it's just around the corner from WorldWay. suppose you meet me there in 30 minutes?"

"where's Griffo's? I mean, what's the address?"

"just tell the cabby — Griffo's."

he hung up. Signo did, that is.

he told the cabby Griffo's. and there they were. he went inside. stood inside the doorway. there were 45 people in the place. which one was Signo?

"Skorski," he heard a voice. "over here!"

it was at a table. Signo. one other. they were having cocktails. when he sat down the waiter came up and placed a cocktail in front of him.

jesus, that was more like it.

"how did you know who I was?" he asked Signo.

"oh, I know," said Signo.

Signo never looked at a man, always over the top of the man's head as if he were waiting for a message or a bird to fly in or a poison dart from a Ubangi.

"this is Strange," said Signo.

"yes, it is," said Dan.

"I mean, this is Mr. Strange, one of our senior editors."

"hello," said Strange, "I've always admired your work."

Strange had it the other way: he was always looking down at the floor as if awaiting something to crawl up between the floorboards — oil seepage or a boxed-in bobcat or an invasion of beer-maddened roaches. nobody said anything. Dan finished his cocktail and waited on them. they drank very slowly, as if it didn't matter, as if it were chalkwater. they had another round and went to the office . . .

they showed him his desk. each desk was partitioned off from the other by these high whiteglass wall-like cliffs. you couldn't see through the glass. and behind your desk was a whiteglass door, closed. and by pressing a button, a shot of glass closed in right in front of your desk and you were all alone. you could lay a secretary in there and nobody would know a damn thing. one of the secretaries had smiled at him. god, what a body! all that flesh, wobbling and trussed-in and just aching to be fucked, and then the smile . . . what a medieval torture.

he played with a sliding ruler on his desk. it was something for measuring picas or micas or something. he didn't know anything about the ruler. he just sat there playing with it. 45 minutes went by. he began to get thirsty. he opened the back door to his desk and then walked between all the rows of desks that had these white glass walls around them. in between each glass wall was a man. some were on telephones. others played with papers. they all seemed to know what they were doing. he found Griffo's. sat at the bar and had two drinks. then went back up. sat down and played with the ruler again. 30 minutes went by. then he got up and went back down to Griffo's. 3 drinks. then back to the ruler. it was down to Griffo's and back. he lost track. but later in the day, as he walked along in front of the desks, each editor pushed his button and the glass front would flip closed in front of him. flip, flip, flip, they went all the way until he got to his desk. only one editor did not close his glass front. Dan stood there and looked at him — he was a huge dying man, with a somehow fat but flabby throat, the tissues sinking in, and the face puffed round, bloated round like a child's beachball with the features dimly scrawled in. the man would not look at him. he stared at the ceiling above Dan's head, and the man was furious — first red, then white, decaying, decaying. Dan walked to his desk, hit the button and locked himself in. there was a knock at his door. he opened the door. it was Signo. Signo looked over his head.

"we've decided we can't use you."

"how about expenses back."

"how much do you need?"

"a hundred and 75 ought to cover."

Signo wrote out a check for 175, dropped it on his desk and walked out . . .

Skorski, instead of planing for L.A., decided on San Deigo. it had been a long time since he'd been to Caliente racetrack. and he had this thing worked out on the 5-10. he felt he could pick 5 for 6 without buying too many combos. he'd rather figure out a weight-distance-speed ratio play that seemed fairly sound. he remained fairly sober on the flight back, stayed one night in San Diego, then took a taxi to Tijuana. he switched taxis at the border and the Mexican cabby found him a good hotel in the center of town. he put his bag of rags in a closet in his room and then went out to check the town. it was about 6 p.m. and the pink sun seemed to soothe the poverty and anger of the town. poor shits, close enough to the U.S. to speak the language and know its corruption, but only able to drain away a little of the wealth, like a suckerfish attached to the belly of a shark.

Dan found a bar and had a tequila. Mexican music was on the juke. 4 or 5 men sat around nursing drinks by the hour. no women around. well, that was no problem in T. and the last thing he wanted right then was a woman, that pussy throbbing and pulsing at him. women always got in the way. they could kill a man in 9,000 different ways. after he hit the 5-10, picked up his 50 or 60 grand, he'd get a little place along the coast, halfway between L.A. and Dago, and then buy an electric typer or get out the paintbrush, drink French wine and take long walks along the oceanfront each night.

the difference between living well and living badly was only a matter of a little luck and Dan felt he had a little luck coming. the books, the balance books owed it to him . . .

he asked the bartender what day it was and the bartender said, "Thursday," so he had a couple of days. they didn't run until Saturday. Aleseo had to wait for the American crowds to suck over the border for their two days of madness after 5 days of hell. Tijuana took care of them. Tijuana took care of their money for them. but the Americans never knew how much the Mexicans hated them; the American money stupified them to fact, and they ran through TJ like they owned it, and every woman was a fuck and every cop was just some kind of character in a comic strip. but the Americans had forgotten that they'd won a few wars from Mexico, as Americans and Texans or whatever the hell else. to the Americans, that was just history in a book; to the Mexicans it was very real. it didn't feel well to be an American in a Mexican bar on a Thursday night. the Americans even ruined the bullfights; the Americans ruined everything.

Dan ordered another tequila.

the bartender said, "you want a nice girl, senor?"

"thanks, friend," he answered, "but I am a writer. I am more interested in humanity in general than I am in pussy in the exact."

it was a self-conscious remark and he felt lousy after saying it, and the bartender moved off.

but it was peaceful there. he drank and listened to the Mexican music. it was good to be removed from U.S. soil for a while. to sit there and feel and listen to the backside of another culture. what kind of word was that? culture. anyhow, it felt good.

he drank 4 or 5 hours and nobody bothered him and he didn't bother anybody and he left a bit loaded and went up to his room, pulled up the shade, stared out at the Mexican moon, stretched, felt fairly damn well decent about everything, and slept . . .

Dan found a cafe the next morning where he could get ham and eggs, refried beans. the ham was tough, the eggs — straight-up — burned around the edges, and the coffee was bad. but he liked it. the place was empty. and the waitress was fat and stupid as a roach, unthinking — she'd never had a toothache, she'd never been constipated even, she never thought about death and only a little about life. he had another coffee and smoked a sugar-sweet Mexican cigarette. Mexican cigarettes burned differently — they burned *hot* as if they were alive.

it was only around noon and really too early to start at the bar but they didn't run until Saturday and he didn't have a typer. he had to write straight off the typer. he couldn't write with a pencil or pen. he liked the machinegun sound of the typer. it helped the writing.

Skorski walked back to the same bar. the Mexican music was playing. the same four or 5 guys seemed to be sitting there. the bartender came up with the tequila. he seemed kinder than the day before. maybe these 4 or 5 guys had a story to tell. Dan remembered sitting around the black bars on Central Ave., alone, long before being pro-black became the intellectual thing to do, became the con-game. and talking to them and coming away short because they talked and thought just like white men — materialistic, very. and he'd fallen drunk across their tables and they hadn't murdered him when he really wanted to be murdered, when death was the only place to go.

now there was this. Mexico.

he got drunk early and began loading his coins into the juke, playing Mexican music. he didn't understand most of it. it seemed to have the same sing-song Romantic jive-shit sleep-toll imbedded within it.

getting bored, he asked for a woman. she came and sat next to him. a little older than he had expected. she had a gold tooth in the center of her mouth and he had absolutely no desire, no desire, to fuck her. he gave her $5 and told her, he thought, in a very kind way to go away. she want away.

more tequila. the five guys and the bartender sat and watched him. he must get at their *souls!* they *must* have souls. how could they lay back like that? like inside of cocoons? or flies on a window-ledge circling in a 4 p.m. lazy sun?

Skorski got up and placed some more coins within the juke.

then he left his seat and began to dance. they laughed and shouted. it was *encouraging.* some life in this place at last!

Dan kept loading the juke and dancing. soon they stopped shouting and laughing and only watched him, silently. he ordered tequila after tequila, he bought drinks for the 5 silent ones, he

bought drinks for the bartender as the sun went down, as night
began to crawl like a wet dirty cat across the soul of Tijuana, Dan
danced. on and on he danced. out of his wig, sure. but it was perfect.
the breakthru. at last. it was Central Ave. all over again in 1955. he
was perfect. he was always there first before the crowds and the
opportunists came along to fuck it up.

he even fought a bull with a chair and the bartender's bar
rag . . .

Dan Skorski awakened in the public park, the plaza, sitting on
a bench. he noticed the sun first. that was good. then he noticed the
glasses on his head. they were hanging by one ear. and one of the
circles of glass had been punched out of the holder, it just hung to a
rim by a small thread. as he reached out to touch it, the touch of his
hand caused the thread to break and the glass fell, the glass fell, after
hanging on all night, it fell to the cement and broke.

Dan took the remainder of the glasses off, put them in his
front shirt pocket. then came the next move which he KNEW would
be useless, useless, useless . . . but he HAD to make it, to find out,
finally . . .

he reached for his wallet.

there was nothing there. his whole bankroll had been in there.

a pigeon walked so idly past his feet. he always hated the way
the neck worked on those fuckers. stupidity. like stupid wives and
stupid bosses and stupid presidents and stupid Christs.

and there was a stupid story he'd never be able to tell them.
the night he was drunk and lived in this neighborhood where they
had THE PURPLE LIGHT. they had this little glass cubicle and in
the middle of this garden of flowers stood this life-sized Christ,
looking a bit sad and a bit seedy, looking downward upon his
toes . . . THE PURPLE LIGHT SHINED UPON HIM.

it bugged Dan. finally, one night quite a bit drunk, the old
ladies sitting around in the garden, looking at their purple Christ,
Skorski had entered drunk. and began working, trying to get Christ
out of his plastic cage. but it was difficult. then a man ran out.

"sir! what are you trying to do?"

". . . jus' tryin' ta free this muthafucka from his cage! ya
mind?"

"I'm sorry, sir, but we have called the police . . ."

"the police?"

Skorski had dropped Christ and run off.

all the way down to the Mexican plaza of nowhere.

there was a young boy tapping his knee. a young boy all dressed in white. beautiful eyes. he'd never seen such beautiful eyes.

"you wanna fuck my *seester?*" asked the boy. "12 years old."

"no, no, not really, not today."

the little boy walked off genuinely sad, head hanging. he'd failed. Dan felt the sadness for him.

then he got up and walked out of the plaza. but not North toward the land of Freedom. but South. deeper into Mexico.

some small boys, when he passed through a back muddy alley to somewhere, threw stones at him.

but it didn't matter. at least, this time, he had shoes on.

and what he wanted was what they would give him.

and what they would give him was what he wanted.

it was all in the hands of the idiots.

passing through one small town, walking, halfway to Mexico City, they say he looked almost like a purple Christ, well, he was BLUE anyhow, which is getting close.

then they never saw him again.

which means, maybe he should have never drank those cocktails so fast in New York City.

or maybe he should have.

TOO SENSITIVE

"show me a man who lives alone and has a perpetually dirty kitchen, and 5 times out of 9 I'll show you an exceptional man."
                                    —Charles Bukowski, 6-27-67, over 19th
                                    bottle of beer.

"show me a man who lives alone and has a perpetually clean kitchen, and 8 times out of 9 I'll show you a man with detestable spiritual qualities."
                                    —Charles Bukowski, 6-27-67, over 20th
                                    bottle of beer.

often, the state of the kitchen is the state of the mind, confused and unsure men, pliable men are the thinkers. their kitchens are like their minds, cluttered with garbage, dirty ware, impurity, but they are aware of their mind-state and find some humor in it. at times, with a violent burst of fire they defy the eternal deities and come up with a lot of shining that we sometimes call creation; just as at times they will get half drunk and clean up their kitchens. but soon again all falls into disorder and they are in the darkness again, in need of **BABO**, pills, prayer, sex, luck and salvation. the man with the ever-orderly kitchen is the freak, however. beware of him. his kitchen-state is his mind-state: all in order, settled, he has let life condition him quickly to a basened and hardened complex of defensive and soothing thought-order. if you listen to him for ten minutes you will know that anything he says in a lifetime will be essentially meaningless and always dull. he is a cement man. there are more cement men than other kinds of men. so if you are looking for a living man, first check his kitchen and save yourself time.

now, the female with the dirty kitchen is another matter — from the male viewpoint. if she is not employed elsewhere and is childless, the cleanliness or dirtyness of her kitchen is almost always (exceptions be granted) in direct ratio to how much she cares for you. some women have theories on how to save the world but can't wash out a coffee cup. if you mention this to them, they will tell you: "washing out coffee cups is not important." unfortunately, it is. especially to a man who has put in 8 hours straight plus 2 overtime on a turret lathe. you begin saving the world by saving one man at a time; all else is grandiose romanticism or politics.

there are good women in the world, I've even met one or 2. then, there's the other kind. at one time the god damned job was killing me so much that at the end of 8 hours or 12 hours, my whole body would be stiffened into one board of pain. I say "board" because that is the only way that I can think of it. I mean, that at the end of the night I couldn't even put on my coat. it was impossible to lift my arms and place them into the sleeves. the pain was too great and the arm could not be lifted that much. any movement at all would cause these red light horror yak explosions of running pain, like insanity. at this time I had run into a series of traffic tickets, most of them at 3 a.m. or 4 a.m. in the morning. on the way home from work, this particular night, trying to protect myself from small technicalities, I attempted to stick out my left arm to indicate a left turn. my blinkers no longer worked, since I had once ripped the whole blinker stick off the wheel while drunk, so I tried to stick out my left arm. I just managed to get my wrist to the window and stick out one little finger. my arm would not lift any more and the pain was ridiculous, so ridiculous that I began to laugh. it seemed funny as hell, that little finger sticking out in obedience to Los Angeles' finest, the night black and empty, nobody around, and me making that chickenshit failing signal to a halfwind. the laughter came and I almost crashed into a parked car while steering, laughing, trying to make it with the other lousy arm. I made it on in. parked, somehow, got key in door and entered my place. ah. home!

there she was in bed, eating chocolates (really!) and going through the New Yorker and the Saturday Review of Literature. it was around Wednesday or Thursday and the Sunday papers were still on the front room floor. I was too tired to eat and I filled the tub only half full so I would not drown. (it is better to choose your time than to have it chosen for you.)

after clambering out of the damned tub inch by inch like a

misplaced centipede I made my way to the kitchen in order to attempt to drink a glass of water, the sink was stopped up. grey and stinking water came to the edge; I gagged. undumped garbage was everywhere. and this woman had some type of hobby of saving empty jars and jar lids. and floating in the water, among the dishes and etc. were these half-filled jars and lids in a kind of gentle and unreasoning mockery of everything.

I washed out a glass and drank some water. then I made my way to the bedroom. you will never know what agony it was to get my body from standing position to the flat position upon the bed. the only way out was not to move, and so there I stayed still like a frozen dumb stupid fucking fish. I heard her pages turning, and wanting to make some human contact, I essayed forth a question:

"well, how did it go at the poetry workshop tonight?"

"oh, I'm worried about Benny Adimson," she answered.

"Benny Adimson?"

"yes, he's the one who writes these funny stories about the Catholic church. he makes everybody laugh. he's never been published except once in a Canadian magazine, and he doesn't send his stuff out anymore. I don't think the magazines are ready for him. but he's really funny, he makes us all laugh."

"what's his problem?"

"well, he lost his job on the delivery truck. I spoke to him outside the church before the reading began. he says he just can't write when he doesn't have a job. he needs to have a job in order to write."

"that's funny," I said, "I did some of my best writing when I wasn't working. when I was starving to death."

"but Benny Adimson," she answered, "Benny Adimson just doesn't write about HIMSELF! he writes about OTHER people."

"oh."

I decided to forget it. I knew that it would be at least 3 hours before I could go to sleep. by then, some of the pains would run out of the bottom of the mattress. and soon it would be time to get up and go back to the same place. I heard her turn some pages of the New Yorker. I felt badly but decided that there WERE other ways of thinking. maybe the poetry workshop did have some writers in it; it was unlikely but it COULD happen.

I waited for my body to untie. I heard another page turn, a chocolate being taken from its wrapper. then she spoke again:

"yes, Benny Adimson needs a job, he needs some base to work from. we are all trying to encourage him to submit to magazines. I do wish you could read his anti-Catholic stories. he used to be a Catholic once, you know."

"no, I didn't know."

"but he needs a job. we are all trying to find him a job so he can be able to write."

there was a space of silence. frankly, I wasn't even thinking of Benny Adimson and his problem. then I tried to think of Benny Adimson and his problem.

"listen," I said, "I can solve Benny Adimson's problem."

"YOU can?"

"yeh."

"what is it?"

"they're hiring down at the postoffice. they're hiring right and left. he can probably get on tomorrow morning. then he will be able to write."

"the postoffice?"

"yeh."

another page turned. then she spoke:

"Benny Adimson is too SENSITIVE to work at the post-office!"

"oh."

I listened but didn't hear either pages or chocolates. she was very interested at the time in some short story writer called Choates or Coates or Chaos or something, who wrote deliberately dull prose that filled the long columns between the liquor and steamship ads with yawns and then always ended up like with say this guy with a complete collection of Verdi and a bacardi hangover murdering a little 3 year old girl in blue jumpers in some dirty New York alley at 4:13 in the afternoon. this was the New Yorker's editors balling and subnormal idea of avant-garde sophistication — meaning death always wins and that there's dirt under our fingernails. this was all done once and better 50 years ago by somebody called Ivan Bunin in something called The Gentleman from San Francisco. since the death of Thurber the New Yorker has been wandering like a dead bat among the ice-cave hangovers of the Chinese red guard. meaning, they've had it.

"good night," I said to her.

there was a long pause. then she decided to give me the difference.

"good night," she finally said.

with the blue screams strumming their banjos, but without a sound, I turned, (a good five minutes work) from back to belly, and waited for morning and another day.

perhaps I have been unkind to this lady, perhaps I have wandered from kitchens to vindictiveness. there is a lot of snot in each of our souls, and plenty in mine. and I become mixed-up on kitchens, mixed-up on most. the lady I have mentioned has very much courage in many ways. it was just not a very good night for her or for me either.

and I hope that that mother with his anti-Catholic stories and his worries has found a job to suit his sensitivities and that we will all be rewarded with his un-submitted (except for Canada) genius.

meanwhile, I write about myself and drink too much.

but you know that.

RAPE! RAPE!

The doctor was giving me some kind of test. It consisted of a triple blood withdrawal — the 2nd ten minutes after the first, the 3rd 15 minutes later. The doctor had made the first two withdrawals and I was out walking around the street waiting for the 15 minutes to go back. As I stood on the street, I noticed a woman sitting on the bus stop across the street. Out of all the millions of women, now and then you see one that brings it all out of you. There is something about the shape of them, the way they are hung together, a special dress that they are wearing, something about them that you cannot overcome. She had her legs crossed high and was wearing a bright yellow dress. The legs tapered into thin delicate ankles, but she had plenty of good calf and fine upper haunches and thighs. Her face had this playful look about it, as if she were laughing at me but trying to conceal it.

I went down to the signal, then crossed the street. I walked toward her on that bus-stop bench. I was in a trance. I had no control. As I got near she stood up and walked down the street. Those buttocks charmed me out of my senses. I walked along behind her listening to her heels click, my eyes eating her body.

What's wrong with me? I thought. I've lost control.

I don't give a damn, something answered me.

She came to a postoffice and walked in. I walked in behind her. The line was 4 or 5 deep. It was a warm and pleasant afternoon. Everybody seemed to be in a dream-state. I certainly was.

I'm an inch away from her, I thought. I could touch her with my hand.

She got a money order for $7.85. I listened to her voice. Even her voice was like something from a special sex machine. She left. I bought a dozen airmail postcards I didn't want. Then I hurried out. She was waiting on the bus and the bus was drawing up. I just made

105

it to the door behind her. Then I found a seat behind her. We rode along a great distance. She must sense that I am following her, I thought, yet she doesn't seem uncomfortable. Her hair was red-yellow. Everything about her was fire.

We must have ridden along for 3 or 4 miles. Suddenly she leaped up and pulled the cord. I watched her tight dress pull up along her body as she jerked the cord.

Christ, I can't stand it, I thought.

She got off the front door and I got off the back. She turned right at the corner and I followed. She never looked back. It was an apartment house district. She looked better than ever. A woman like that should never walk the streets.

Then she walked into a place called "Hudson Arms." I stood outside as she waited on the elevator. I saw her get in, the door closed and then I went in and stood at the bottom of the elevator. I heard it going up, the doors open, and she got out. As I pressed the button to get it down, I heard it move on down and I took a count in estimated seconds:

one, two, three, four, five, six . . .

When it got to the bottom I had an estimated 18 seconds on the descent.

I got in and hit the top button, 4th floor. Then I counted. When I got to the 4th floor I had 24 seconds. That meant she was on the 3rd floor. Somewhere. I pushed the 3. 6 seconds. Then I got out.

There were quite a number of apartments up there. Figuring it would be too easy if she were in the first apartment, I let that door go and knocked on the second one.

A bald man in undershirt and suspenders opened the door.

"I'm from the Concord Life Insurance Co. Do you have adequate coverage?"

"Go away," said Baldy and closed the door.

I tried the next door. A woman of about 48, quite wrinkled and fat, opened the door.

"I'm from the Concord Life Insurance Co. Do you have adequate coverage, mam?"

"Please come in, sir," she said.

I walked in.

"Listen," she said, "my boy and I are starving. My husband

dropped dead in the streets two years ago. Dead in the streets he dropped. I can't make it on one hundred and 90 dollars a month. My boy is hungry. Do you have some money so I can buy my boy an egg?"

I looked her over. The boy was standing in the center of the room, grinning. A very large lad, about 12 years old and somewhat subnormal. He kept grinning.

I gave the woman a dollar.

"Oh thank you, sir! Oh, thank you!"

She reached her arms around me and kissed me. Her whole mouth was wet, watery, soft. Then she punched her tongue into my mouth. I almost gagged. It was a fat tongue full of saliva. Her breasts were large, very soft, pancake style. I broke loose.

"Listen, don't you ever get lonely? Don't you need a woman? I'm a good clean woman, I really am. You don't have to worry about no diseases with me."

"Look, I've got to go," I said. I got out of there.

I tried 3 more doors. No good.

Then at the 4th door, it was her. It was open about 3 inches. I leaned forward and pushed in, closed the door behind me. It was a nice apartment. She stood looking at me. When is she going to scream? I thought. I had this large thing in front of me.

I walked up to her, grabbed her by the hair and ass and kissed her. She pushed against me, fighting me. She still had on that tight yellow dress. I pulled back and slapped her hard, 4 times. When I grabbed again there was less resistance. We staggered across the floor. I ripped her dress at the throat, ripped it down the front, tore off her brassiere. Volcanic, immense breasts. I kissed her breasts then got her mouth. I had her dress up, working at the panties. Then they were down. And I had it in. I took her standing up. After I made it, I threw her back against the couch. Her pussy looked at me. It still looked good.

"Go to the bathroom," I told her. "Clean up."

I went to the refrigerator. There was a bottle of good wine. I found two glasses. Poured two drinks. When she came out I handed her a drink, sat on the couch next to her.

"What's your name?"

"Vera."

"Did you enjoy it?"

"Yes. I like being raped. I knew you were following me. I was hoping. When I got on the elevator without you, I thought you had lost your nerve. I've only been raped once before. It's hard for a beautiful woman to get a man. Everybody thinks she's unaccessible. It's hell."

"But the way you look and dress. You realize that you are torturing men on the streets?"

"Yes. I want you to use your belt next time."

"My belt?"

"Yes, against my ass, my thighs, my legs. Hurt me, then put it in. Tell me that you are going to rape me!"

"O.k., I'm going to beat you, I'm going to rape you."

I grabbed her by the hair, kissed her violently, bit her lip.

"Fuck me!" she said, "fuck me!"

"Wait," I said, "I have to rest up!"

She unzipped my fly and took my penis out.

"He's beautiful. All purple and bent!"

She put it in her mouth. She began working. She was very good at it.

"Oh shit," I said, "oh shit!"

She had me. She worked a good 6 or 7 minutes, then it began pumping. She nipped her teeth just below the head and sucked the marrow out of me.

"Listen," I said, "it looks as if I'll be here all night. I'm going to need strength. What say I take a bath and you fix me something to eat?"

"All right," she said.

I went into the bathroom and closed the door, let the hot water run. I hung my clothes on the door hook.

I had a good hot bath, then came out with a towel on.

Just as I did, two cops walked in the door.

"That son of a bitch raped me!" she told the cops.

"Now wait a minute," I said.

"Get your clothes on, buddy," the biggest cop said.

"Look, Vera, this is some kind of joke, isn't it?"

"No, you raped me! You raped me! And then you forced me to have oral intercourse!"

"Get your clothes on, buddy," said the big cop, "I'm not going to tell you again!"

I walked into the bathroom and began dressing. When I came out they handcuffed me.

Vera said it again: "Rapist!"

We went down the elevator. As we walked through the lobby several people looked at me. Vera had stayed in her apartment. The cops threw me roughly into the rear seat.

"What's the matter, buddy?" one of them asked, "You got to ruin your life over a piece of snatch? It ain't sensible."

"It wasn't exactly a rape," I said.

"Few of them are."

"Yeah," I said, "I think you're right."

I went through the booking. Then they put me in a cell.

It's just a woman's word they go by, I thought. Where's the equality?

Then I thought, did you rape her or didn't you rape her?

I didn't know.

I finally slept. In the morning there was grapefruit, mush, coffee and bread. Grapefruit? A real class place. Yeah.

I was in my cell about 15 minutes when they opened the door.

"You're lucky, Bukowski, the lady dismissed the charges."

"Great! Great!"

"But watch your step."

"Sure, sure!"

I got my property and walked out of there. I got on the bus, transferred, got off in the apartment house area and then I was standing in front of the "Hudson Arms." I didn't know what to do. I must have stood there 25 minutes. It was Saturday. She was probably in. I walked to the elevator, got in and pushed the button for the 3rd. floor. Then I got out. I knocked on the door. She was there. I pushed in.

"I got another dollar for your boy," I said.

She took it.

"Oh, thank you! Thank you!"

She put her mouth up against mine. It was like a wet rubber vacuum. Out came the fat tongue. I sucked on it. Then I lifted her dress. She had a nice big ass. Plenty of ass. Blue wide panties with a

109

little hole on the left side. We were in front of a full length mirror. I grabbed that big ass and then I stuck my tongue into that vacuum mouth. Our tongues circled like crazy snakes. I had something big in front of me.

The idiot son stood in the center of the room and grinned at us.

AN EVIL TOWN

Frank walked down the steps. He didn't like elevators.

He didn't like many things. He *disliked* steps less than he disliked elevators.

The desk clerk called to him: "Mr. Evans! Would you step over here, please?"

The desk clerk's face looked like cornmeal mush. It was all Frank could do to keep from hitting him. The desk clerk looked about the lobby, then leaned very close.

"Mr. Evans, we've been watching you."

The desk clerk again looked about the lobby, saw that there wasn't anybody near, then leaned forward again.

"Mr. Evans, we've been watching you and we believe that you're losing your mind."

The desk clerk leaned back then and looked right at Frank.

"I feel like going to a movie," said Frank. "You know of any good movies in town?"

"Let's stick to the subject, Mr. Evans."

"O.k., I'm losing my mind. Anything else?"

"We want to help you, Mr. Evans. I believe we've found a piece of your mind. Would you like it back?"

"All right, give me a piece of my mind back."

The clerk reached under the counter and came up with something wrapped in cellophane.

"Here it is, Mr. Evans."

"Thank you."

Frank dropped it in his coat pocket and walked outside. It was a cool autumn night and he walked down the street, west. He stopped at the first alley, stepped in. He reached into his coat and got the wrapped-up thing, peeled the cellophane off. It looked like cheese. It smelled like cheese. He took a bite. It tasted like cheese. He

111

ate it all, then stepped out of the alley and walked down the street again.

He turned into the first movie house he saw, bought his ticket and walked into the darkness. He took a seat in the back. There weren't many people in there. The whole place smelled like urine. The women on the screen dressed as they did in the '20's and the men wore vaseline on their hair, combed it back hard and straight. Their noses seemed very long and the men also seemed to have mascara under their eyes. It wasn't even a talkie. Words showed under the film: BLANCHE WAS NEW IN THE BIG CITY. A guy with straight greasy hair was making Blanche drink from a bottle of gin. Blanche appeared to be getting drunk. BLANCHE GREW DIZZY. SUDDENLY HE KISSED HER.

Frank looked around. Everywhere heads seemed to be bobbing. There weren't any women in the place. The guys seemed to be sucking each other off. They went at it and at it. They never seemed to get tired. The men sitting alone seemed to be jacking-off. The cheese had been good. He wished the clerk had given him more cheese.

HE BEGAN TO DISROBE BLANCHE.

And every time he looked around this guy was getting nearer to him. Then when Frank looked back at the movie the guy would move 2 or 3 seats nearer to him.

HE MADE LOVE TO BLANCHE WHILE SHE WAS HELP-LESSLY INTOXICATED.

He looked again. The guy was 3 seats away. Breathing heavily. Then the guy was in the seat next to him.

"Oh shit," the guy said, "O, my shit, ooo, ooo,oooo. ah, ah! eeeyew! oh!"

WHEN BLANCHE AWAKENED THE NEXT MORNING SHE REALIZED THAT SHE HAD BEEN RAVISHED.

The guy smelled as if he had never wiped his ass. The guy was leaning toward him, bits of spit drooling from the sides of his mouth.

Frank hit the button of the switchblade:

"Careful!" he told the guy. "You get any closer you might hurt yourself on this!"

"Oh, my god!" said the guy. He got up and ran down the row

of seats to the aisle, then walked quickly down the aisle to the front
row. Two guys were at it. One guy was jacking-off the other guy as
the guy went down on him. The guy who had been bothering Frank
sat there and watched them.

SOON AFTER, BLANCHE WAS IN A HOUSE OF PROSTI-
TUTION.

Then Frank had to urinate. He got up and walked toward the
sign: MEN. He went in. It really stank in there. He gagged, opened
the toilet door, went in. He took out his penis and started to piss.
Then he heard some sounds.

"Oooooh shit ooooo shit ooooh oooooh my god it's a snake a
cobra o my god jesus oooh oooh!"

There was a hole cut into the partition separating the toilets.
He saw some guy's eye. He took his pecker and switched it around
and pissed in the guy's eye.

"Oooooh ooooh, you filthy fuck!" said the guy. "oooh you
beastly fiendish piece of shit!"

He heard the guy ripping off toilet paper and wiping his face.
Then the guy began to cry. Frank stepped out of the toilet, washed
his hands. He didn't want to see any more of the movie. Then he was
out on the street, walking back toward his hotel. Then he was in the
lobby. The desk clerk nodded him over.

"Yeah?" asked Frank.

"Look, Mr. Evans, I'm sorry. I was just kidding you."

"About what?"

"You know."

"No, I don't know."

"Well, about losing your mind. I've been drinking, you know.
Don't tell anybody or I'll lose my job. But I've been drinking. I
know that you're not losing your mind. I was just joking."

"But I am losing my mind," said Frank, "and thanks for the
cheese."

Then he turned and walked up the stairway. When he got to
his room he sat down at the writing desk. He took out the switchblade, hit the button, looked at the knifeblade. It was well sharp-
ened down one entire side. It could stab or slice. He hit the button
and put the knife back in his pocket. Then Frank found pen and
paper and began to write:

"Dear Mother:

This is an evil town. The Devil is in control. Sex is everywhere and it is not being used as an instrument of Beauty as God meant it to be, but as an instrument of Evil. Yes, it has most certainly fallen into the devil's hands, into Evil hands. Young girls are forced to drink gin, then they are deflowered by these beasts and forced into houses of prostitution. It is terrible. It is unbelievable. My heart is torn.

I walked along the shore yesterday. Not along the shore, really, but up along on top of cliffs and then I stopped and sat there while breathing in the Beauty. The sea, the sky, the sand. Life became the Eternal Bliss. Then a most miraculous thing happened. 3 small squirrels saw me from way down below and they began to climb the cliffs. I saw their little faces peeking at me from behind rocks and crevices in the cliffs as they climbed toward me. Finally they were at my feet. Their eyes looked at me. Never, Mother, have I seen more beautiful eyes — undiluted by Sin: the whole sky, the whole sea, Eternity was in those eyes. Finally I moved and they . . ."

There was a knock on the door. Frank got up, walked over, opened it. It was the desk clerk.

"Mr. Evans, please, I must speak to you."

"All right, come in."

The desk clerk closed the door and stood in front of Frank. The desk clerk smelled like wine.

"Mr. Evans, please don't tell management about our misunderstanding."

"I don't know what you're talking about."

"You're a great guy, Mr. Evans. You know, I've been drinking."

"You are forgiven. Now go."

"Mr. Evans, there's something I've got to tell you."

"Very well. What is it?"

"I'm in love with you, Mr. Evans."

"Oh, you mean my *spirit*, eh, my boy?"

"No, your body, Mr. Evans."

"What?"

"Your body, Mr. Evans. Please don't be offended, but I want you to ream me!"

"What?"

"REAM ME, Mr. Evans! I've been reamed by half the United States Navy! Those boys know what's good, Mr. Evans. There's nothing like a bit of clean round-eye!"

"You will leave my room immediately!"

The desk clerk threw his arms about Frank's neck, then his mouth was on Frank's mouth. The desk clerk's mouth was very wet and cold, it stank. Frank pushed him away.

"You rotten bastard! YOU KISSED ME!"

"I love you, Mr. Evans!"

"You filthy swine!"

Frank had the knife, hit the button, the blade jumped out and he stuck it into the desk clerk's stomach. Then pulled it out.

"Mr. Evans . . . my god . . ."

The clerk fell to the floor. He was holding both hands over the wound trying to stop the blood.

"You bastard! YOU KISSED ME!"

Frank reached down and unzipped the desk clerk's fly. Then he got the clerk's penis, pulled it straight up toward him and sliced it off three-quarters of the way down.

"Oh, my god my god my god my god . . ." said the clerk.

Frank walked to the bathroom, took the thing and threw it into the toilet. Then he flushed the toilet. Then he washed his hands very well with soap and water. He came out, sat down to the desk again. He picked up the pen.

". . . ran away but I had seen Eternity.

Mother, I must move from this city, from this hotel – the Devil is in control of almost all the bodies. I will write you again from the next city – perhaps San Francisco, Portland or Seattle. I feel like moving north. I think of you continually and hope that you are happy and in good health, and may the good Lord be with you always.

love,
your son,
Frank"

He wrote the address on the envelope, sealed it, added stamp and then walked over and put it in the inside pocket of his coat which was hanging in the closet. Then he took a suitcase from the closet, put it on the bed, opened it and began to pack.

LOVE IT OR LEAVE IT

I walked along in the sun wondering what to do. I kept walking, walking. I seemed to be on the outer edge of something. I looked up and there were railroad tracks and by the edge of the tracks was a little shack, unpainted. It had a sign out:

HELP WANTED

I walked in. A little old guy was sitting there in blue-green suspenders and chewing tobacco.

"Yeah?" he asked.

"I, ah, I ah, I . . ."

"Yeh, come on, man, spit it out! Whatcha want?"

"I saw . . . your sign . . . help wanted."

"Ya wanna sign on?"

"Sign on? What?"

"Well, shit, it ain't a spot as a chorus girl!"

He leaned over and spit into his filthy spitoon, then worked at his wad again, drawing his cheeks in over his toothless mouth.

"What do I do?" I asked.

"You'll be *tole* what to do!"

"I mean, what is it?"

"Railroad track gang, someplace west of Sacramento."

"Sacramento?"

"You heard me, god damn it. Now I'm a busy man. You wanna sign or not?"

"I'll sign, I'll sign . . ."

I signed the list he had on the clipboard. I was # 27. I even signed my own name.

He handed me a ticket. "You show up at gate 21 with your gear. We got a special train for you guys."

I slipped the ticket into my empty wallet.

He spit again. "Now, well, look, kid, I know you're a little

117

goofy. This line takes care of a lot of guys like you. We help humanity. We're nice folks. Always remember old − − − − − − − − − Lines and put in a good word for us here and there. And when you get out on those tracks, listen to your foreman. He's on your side. You can save money out on that desert. God knows, there's no place to spend it. But on Saturday night, kid, on Saturday night . . ."

He leaned to his spitoon again, came back:

"Why hell, on a Saturday night you go to town, get drunk, catch a cheap blowjob from a wetback Mexican senorita and come back in feeling good. Those blowjobs suck the misery right out of a man's head. I started on the gang, now I'm here. Good luck to you, kid."

"Thank you, sir."

"Now get the hell out of here! I'm busy! . . ."

I arrived at gate 21 at the time instructed. By my train were all these guys standing there in rags, stinking, laughing, smoking rolled cigarettes. I went over and stood behind them. They needed haircuts and shaves and they acted brave and were nervous at the same time.

Then a Mexican with a knife scar on his cheek told us to get on. We got on. You couldn't see through the windows.

I took the last seat in the back of our car. The others all sat up in front, laughing and talking. One guy pulled out a half pint of whiskey and 7 or 8 of them each had a little suck.

Then they began looking back at me. I began hearing voices and they weren't all in my head:

"What's wrong with that sona bitch?"

"He think he's better than us?"

"He's gonna hafta work with us, man."

"Who's he think he is?"

I looked out the window, I tried to, the thing hadn't been cleaned in 25 years. The train began to move out and I was on there with them. There were about 30 of them. They didn't wait very long. I stretched out on my seat and tried to sleep.

"SWOOSH!"

Dust blew up into my face and eyes. I heard somebody under my seat. There was the blowing sound again and a mass of 25 year old dust rose up into my nostrils, my mouth, my eyes, my eyebrows.

I waited. Then it happened again. A real good blast. Whoever was under there was getting damed good at it.

I leaped up. And I heard all this sound from under my seat and then he was out from under there and running up toward the front. He threw himself into a seat, trying to be part of the gang, but I heard his voice:

"If he comes up here I want you fellows to help me! Promise to help me if he comes up here!"

I didn't hear any promises, but he was safe: I couldn't tell one from the other.

Just before we got out of Louisiana I had to walk up front for a cup of water. They watched me.

"Look at him. Look at him."

"Ugly bastard."

"Who's he think he is?"

"Son of a bitch, we'll get him when we get him out over those tracks alone, we'll make him cry, we'll make him suck dick!"

"Look! He's got that paper cup *upsidedown!* He's drinking from the *wrong* end! Look at him! He's drinking from the *little* end! That guy's *nuts!*"

"Wait'll we get him over those tracks, we'll make him suck dick!"

I drained the paper cup, refilled it and emptied it again, wrongsideup. I threw the cup into the container and walked back. I heard:

"Yeah, he acts nuts. Maybe he had a split-up with his girlfriend."

"How's a guy like that gonna get a girl?"

"I dunno. I seen crazier things than that happen." . . .

We were over Texas when the Mexican foreman came through with the canned food. He handed out the cans. Some of them didn't have any labels on them and were badly dented-up.

He came back to me.

"You Bukowski?"

"Yes."

He handed me a can of *Spam* and wrote "75" under column "F." I could see that I was charged with "$45.90" under column "T." Then he handed me a small can of beans. "45" he wrote down under column "F."

119

He walked back toward the front of the car.

"Hey! Where the hell's a can opener? How can we eat this stuff without a can opener?" somebody asked him.

The foreman swang through the vestibule and was gone.

There were water stops in Texas, bunches of green. At each stop 2 or 3 or 4 guys leaped off. When we got to El Paso there were 23 left out of the 31.

In El Paso they pulled our traincar out and the train went on. The Mexican foreman came through and said, "We must stop at El Paso. You will stay at this hotel."

He gave out tickets.

"These are your tickets to the hotel. You will sleep there. In the morning you will take traincoach #24 to Los Angeles and then on to Sacramento. These are your hotel tickets."

He came up to me again.

"You Bukowski?"

"Yes."

"Here's your hotel."

He handed me the ticket and wrote in "12.50" under my "L" column.

Nobody had been able to get their cans of food open. They would be picked up later and given to the next crew across.

I threw my ticket away and slept in the park about two blocks from the hotel. I was awakened by the roaring of alligators, one in particular. I could see 4 or 5 alligators in the pond, and perhaps there were more. There were two sailors dressed in their whites. One sailor was in the pond, drunk, pulling at the tail of an alligator. The alligator was angry but slow and could not turn its neck enough to get at the sailor. The other sailor stood on the shore, laughing, with a young girl. Then while the sailor in the pond was still fighting the alligator, the other sailor and the girl walked away. I turned over and slept.

On the ride to Los Angeles, more and more of them jumped off at the waterstops. When we reached Los Angeles there were 16 left of the 31.

The Mexican foreman came through the train.

"We will be in Los Angeles for two days. You will catch the 9:30 a.m. train, gate 21, Wednesday morning, traincoach 42. It is written upon the cover which goes around your hotel tickets. You are also being issued food-ration coupons which can be honored at French's Cafe, Main Street."

He handed out 2 little booklets, one labeled ROOM, the other FOOD.

"You Bukowski?" he asked.

"Yes," I said.

He handed me my booklets. And added under my "L" column: 12.80 and under my "F" column, 6.00

I came out of Union Station and while I was cutting across the plaza I noticed 2 small guys who had been on the train with me. They were walking faster than I and cut across to my right. I looked at them.

They both got these big grins on and said, "Hi! How ya doin'?"

"I'm doin' all right."

They walked faster and slid across Los Angeles street toward Main . . .

In the cafe the boys were using their food coupons for beer. I used my food coupons for beer. Beer was just ten cents a glass. Most of them got drunk very fast. I stood down at the end of the bar. They didn't talk about me anymore.

I drank up all my coupons and then sold my lodging tickets to another bum for 50 cents. I had 5 more beers and walked out.

I began walking. I walked north. Then I walked east. Then north again. Then I was walking along the junkyards where all the broken-down cars were stacked. A guy had once told me, "I sleep in a different car each night. Last night I slept in a Ford, the night before in a Chevy. Tonight I am going to sleep in a Cadillac."

I found a place with the gate chained but the gate door was bent and I was thin enough to slide my body between the chains and the gate and the lock. I looked around until I found a Cadillac. I didn't know the year. I got into the back seat and slept.

It must have been about 6 a.m. in the morning when I heard this kid screaming. He was about 15 years old and had this toy base-ball bat in his hand:

"Get out of there! Get out of our car, you dirty bum!"

The kid looked frightened. He had on a white t shirt and tennis shoes and there was a tooth missing from the center of his mouth.

I got out.

"Stand back!" he yelled. "Stand back, stand back!" He pointed the bat at me.

I slowly walked toward the gate, which was then open but not very far.

Then an old guy, about 50, fat and sleepy, stepped out of a tarpaper shack.

"Dad!" The kid yelled, "This man was in one of our cars! I found him in the back seat asleep!"

"Is that right?"

"Yeah, that's right, Dad! I found him asleep in the back seat of one of our cars!"

"What were you doing in our car, Mr.?"

The old guy was nearer to the gate than I was but I kept moving toward it.

"I asked you, 'What were you doing in our car?' "

I moved closer to the gate.

The old guy grabbed the bat from the kid, ran up to me and jammed the end of it into my belly, hard.

"Oof!" I went, "god o mighty!"

I couldn't straighten up. I backed away. The kid took courage when he saw that.

"I'll get him, Dad! I'll get him!"

The kid grabbed the bat from the old man and began swinging it. He hit me almost everywhere. On the back, the sides, all along both legs, on the knees, the ankles. All I could do was protect my head. I kept my arms up around my head and he beat me on the arms and elbows. I backed up against the wire fence.

"I'll get him, Dad! I'll get him!"

The kid wouldn't stop. Now and then the bat got through to my head.

Finally the old man said, "O.k., that's enough son."

The kid kept swinging the bat.

"Son, I said, 'That's enough.' "

I turned and held myself up by the wires of the fence. For a moment I couldn't move. They watched me. I finally let go and was able to stand. I limped toward the gate.

"Let me get him again, Dad!"

"No, son."

I got through the gate and walked north. As I began to walk, everything began to tighten. Everything was beginning to swell. My steps became shorter. I knew that I wouldn't be able to move much further. There were only more junkyards. Then I saw a vacant lot between two of them. I walked into the lot and turned my ankle in a hole, right off. I laughed. The lot sloped downwards. Then I tripped over a hard brush branch which would not give. When I got up again my right palm had been cut by the edge of a piece of green glass. Winebottle. I pulled the glass out. The blood came through the dirt. I brushed the dirt off and sucked against the wound. When I fell the next time, I rolled over on my back, screamed once with pain, then looked up into the morning sky. I was back in my hometown, Los Angeles. Small gnats whirled about my face. I closed my eyes.

A DOLLAR AND 20 CENTS

he liked the end of Summer best, no Fall, maybe it was Fall, anyhow, it got cold down at the beach and he liked to walk along the water right after sundown, no people around and the water looked dirty, the water looked deathly, and the seagulls didn't want to sleep, hated to sleep. the seagulls came down, flew down wanting his eyes, his soul, what was left of his soul.

if you don't have much soul left and you know it, you still got soul.

then he'd sit down and look across the water and when you looked across the water, everything was hard to believe. say like there was a nation like China or the U.S. or someplace like Vietnam. or that he'd once been a child. no, come to think of it, that wasn't so hard to believe; he'd had a hell of a childhood, he couldn't forget that. and the manhood: all the jobs and all the women, and then no woman, and now no job. a bum at 60. finished. nothing. he had a dollar and 20 cents in cash. a week's rent paid. the ocean .... he thought back over the women. some of them had been good to him. others had simply been shrews, scratchers, a little crazy and terribly hard. rooms and beds and houses and Christmases and jobs and singing and hospitals, and dullness, dull days and nights and no meaning, no chance.

now 60 years worth: a dollar and 20 cents.

then he heard them behind him laughing. they had blankets and bottles and cans of beer, coffee and sandwiches. they laughed, they laughed. 2 young boys, 2 young girls. slim, pliable bodies. not a care. then one of them saw him.

"Hey, what's THAT?"
"Jesus, I dunno!"
he didn't move.
"is it human?"

"does it breathe? does it screw?"

"screw WHAT?"

they all laughed.

he lifted his wine bottle. there was something left. it was a good time for it.

"it MOVES! look, it MOVES!"

he stood up, brushed the sand from his pants.

"it has arms, legs! it has a face!"

"a FACE?"

they laughed again. he could not understand. kids were not this way. kids were not bad. what were these?

he walked up to them.

"there's no shame in old age."

one of the young boys was finishing off a beercan. he threw it to one side.

"there's a shame in wasted years, pops. you look like waste to me."

"I'm still a good man, son."

"supposin' one of these girls put some pussy on you, pops, what would you do?"

"Rod, don't TALK that way!"

a young girl with long red hair spoke. she was arranging her hair in the wind, she seemed to sway in the wind, her toes hooked into the sand.

"how about it, pops? what would you do? huh? what would you do if one of these girls laid it on you?"

he started to walk, he walked around their blanket up the sand toward the boardwalk.

"Rod, why'd you talk to that poor old man that way? sometimes I HATE you!"

"COM'ERE, baby!"

"NO!"

he turned around and saw Rod chasing the girl. the girl screamed, then laughed. then Rod caught her and they fell in the sand, wrestling and laughing. he saw the other couple standing upright, kissing.

he made the boardwalk, sat on a bench and brushed the sand from his feet. then he put on his shoes. ten minutes later he was back in his room. he took off his shoes and stretched out on the bed. he didn't turn on the light.

there was a knock on the door.

"Mr. Sneed?"

"yes?"

the door opened. it was the landlady, Mrs. Conners. Mrs. Conners was 65, he couldn't see her face in the dark. he was glad he couldn't see her face in the dark.

"Mr. Sneed?"

"yes?"

"I made some soup. I made some nice soup. Can I bring you a bowl of soup?"

"no, I don't want any."

"oh, come on, Mr. Sneed, it's nice soup, real nice soup! let me bring you a bowl!"

"oh, all right."

he got up and sat in a chair and waited. sne had left the door open and the light came in from the hall. a shot of light, a beam of it across his legs and lap. and that's where she sat the soup. a bowl of soup and a spoon.

"you're gonna like it, Mr. Sneed. I make good soup."

"thank you," he said.

he sat there looking at the soup. it was piss-yellow. it was chicken soup. without meat. he sat looking at the little bubbles of grease in the soup. he sat for some time. then he took the spoon out and put it on the dresser. then he took the soup to the window, unhooked the screen and quietly spilled the soup onto the ground. there was a small rise of steam. then it was gone. he put the bowl back on the dresser, closed the door and got back on the bed. it was darker than ever, he liked the dark, the dark made sense.

by listening very carefully he heard the ocean. he listened to the ocean for some time. then he sighed, he sighed one large sigh and died.

NO STOCKINGS

Barney got her in the ass while she sucked me off; Barney finished first, put his toe in her ass, wiggled it, asked, "how ya like that?" she couldn't answer right then. she finished me off. then we drank an hour or so. then I switched to the bunghole. Barney took the mouth. after that, he went to his place. I went to mine. I drank myself to sleep.

it must have been 4:30 in the afternoon, the doorbell rang. it was Dan. it was always Dan when I was sick or needed sleep. Dan was kind of a commie intellectual who ran a poetry workshop, had a knowledge of classical music; he had a snip of a beard and always came up with these drab little quips throughout his conversation, and worse than that – he wrote rhyming poetry.

I looked at him. "oh shit," I said.

"sick again, Buk? oh, Buke, he will puke!"

how right. I ran into the bathroom and let go.

when I came back he was sitting on my couch looking quite pert.

"yeah?" I asked.

"well, we need some of your poems for the Spring reading."

I never showed at his readings nor did I have interest in them but he had been coming around for years and I didn't know how to decently shut him off.

"Dan, I don't have any poems."

"you used to have closetsful."

"I know."

"mind if I look in the closet?"

"go ahead."

I went into the refrigerator and came out with a beer. Dan was sitting with some wrinkled papers.

"say, this one's not bad. humm. oh, this one's shit! and this one's shit. and this one is too. heeheeee! what's happened to you, Bukowski?"

"I dunno."

"hmmmmmm. this one's not *too* bad. oooh, this one's shit! and this one!"

I don't know how many beers I drank while he commented on the poems. but I began to feel a little better.

"this one's . . ."

"Dan?"

"yes, yes?"

"do you know any pussy?"

"what?"

"do you know any women laying around panting for 4 or 5 inches only?"

"these poems . . ."

"fuck the poems! pussy, man, pussy!"

"well, there's Vera . . ."

"let's go!"

"I'd like some of these poems . . ."

"take them. care for a beer while I dress?"

"well, one wouldn't hurt."

I gave him one while I got out of my torn robe and into my worn clothes. a rhymer. one pair of shoes, ripped shorts, zipper in pants that only pulled 3/4's up. we went out the door, got into the car. I stopped for a fifth of scotch.

"I have never seen you eat," said Dan, "don't you ever eat?"

"only certain items."

he directed the way to Vera's. we got out, fifth, me, Dan. rang a doorbell of a fairly expensive apartment.

Vera opened the door. "ooh, hello, Dan."

"Vera, this . . . Charles Bukowski."

"oooh, I always wondered what Charles Bukowski looked like."

"yeh. me too." I pushed in past her. "got any glasses?"

"oooh, yes."

Vera came out with the glasses. there was some guy sitting on the couch. I filled 2 glasses with scotch, gave one to Vera, one to myself, then sat myself on the couch in between Vera and the guy who was sitting there. Dan sat across the way.

"Mr. Bukowski," said Vera, "I've read your poetry and . . ."

"fuck poetry," I said.

"oooh," said Vera.

I drank the scotch down, reached over, flipped the dress higher over Vera's knees. "you have beautiful legs," I told her.

"I think I'm a little fat," she said.

"oh, no! just right!"

I poured myself another scotch, leaned over and kissed one of her knees. I had a little sip more, then kissed a little higher up the leg.

"oh hell, I'm going!" said the guy who was at the other end of the couch. he got up and walked out.

I interspersed my kissing movements with bits of dull conversation. filled her glass again. soon I had her dress up around her ass. I saw the panties. they were wonderful panties. they were not made out of that usual pantystuff, but they looked more like an old-fashioned bed quilt — high, raised and separate squares of this silky soft stuff; just like a miniature bed quilt shaped into panties — and delicious colors: green and blue and gold and lavender. truly, she must have had hot pants.

I pulled my head from between her legs and there sat Dan across from us, glistening. "Dan, my boy," I said, "I think it's time for you to go."

Dan, my boy, left with much seeming reluctance, a peepshow improved a handjob later on. but it was hard for him to leave anyhow. it was hard for me too. nice and.

I straightened up and had another drink. she waited. I drank slowly.

"Charles," she said.

"look," I said, "I like my booze. don't worry now, I'll get around to you."

Vera sat there with her dress up around her ass waiting. "I'm too fat," she said, "really, don't you think so?"

"oh no, perfect. I could rape you for 3 hours. you're just kind of buttery. I could melt into you forever."

I drained my scotch, poured another.

"Charles," she said.

"Vera," I said.

"what?" she asked.

"I am the world's greatest poet," I told her.

"living or dead?" she asked.

"dead," I said. I reached over and grabbed a breast. "I'd like to jam a live codfish up your ass, Vera!"

"why?"

"hell, I dunno."

she pulled her dress down. I finished off the scotch glass.

"you piss outa your pussy, don't you?"

"I guess so."

"well, that's what's wrong with alla you women."

"Charles, I'm afraid I'm going to have to ask you to go. I have to go to work early tomorrow morning."

"work. smerk. the Turk lurked and jerked."

"Charles," she said, "please leave."

"please don't worry. I'm going to fuck you! I just want a little more to drink. I am a man who loves his drink."

I saw her get up, and forgot it, poured another drink. then I looked up and there was Vera and another woman. the other woman looked all right too.

"sir," said the other woman, "I am a friend of Vera's. you've frightened her and she must get up early in the morning. I'll have to ask you to leave!"

"LISTEN, YOU LOUSY CUNTS, I'LL FUCK THE BOTH OF YOU, I PROMISE! JUST LEMME HAVE A FEW MORE DRINKS, THAT'S ALL I ASK! YOU BOTH GOT 8 GOOD INCHES WAITING ON YOU!"

I was sitting there fairly close to the bottom of the fifth when the two cops came in. I was sitting in my shorts on the couch with my shoes and stockings off. I liked it there. quite a nice apartment.

"gentlemen?" I asked, "are you from the Nobel Prize Committee? or is it the Pulitzer?"

"get your shoes and pants on," said one of them. "NOW!"

"gentlemen, do you realize you are addressing Charles Bukowski?" I asked.

"we'll get your I.D. down at the station. now get your shoes and pants on."

they handcuffed me behind my back, hard as usual, the little notches on the bracelets biting into the veins. then they hustled me fast, outside, down a slanting drive, moving me a little faster than the legs could go. I felt as if the whole world were watching, and I felt also, strangely, ashamed of something. guilty, crappy, incomplete, like a pissant, like a wasted machinegun bullet.

"you're a great lover, eh?" one of them asked me.

I thought that this was a strangely friendly and human remark. "it was a nice apartment," I said, "and you should have seen the panties."

"shut up!" the other one said.

they threw me in the back without too much care. I stretched out and listened to their comfortable and superior and godly radio. I always got the idea, at such times, that the cops were better than I was. and there was some truth in it . . .

down at the station — the usual photographs, confiscation of pocket materials. things kept changing. modernizing. then a guy in civvies. after the difficult fingerprinting where I always had trouble with the left thumb: "RELAX! NOW, RELAX!" always this guilt with the rolling thumb. but how could you RELAX in jail?

the guy in civvies. asking various questions for a lined-green paper. he kept smiling.

"these men are beasts," he said in a low voice. "I like you. give me a call when you get out." he gave me a slip of paper. "beasts," he said, "they are. be careful."

"I'll phone you," I lied, thinking it might help. when you get in there, any sympathetic voice seems wonderful . . .

"you've got one phone call," said the screw, "make it now."

they let me out of the drunktank where they all slept on boards and seemed quite comfortable, bumming cigarettes, snoring, laughing, pissing. the Mexicans seemed most relaxed as if they were in their own bedroom. I was jealous of their easiness.

I went out and looked through the phonebook. it was then that I realized that I didn't have any friends. I kept turning pages.

"listen," said a screw, "how long's it gonna take you? you been out here 15 minutes."

I made a hasty surmise and called a number. all I got was a lot of shit from somebody's mother, who answered the phone, she said I'd once forced him (her son) to go to jail by my insistence that I thought it would be funny to go to sleep on some mortuary steps on the main boulevard of Inglewood, Calif. while we were drunk. the old bitch had no sense of humor. the screw put me back in.

it was then I noticed that I was the *only* guy in jail without stockings on. there must have been 150 of them in that tank and 149 wore stockings. many of them just off of boxcars. I was the only one without. you could hit bottom and then find another bottom. balls.

each time I found a new screw I asked if I might be allowed to make my one phone call. I don't know how many people I phoned. finally I gave up and decided just to rot there. Then the cell door opened and my name was called.

"you made bail," the screw said.

"jesus christ," I said.

all during the bailing-out process, which takes about an hour, I wondered who the angel was. I thought of everybody. I thought of who might be my friend. when I got out I found it was a guy and his wife who I had thought had hated me. they were waiting on the sidewalk.

they drove me to my place where I paid them off the bail money. I walked them back down to their car and just as I got in the door, the phone rang. it was a woman's voice. it sounded good. "Buk?"

"yeah, baby. who are you? I just got out of jail."

it was a long distance call from some cunt in Sacramento. but I couldn't reach her with my cock and I still didn't have any stockings on.

"sometimes I read your books of poetry all over again, Buke, and all the poems stand up. Buke, I think of you all the time."

"thanks, Ann, thanks for calling, you're a sweet kid but I've got to go out and get a touch to drink."

"love you, Buke."

"me too, Ann . . ."

I went out and got a tall 6 pack and a pint of scotch. I was pouring the first scotch when the phone rang again. I took half a glass straight down, then answered.

"Buke?"

"yeah. Buk. I just got out of jail." Buk.

"yes, I know. this is Vera."

"you lousy cunt. you called the cops."

"you were horrible. horrible. they asked me if I wanted to prefer rape charges. I told them I didn't."

she had the chain on the door but I could see on in through there. the pint of scotch and the tall 6-pack rode on inside of me. she had on a robe and the robe was open and I could see one very fulsome breast trying very hard to work out toward my mouth.

"Vera, baby," I said, "I think that we could be nice friends, very nice friends. I forgive you for phoning the cops. let me in."

"no, no, Buke, we can never be friends! you are a horrible person!"

the breast kept pleading to me.

"Vera! . . ."

"no, Buke, take your stuff and go, please, please!"

I snatched the wallet and stockings. "o.k., fatty, jam it up your jello ass!"

"ooooh!" she said, and then slammed the door.

as I examined the wallet for the 35, I heard her put on Aaron Copeland. what a phony.

I walked on down the drive this time without police escort. I found the car a little further down. got in. it started. I let it warm. good old baby. I took off my shoes, put on my socks, put my shoes back on again, and then being a decent citizen once more, I put it in reverse, backed out between the two cars, swung it clear, moved up the dark street North North north . . .

toward myself toward my place toward something, the old car had it, then I had it, and the way, and at a signal I found a half an old cigar in the tray, lit it, burned my nose a little, signal changed, I inhaled, blew out blue smoke, nothing was ever dead that didn't take a chance, lose, come back to the same place.

odd: sometimes no-fuck beats some fuck.

though I might be wrong. they say that I usually am.

A QUIET CONVERSATION PIECE

people who come by my place are a bit odd, but then almost everybody's a bit odd; the world is shaking and trembling more than ever and its effects are obvious.

there's this one who is a bit fat, has now grown a tyke of a beard, and he looks fairly well. he wants to read one of my poems at a reading. I tell him o.k. and then I tell him HOW to read it and he gets a bit nervous.

"where's the beer? jesus christ, don't you have anything to drink?"

he picks up 14 sunflower seeds, puts them in his mouth, chews like a machine. I go get the beer. this kid, Maxie, has never worked. he keeps going to college in order to stay out of Vietnam. now he is studying to be a rabbi. he'll make a hell of a rabbi. he's lusty enough and full of shit. he'll make a good one. but he's really not anti-war. he, like most people, divides wars into good wars and bad wars. he wanted to get into the Israeli-Arab war but before he could get packed the damn thing was over. so it's obvious that men will still shoot at each other; all you have to do is give them this little thing that will click in their reasoning process. not good to shoot a North Vietnamese: o.k. to shoot an Arab. he'll make a hell of a rabbi.

he snatches the beer from my hand, gives those sunflower seeds a little water.

"jesus," he says.

"you killed jesus," I say.

"oh don't start all that!"

"I won't. I'm not that way."

"I mean, jesus, I hear you got good royalties from TERROR STREET."

"yeah, I'm his best seller. I outsell his Duncan, Creeley and Levertov series all put together. but it might not mean anything —

134

they sell a lot of copies of the *L.A. Times* each night too but there's nothing in the *L.A. Times.*"

"yeah."

we work at the beer.

"how's Harry?" I ask. Harry's a kid, Harry WAS a kid out the madhouse. I wrote the foreword to Harry's first book of poems. they were quite good. they almost screamed. then Harry fell into a job I refused to take — writing for the girlie mags. I told the editor "no" and sent Harry over. Harry was a mess; he was taking jobs as a babysitter. now he doesn't write poems anymore.

"oh, Harry. he has FOUR motorcycles. on the 4th of July he took the crowd out into the backyard and shot off $500 worth of firecrackers. in 15 minutes the $500 was gone into the sky."

"Harry's come quite a way."

"he sure has. fat as a pig. drinking that good whiskey. eating all the time. he married this gal who got 40,000 dollars when her husband died. he had an accident while skin diving. I mean, he drowned. now Harry's got a skin diving outfit."

"beautiful."

"he's jealous of you, though."

"why?"

"I don't know. just mention your name and he starts raving."

"I'm just hanging by a string. it's about up with me."

"they each have sweaters with each other's names on them. she thinks Harry's a great writer. she hasn't been around much. they're busting out one of the walls to make a writing studio for Harry. soundproof like Proust. or was it Proust?"

"who had the cork-lined room?"

"yeah, I think so. anyhow, it's going to cost them 2 grand. I can see the great writer in his cork-lined room now writing, 'Lilly lithely leaped farmer John's fence . . .' "

"let's get off that guy. he's so funny he's drowning in money."

"yeah. well, how's the little girl? what's her name? Marina?"

"Marina Louise Bukowski. yeah. she saw me getting out of the bathtub the other day. she's 3 and one half. know what she said?"

"no."

"she said, 'Hank, look at your silly self. you got all that hanging out the front and you've got nothing hanging out the back!' "

135

"too much."

"yeah, she expected dick at both ends."

"might not be a bad idea."

"not for me. I can't get work enough for one."

"you got any more beer?"

"sure. sorry."

I bring them out.

"Larry was by," I tell him.

"yeah?"

"yeah. he thinks the revolution is tomorrow morning. it might be, it might not be. nobody knows. I tell him that the problem with revolutions is that they must begin from the INSIDE-out, not from the outside-IN. the first thing these people do in a riot is run and grab a color tv set. they want the same poison that made the enemy a half-wit. but he won't listen. he's packing his rifle around. went to Mexico to join the revolutionaries. the revolutionaries were drinking tequila and yawning. then, there's the language barrier. now it's Canada. they have a hideout of food and guns in one of the northern states. but they don't have the atom-bomb. they're fucked. and no air-power."

"neither have the Vietnamese. they're doing all right."

"that's because we can't use the a-bomb on account of Russia and China. but suppose we decided to bomb a hideout in Oregon full of Castros? that would be our business, wouldn't it?"

"you talk like a good American."

"I don't have any politics. I'm an observer."

"it's a good thing everybody isn't an observer or we would never get anywhere."

"have we gotten somewhere?"

"I don't know."

"neither do I. but I do know that a lot of revolutionaries are real pricks, and DULL, very dull to top it all off. man, I'm not saying that the poor man should not get help, that the uneducated should not get educated, that the sick should not have hospitalization, so forth. what I'm saying is that we are putting a lot of priests' robes on some of these revolutionaries, and some of them are very sick fellows bothered with acne, deserted from by their wives and wearing these bloody little Peace Symbols from strings around their

136

necks. a lot of them are merely opportunists of the moment and they'd do just as well working for the Ford Co. if they could get their foot in the door. I don't want to go from one bad leadership to another bad leadership — we've been doing that every election."

"I still think a revolution would get rid of a lot of shit."

"win or lose, it will. it'll get rid of a lot of good things and bad. human history moves very slowly. me, I'll settle for a birdbath."

"the better to observe from."

"the better to observe from. have another beer."

"you still sound like a reactionary."

"listen, Rabbi, I'm trying to see the thing from all sides, not just my side. the Establishment is very cool. you've got to give them that. I'll talk with the Establishment any time. I know that I'm dealing with a tough boy. look at what they did to Spock. both Kennedys. King. Malcolm X. you make your list. it's a long one. you can't move too fast on the big boys or you'll find yourself whistling Dixie through a cardboard toiletpaper holder at Forest Lawn. but things are changing. the young are thinking better than the old used to think and the old are dying. there's still a way to do it without everybody getting murdered."

"they've got you backtracking. with me, 'Give me Victory or Death.' "

"that's what Hitler said. he got death."

"what's wrong with death?"

"the question before us tonight is what's wrong with life."

"you write a book like TERROR STREET and then you want to sit around and shake hands with killers."

"have we shaken hands, Rabbi?"

"you talk out of the side of your mouth while cruelties are happening at this very moment."

"you mean the spider with the fly or the cat with the mouse?"

"I mean Man against Man when Man has the facility to know better."

"there's something in what you say."

"Hell yes. you're not the only one with a mouth."

"then what do you say we do? burn the town?"

"no, burn the nation."

"like I say, you'll be a hell of a Rabbi."

"thank you."

"and after we burn the nation, we replace it with what?"

"would you say that the American Revolution failed, that the French Revolution failed, that the Russian Revolution failed?"

"not entirely. but they sure fell short."

"it was a try."

"how many men must we kill in order to move forward one inch?"

"how many men are killed by not moving at all?"

"sometimes I feel like I'm talking with Plato."

"you are: Plato with a Jewish beard."

it gets quiet then and the problem hangs between us. meanwhile, the skidrows are filled with the disenchanted and the discarded; the poor die in charity wards among a scarcity of doctors; the jails are so filled with the disorded and the lost that there are not enough bunks and the prisoners must sleep on the floor. to get on relief is an act of mercy that may not last and the madhouses are stuffed wall to wall because of a society that uses people like chess pawns . . .

it's damned pleasant to be an intellectual or a writer and to observe these niceties as long as your OWN ass is not in the wringer. that's ONE thing that's wrong with intellectuals and writers — they don't feel a hell of a lot except their own comfort or their own pain. which is normal but shitty.

"and congress," says my friend, "believes they can solve something with a gun-control bill."

"yeah. actually we know who has been shooting most of the guns. but we are not so sure who has been shooting some of the others. is it the army, the police, the state, or some other madmen? I'm afraid to guess for I may be next and I have a few more sonnets I'd like to finish."

"I don't think that you are important enough."

"thank god for that, Rabbi."

"I think, though, that you have a bit of the coward in you."

"yes, I do. a coward is a man who can foresee the future. a brave man is almost always without imagination."

"sometimes I think YOU would make a good Rabbi."

"not so. Plato had no Jewish beard."

"grow one."

"have a beer."

"thank you."

and so, we become quiet. it is another strange evening. the people come to me, they talk, they fill me: the future Rabbis, the revolutionaries with their rifles, the FBI, the whores, the poetesses, the young poets from Cal State, a professor from Loyola going to Michigan, a prof from the University of Cal at Berkeley, another who lives in Riverside, 3 or 4 boys on the road, plain bums with Bukowski books stashed in their brains . . . and for a while I thought that this gang would intrude upon and murder my fair and precious moments, but I've been lucky lucky for each man and each woman has brought me something and left me something, and I no longer must feel like Jeffers behind a stone wall, and I've been lucky in another way for what fame I have is largely hidden and quiet and I'll hardly ever be a Henry Miller with people camping on my front lawn, the gods have been very good to me, they've kept me alive and even, still kicking, taking notes, observing, feeling the goodness of good people, feeling the miracle run up my arm like a crazy mouse. such a life, given to me at the age of 48, even though tomorrow does not know is the sweetest of the sweet dreams.

the kid gets up a bit full of beer, tomorrow's Rabbi thundering across Sunday morning breakfasts.

"got to make it. class tomorrow."

"sure, kid, are you all right?"

"yeah. I'm all right. my dad says to say hello to you."

"you tell Sam I said to hang it in. we've all got to make it."

"you got my phone number?"

"yeah. right over my left tit."

I watch him leave. down the steps. a little fat. but good that way. power. excess power. he is glowing and rumbling. he will make a fine Rabbi. I like him very much. then he is gone, out of vision, and I sit down to write you this. cigarette ashes all across the type-writer. to let you know how it goes and what's next. next to my typewriter are 2 small white doll's shoes about half an inch long. my daughter, Marina, left them there. she's in Arizona, somewhere, about now, with a revolutionary mother. it's July 1968 and I hit the machine as I wait for the door to break down and see the two green-faced men with eyes the shade of stale jelly, air-cooled hand m.g.'s. I hope they don't show. it's been a lovely evening. and only a few lone partridges will remember the roll of the dice and the way the walls smiled. good night.

BEER AND POETS AND TALK

it was a hell of a night. Willie had slept in the weeds outside Bakersfield the night before. Dutch was there, and a buddy. the beer was on me. I made sandwiches. Dutch kept talking about literature, poetry; I tried to get him off it but he laid right in there. Dutch runs a bookshop around Pasadena or Glendale or somewhere. then talk about the riots came up. they asked me what I thought about the riots and I told them that I was waiting, that the thoughts would have to come by themselves. it was nice to be able to wait. Willie picked up one of my cigars, took the paper off, lit it.

somebody said, "how come you're writing a column? you used to laugh at Lipton for writing a column, now you're doing the same thing."

"Lipton writes a kind of left-wing Walter Winchell thing. I create Art. there's a difference."

"hey, man, you got any more of these green onions?" asked Willie.

I went into the kitchen for more green onions and beer. Willie was one right out of the book — a book that hadn't been written yet. he was a mass of hair, head and beard. bluejeans with patches. one week he was in Frisco. 2 weeks later he was in Albuquerque. then, somewhere else. he carried with him, everywhere, this batch of poems he had accepted for his magazine. whether the crazy magazine ever evolved or not was anybody's guess. Willie the Wire, slim, bouncy, immortal. he wrote very well. even when he put the knock on somebody it was a kind of without hatred knock. he just laid the statement down, then it was yours. a graceful carelessness.

I cracked some new beers. Dutch was still on literature. he had just published "18th Dynasty Egyptian Automobile Turnon" by D. R. Wagner. and a nice job too. Dutch's young buddy just listened — he was the new breed: quiet but very much there.

141

Willie worked on an onion. "I talked to Neal Cassady. he's gone completely crazy."

"yeah, he's begging for busts. it's stupid. building a forced myth. being in Kerouac's book screwed up his mind."

"man," I said, "there's nothing like a bit of dirty literary gossip, is there?"

"sure," said Dutch, "let's talk shop. everybody talks shop."

"listen, Bukowski, do you think that there's any poetry being written now? by anybody? Lowell made time, you know."

"almost all the great names have died recently — Frost, cummings, Jeffers, W. C. Williams, T. S. Eliot, the rest. a couple of nights ago, Sandburg. in a very short period, they all seemed to die together, throw in Vietnam and the ever-riots and it has been a very strange and quick and festering and new age. look at those skirts now, almost up around the ass. we are moving very quickly and I like it, it is not bad. but the Establishment is worried about its culture. culture is a steadier. there's nothing as good as a museum, a Verdi opera or a stiff-neck poet to hold back progress. Lowell was rushed into the breach, after a careful check of credentials. Lowell is interesting enough not to put you to sleep but diffuse enough so as not to be dangerous. the first thoughts you have after reading his work is, this baby has never missed a meal or even had a flat tire or a toothache. Creeley is a near similarity, and I imagine the Establishment balanced Creeley and Lowell for some time but had to finally come up with Lowell because Creeley just didn't seem like such a very good dull guy, and you couldn't trust him as much — he might even show up at the president's lawn party and tickle the guests with his beard. so, it had to be Lowell, and so it's Lowell we've got."

"so who's writing it? where are they?"

"not in America. and there are only 2 that I can think of. Harold Norse who is nursing his melancholia-hypochondria in Switzerland, taking handouts from rich backers, and having the running shits, fainting spells, the fear of ants, so forth. and writing very little now, kind of going crazy like the rest of us. but then WHEN he writes, it's all there. the other guy is Al Purdy. not Al Purdy the novelist, I mean Al Purdy the poet. they are not the same people. Al Purdy lives in Canada and grows his own grapes which he squeezes into his own wine. he is a drunk, an old hulk of a man who must now be somewhere in his mid-forties. his wife supports him so he can write his poetry, which, you've got to admit, is some wonderful kind of wife. I've never met one like that or have you. but, anyhow, the Canadian government is always laying some kind of grant on him, $4,000 here and there, and they send him up to the Pole to write about life there, and he does it, crazy clear poems about birds and people and dogs. god damn, he wrote a book of poems once called "Songs for All the Annettes" and I almost cried all the way through the book reading it. it's nice to look up sometimes, it's nice to have heroes, it's nice to have somebody else carrying some of the load."

"don't you think you write as well as they?"

"only at times. most of the time, no."

the beer ran out and I had to take a shit. I gave Willie a five and told him it'd be good if he got 2 six packs, tall, Schlitz (this is an advertisement), and all 3 of them left and I went in and sat down. it wasn't bad to be more or less asked questions of the age. it was better yet to be doing what I was doing. I thought about the hospitals, the racetracks, some of the women I used to know, some of the women I had buried, outdrunk, outfucked but not outargued. the alcoholic madwomen who had brought love to me especially and in their own way. then I heard it through the wall:

"listen, Johnny, you ain't even kissed me in a week. what's wrong, Johnny? listen, talk to me, I want you to talk to me."

"god damn you, get away from me. I don't want to talk to you. LEAVE ME ALONE, WILL YOU? GOD DAMN YOU, LEAVE ME ALONE!"

"listen, Johnny, I just want you to talk to me, I can't stand it. you don't have to touch me, just talk to me, jesus christ Johnny I can't stand it, I CAN'T STAND IT, JESUS!"

"GOD DAMN IT, I TOLD YOU TO LEAVE ME ALONE! LEAVE ME ALONE, GOD DAMN YOU, LEAVE ME ALONE, LEAVE ME ALONE, LEAVE ME ALONE, WILL YOU?"

"Johnny . . ."

he hit her a good one. open hand. a real good one. I almost fell off the stool. I heard her choking off the crap and walking off.

then Dutch and Willie and crew were back. they ripped open the cans. I finished my business and walked back in.

143

"I'm gonna get up an anthology," said Dutch, "an anthology of the best living poets, I mean the real best."

"sure," said Willie, "why not?" then he saw me: "enjoy your crap?"

"not too much."

"no?"

"no."

"you need more roughage. you ought to eat more green onions."

"you think so?"

"yeah."

I reached over and got 2 of them, jammed them down. maybe next time would be better. meanwhile there were riots, beer, talk, literature, and the lovely young ladies were making the fat millionaires happy. I reached over, got one of my own cigars, took off the paper, took off the cigar band, jammed the thing into my screwed-up and complex face, then lit it, the cigar. bad writing's like bad women: there's just not much you can do about it.

I SHOT A MAN IN RENO

Bukowski cried when Judy Garland sang at the N.Y. Philharmonic, Bukowski cried when Shirley Temple sang "I Got Animal Crackers in my Soup"; Bukowski cried in cheap flophouses, Bukowski can't dress, Bukowski can't talk, Bukowski is scared of women, Bukowski has a bad stomach, Bukowski is full of fears, and hates dictionaries, nuns, pennies, busses, churches, parkbenches, spiders, flies, fleas, freaks; Bukowski didn't go to war. Bukowski is old, Bukowski hasn't flown a kite for 45 years; if Bukowski were an ape they'd run him out of the tribe . . .

my friend is so worried about tearing the meat of my soul from my bones that he hardly seems to think of his own existence.

"but Bukowski pukes real neat and I've never seen him piss on the floor."

so I do have charm after all, you see. then he throws open a little door and there in a 3 by 6 room stacked with papers and rags is an out.

"you can always stay here, Bukowski. you'll never want."

no window, no bed, but I'm next to the bathroom. it still looks good to me.

"but you may have to wear earplugs because of the music I keep playing."

"I can pick up a set, I'm sure."

we walk back into his den. "you wanna hear some Lenny Bruce?"

"no, thanks."

"Ginsberg?"

"no, no."

he just has to keep that tape machine going, or the record player. they finally hit me with Johnny Cash singing to the boys at Folsom.

145

"I shot a man in Reno just to watch him die."

it seems to me that Johnny is giving them a little shit just like I suspect Bob Hope does to the boys at Viet during Xmas, but I have this kind of mind. the boys holler, they are out of their cells but I feel like it's something like tossing meatless bones instead of biscuits to the hungered and the trapped. I don't feel a damn thing holy or brave about it. there's only one thing to do for men in jail: let 'em out. there's only one thing to do for men at war: stop the war.

"turn it off," I ask.

"whatsa matta?"

"it's a trick. a publicity man's dream."

"you can't say that. Johnny's done time."

"a lot of people have."

"we think it's good music."

"I like his voice. but the only man who can sing in jail, really, is a man who is in jail, really."

"we still like it."

his wife is there and a couple of young black men who play combo in some band.

"Bukowski likes Judy Garland. Somewhere Over the Rainbow."

"I liked her that one time in N.Y. her soul was up. you couldn't beat her."

"she's overweight and a lush."

it was the same old thing — people tearing meat and not getting anywhere. I leave a little early. as I do, I hear them put J. Cash back on.

I stop for some beer and just make it in as the phone is ringing.

"Bukowski?"

"yeah?"

"Bill."

"oh, hello, Bill."

"what are you doing?"

"nothing."

"what are you doing Saturday night?"

"I'm tied then."

"I wanted you to come over, meet some people."

"not this time."

"you know, Charley, I am going to get tired of calling."
"yeah."
"do you still write for that same scurrilous rag?"
"what?"
"that hippie paper . . ."
"have you ever read it?"
"sure. all that prot st stuff. you're wasting your time."
"I don't always write to the paper's policy."
"I thought you did."
"I thought you had *read* the paper?"
"by the way, what have you heard from our mutual friend?"
"Paul?"
"yes, Paul."
"I haven't heard from him."
"you know, he admires your poetry very much."
"that's all right."
"personally, I don't like your poetry."
"that's all right too."
"you can't make it over Saturday."
"no."
"well, I'm going to get tired of calling. take care."
"yeah, good night."

another meat tearer. what the hell did they want? well, Bill
lived in Malibu and Bill made money writing – philosophical sex shit
potboilers full of typos and undergraduate Art work – and Bill
couldn't write but Bill couldn't stay off the telephone either. He'd
phone again. and again. and fling his little scrubby shit turds at me. I
was the old man who hadn't sold his balls to the butcher and it
drove them screwy. their final victory over me could only be a
physical beating and that could happen to any man at any place.

Bukowski thought Mickey Mouse was a nazi; Bukowski made
an ass out of himself at Barney's Beanery; Bukowski made an ass out
of himself at Shelly's Manne-Hole; Bukowski is jealous of Ginsberg,
Bukowski is jealous of the 1969 Cadillac, Bukowski can't understand
Rimbaud; Bukowski wipes his ass with brown hard toilet paper,
Bukowski will be dead in 5 years, Bukowski hasn't written a decent
poem since 1963, Bukowski cried when Judy Garland . . . shot a
man in Reno.

I sit down. stick the sheet in the typer. open a beer. light a smoke.

I get one or two good lines and the phone rings.

"Buk?"

"yeah?"

"Marty."

"hello, Marty."

"listen, I just ran across your last 2 columns. it's good writing. I didn't know you were writing so well. I want to run them in book form. have they come back from GROVE yet?"

"yeah."

"I want them. your columns are as good as your poems."

"a friend of mine in Malibu says my poems stink."

"to hell with him. I want the columns."

"they're with − − − −   − − − −."

"hell, he's a pornie-man. if you go with me you'll hit the universities, the best book stores. when those kinds find you out, it's all over; they're tired of that involute shit they've been getting for centuries. you'll see; I can see bringing out all your back and unavailable stuff and selling it for a buck, or a buck and a half a copy and going into the millions."

"aren't you afraid that will make a prick out of me?"

"I mean, haven't you always been a prick, especially when you've been drinking . . . by the way, how've you been doing?"

"they say I grabbed a guy at Shelly's by the lapels and shook him up a bit. but it could have been worse, you know."

"how do you mean?"

"I mean, he could have grabbed me by the lapels and shook me up a bit. a matter of pride, you know."

"listen, don't die or get killed until we get you out in those buck and a half editions."

"I'll try not to, Marty."

"how's the 'Penguin' coming?"

"Stanges says January. I just got the page proofs. and a 50 pound advance which I blew on the horses."

"can't you stay away from the track?"

"you bastards never say anything when I win."

"that's right. well, let me know on the columns."

"right. good night."

"good night."

Bukowski, the big-time writer; a statue of Bukowski in the Kremlin, jacking off; Bukowski and Castro, a statue in Havana in the sunlight covered with birdshit, Bukowski and Castro riding a tandem racing bike to victory — Bukowski in the rear seat; Bukowski bathing in a nest of orioles; Bukowski lashing a 19-year-old high-yellow with a tiger whip, a high-yellow with 38 inch busts, a high-yellow who reads Rimbaud; Bukowski kukoo in the walls of the world, wondering who shut off the luck . . . Bukowski going for Judy Garland when it was too late for everybody.

then I remember the time and get back in the car. just off Wilshire Boulevard. there's his name on the big sign. we once worked the same shit job. I am not too crazy about Wilshire blvd. but I am still a learner. I don't block out anything. he's half-colored, from a white mother, black father combo. we fell together on the shit job, something mutual. mostly not wanting to wade in shit forever, and although shit was a good teacher there were only so many lessons and then it could drown you and kill you forever.

I parked in back and beat on the back door. he said he'd wait late that night. it was 9:30 p.m. the door opened.

TEN YEARS. TEN YEARS. ten years. ten years. ten. ten fucking YEARS.

"Hank, you son of a bitch!"

"Jim, you lucky mother . . ."

"come on up."

I followed him in. jesus, so you don't buy all that. but it's nice especially with the secretaries and staff gone. I block nothing. he has 6 or 8 rooms. we go in to his desk. I rip out the two 6 packs of beers.

ten years.

he is 43. I am 48. I look at least 15 years older than he. and feel some shame. the sagging belly. the hang-dog air. the world has taken many hours and years from me with their very dull and routine tasks; it tells. I feel shame for my defeat; not his money, my defeat. the best revolutionary is a poor man; I am not even a revolutionary, I am only tired. what a bucket of shit was mine! mirror, mirror on the wall . . .

he looked good in a light yellow sweater, relaxed and really happy to see me.

"I've been going through hell," he said, "I haven't talked to a real human being in months."

"man, I don't know if I qualify."

"you qualify."

that desk looks twenty feet wide.

"Jim, I been fired from so many places like this. some shit sitting in a swivel. like a dream upon a dream upon a dream, all bad. now I sit here drinking beer with a man behind a desk and I don't know anymore now than I did then."

he laughed. "baby, I want to give you your own office, your own chair, your own desk. I know what you're getting now. I want to double that."

"I can't accept it."

"why?"

"I want to know where my value would be to you?"

"I need your brain."

I laughed.

"I'm serious."

then he laid out the plan. told me what he wanted. he had one of those stirring motherfucking brains that dreamed that sort of thing up. it seemed so good I had to laugh.

"it'll take 3 months to set it up," I tell him.

"then a contract."

"o.k. with me. but these things sometimes don't work."

"it'll work."

"meanwhile I've got a friend who'll let me sleep in his broom closet if the walls fall in."

"fine."

we drink 2 or 3 more hours then he leaves to get enough sleep to meet his friend for a yachting next morning (Saturday) and I tool around and drive out of the high rent district and hit the first dirty bar for a closer or two. and son of a bitch if I don't meet a guy I used to know down at a job we both used to have.

"Luke!" I say, "son of a bitch!"

"Hank, baby!"

another colored (or black) man. (what do the white guys do at night?)

he looks low so I buy him one.

"you still at the place?" he asks.

"yeah."

"man, shit," he says.

"what?"

"I couldn't take it anymore where you're at, you know, so I quit. man, I got a job right away. wow, a change, you know. that's what kills a man: lack of change."

"I know, Luke."

"well, the first morning I walk up to the machine. it's a fibre glass place. I've got on this open neck shirt with short sleeves and I notice people staring at me. well, hell, I sit down and start pressing the levers and it's all right for a while and next thing you know I start itching all over. I call the foreman over and I say, 'hey, what the hell's this? I'm itching all over! my neck, my arms, everywhere!' he tells me, 'it's nothing, you'll get used to it.' but I notice he has on this scarf buttoned up all the way around his throat and this long-sleeved working shirt. well, I come in the next day all scarfed-up and oiled and buttoned but it's still no good − this fucking glass is shiving off so fine you can't *see* it and it's all little glass arrows and it goes right through the clothing and into the skin. then I know why they make me wear the protective glasses for my eyes. could blind a man in half an hour. I had to quit. went to a foundry. man, do you know that men POUR THIS WHITE HOT SHIT INTO MOLDS? they pour it like bacon-grease or gravy. Unbelievable! and hot! shit! I quit. man, how you doing?"

"that bitch there, Luke, she keeps looking at me and grinning and pulling her skirt higher."

"don't pay any attention. she's crazy."

"but she has beautiful legs."

"yes, she has."

I buy another drink, pick up, walk over to her.

"hello, baby."

she goes into her purse, comes out, hits the button and she's got a beautiful 6 inch swivel. I look at the bartender who looks blank-faced. the bitch says, "one step closer and you got no balls!"

I knock her drink over and when she looks at that I grab her wrist, twist the swivel out, fold it, put it into my pocket. the bartender still looks neutral. I go back to Luke and we finish our drinks. I notice it's ten to 2 and get 2 six packs from the barkeep. we go out to my car. Luke's without wheels. she follows us. "I need a ride." "where?" "around Century." "that's a long way." "so what, you motherfuckers got my knife."

by the time I am halfway to Century I see those female legs lifting in the back seat. when the legs come down I pull down a long dark corner and tell Luke to take a smoke. I hate seconds but when firsts haven't been for a time and you are supposed to be a great Artist and an understander of Life, seconds just HAVE to do, and like the boys say, with some, seconds are better. it was good. when I dropped her off I gave her the switchblade back wrapped in a ten. stupid, of course. but I like to be stupid. Luke lives around 8th and Irola so it's not too far in for me.

as I open the door the phone begins ringing. I open a beer and sit in the rocker and listen to it ring. for me, it's been enough — evening, night and morning.

Bukowski wears brown b.v.d.'s. Bukowski is afraid of airplanes. Bukowski hates Santa Claus. Bukowski makes deformed figures out of typewriter erasers. when water drips, Bukowski cries. when Bukowski cries, water drips. o, sanctums of fountains, o scrotums, o fountaining scrotums, o man's great ugliness everywhere like that fresh dogturd that the morning shoe did not see again; o, the mighty police, o the mighty weapons, o the mighty dictators, o the mighty damn fools everywhere, o the lonely lonely octopus, o the clock-tick seeping each neat one of us balanced and unbalanced and holy and constipated, o the bums lying in alleys of misery in a golden world, o the children to become ugly, o the ugly to become uglier, o the sadness and sabres and the closing of the walls — no Santa Claus, no Pussy, no Magic Wand, no Cinderella, no Great Minds Ever; kukoo — just shit and the whipping of dogs and children, just shit and the wiping away of shit; just doctors without patients just clouds without rain just days without days, o god o mighty that you put this upon us.

when we break into your mighty KIKE palace and timecard angels I want to hear Your voice just saying once

MERCY

MERCY

MERCY

152

FOR YOURSELF and for us and for what we will do to You, I turned off of Irola until I hit Normandie, that's what I did, and then came in and sat and listened to the telephone ring.

A RAIN OF WOMEN

yesterday, which was Friday, was dark and rainy, and I kept saying, stay sober, man, don't fall to pieces, and I walked out the door and out onto the landlord's lawn and ducked just in time to avoid a football thrown by a future S.C. quarterback, 1975 — 1975?, and I thought, jesus, we are not too far from 1984 I remember when I read that book, I thought, well, 1984, that's ten million miles to China, and here it was almost here, and I was almost dead, getting ready, chewing on the pulpy gig, getting ready to spit it out. dark and rainy — a death closet, a dark stinking death closet: Los Angeles, Calif., late afternoon, Friday, China 8 miles away, rice with eyes, vomiting dogs of mourning — dark and rainy, ah shit! — and I remembered when I was a kid, I thought, I'd like to live to see the year 2,000, I thought that would be the magic thing, with my old man beating hell out of me everyday I wanted to live to be 80 and see the year 2,000; now with everything beating hell out of me I no longer have that desire — it's a day at a time, WAR, dark and rainy — stay sober, man, don't fall to pieces, and I got into the car, used, me and it, and went up and made the 5th of 12 payments, and then I drove down Hollywood Blvd., west, the most depressive of all the streets, jammed glass nothing of nothing, it was the only street that really made me angry, and then I remembered I wanted Sunset which was just about as bad, and I turned south, everybody with their wipers going going going and behind that glass those FACES! — bah! — and I made Sunset, drove a block further west, found M. C. Slum's, pulled up beside a red Chevy with a pale blonde in it and the pale blonde and I stared at each other listlessly and hatefully — I'd fuck her, I thought, on a desert with nobody around, and she looked at me and thought, I'd fuck him inside a dead volcano with nobody around, and I said "SHIT!", started the engine, put it in reverse and drove on out of there, dark and rainy, no service, you could sit there for hours and nobody would ask you what you wanted, you'd just see a mechanic now and then, chewing gum, his head popping up out of the hole, oh what a wonderful person he was! — and if you asked him anything he'd get pissed — you were supposed to see the service manager but the service manager was always hiding somewhere — he was afraid of the mechanic too and didn't want to put too much work on him. actually, the whole horrible answer was that NOBODY COULD DO ANYTHING — poets couldn't write poetry, mechanics couldn't fix cars, dentists couldn't pull teeth, barbers couldn't cut hair, surgeons fucked up with the knife, laundries ripped your shirts and sheets and lost your socks; bread and beans had little stones in them that broke the teeth; football players were cowards, telephone repairmen were molesters of children; and mayors, governors, generals, presidents had as much sense as slugs caught in spider webs. and on and on. dark and rainy, stay sober, don't fall to pieces, I drove into the Bier's garage lot and a big black bastard with a cigar ran up to me: "HEY! YOU! YOU THERE! YOU CAN'T PARK IN HERE!"

"listen, I know I can't park in here! I just wanna see the service manager. are you the service manager?"

"NO! NO, MAN! I'M NOT THE SERVICE MANAGER! MAN, YOU CAN'T PARK IN HERE!"

"well, where is the service manager? in the men's room playing with his pud?"

"YOU'VE GOT TO BACK ON OUT AND PARK IN THAT LOT THERE!"

I backed on out and parked in that lot there. I got out and walked over and stood by the little pulpit that said "Service Manager." a woman drove in, a bit dizzy, big new car, door half open, car stalling, she looked wild, got out, car bucking, short short skirt, long grey stockings, her dress up around her hips climbing out the door, I stared at those legs, stupid bitch, what legs, umm, and she stood there stupid and dizzy and here CAME the service manager out of the men's room, "CAN I HELP YOU, MAM? AH, WHAT'S THE TROUBLE? YOUR BATTERY? DEAD BATTERY?" and he ran off to get the jumper and he ran back with the battery on wheels, asked her how to unhook the hood, and I stood there as they played with the hood, me looking at her legs and ass, thinking, the stupid ones are the best lays because you hate them — they have the gift of flesh and the brains of a fly.

they finally got the hood up and he hooked the battery up to his battery and told her to start the car. she got it started on the 3rd or 4th try, then put it in drive and tried to run him over as he was unhooking the cables. she almost made it, but he was a little too good on his feet. "PUT YOUR BRAKE ON! LEAVE IT IN NEUTRAL!" real stupid wench, I thought, wonder how many men she has killed? big earrings. red mouth like airmail stamps. intestines full of shit.

"O.K., NOW BACK IT UP AROUND THE SIDE OF THE BUILDING! WE'LL CHARGE IT FOR YOU!"

he ran along beside the car, sticking his head in the window and staring at her legs as she backed up. "AT'S RIGHT, AT'S RIGHT, BACK IT UP, BACK IT UP!", looking, looking. she went around the corner and he stood there.

the service manager and I both had hard dicks. I came off from against the wall where I had been leaning. "HEY!"

"WHATZU?" he said.

"I NEED HELP!" I said walking up with my hard dick. he looked at me strangely.

"WHAT KINDA HELP?"

"rotation, realignment and balance."

"HEY! HERITITO!"

a little Japanese ran up.

"rotation, realignment and balance," I told Heritito.

"gimme your keys."

I gave Heritito the keys. it didn't bother me. I always carried 2 or 3 sets of keys. I was a neurotic.

"62 Comet," I told him.

Heritito went toward the 62 Comet as the service manager went to the men's room. I went back to the wall and watched the traffic go by; it was jammed and frightened and tired in the dark Los Angeles fizzling, drizzling rain, dark, 1984 20 years past already, the whole sick sweet society quite mad as a birthday cake given to the ants and the roaches, dark shit rain, Heritito ran my blue Comet, 5 of 12 payments up on the rack and my dick went down.

I saw him take off the wheels and went for a walk. I walked around the block twice, passed 200 people and failed to see a human

156

being. I looked in the store windows and there was nothing in the store windows that I wanted at all. yet each thing had a price. a guitar. now what in the hell would I do with a guitar? I could burn it. a record player. a t.v. a radio. useless, useless. gut-junk. stuff to clog the mind-gut with. slug you like a red 6 ounce glove. pop. you had it.

Heritito was pretty good. a half hour later he had it down from the rack. parked.

"hey, that's good, now where do I pay?"

"oh no, that was just the wheel balance and rotation. we got to put it on the alignment rack yet. there's just one car ahead of you."

"oh."

they were racing at night and I was hoping to make the first post, 7:30 p.m., I needed the money and was going good, but it also took me about an hour before the races to set up my plays, that meant I had to have 6:30. rain, dark rain, failure. on the 13th, rent. on the 14th, child support. on the 15th. car payment. I had to have the horses; without them, I might as well toss in. I don't know how the hell anybody ever made it. well, shit. while waiting I walked over to the store and bought 4 pairs of shorts for $5. got back, threw them in the trunk, locked the trunk, jesus christ, found out I only had ONE key to the trunk! no good for a neurotic. I walked toward the keyman's shack. almost got run over by a woman backing out. I stuck my head in the window and stared at her legs. she had purple garters and very white flesh: "watch out where you are going," I said to her legs, "you damn near killed me!" I never saw her face. I pulled my head out and walked to the keyman's shack. got another key made. while I was paying, an old woman ran up. "hey, I'm blocked in by a truck! I can't get out!"

"well, that's no hair of mine," said the keyman.

she was just too old. flat shoes. insane look in eye. big flat false teeth. skirt halfway to ankles. love, love, love your grand-mother's warts.

she looked at me, "what'll I do, Mr.?"

"try Kool-ade," I said and walked off. maybe 20 years ago. well, I had my little key. it was still raining. I was standing trying to fit the key on the keyring when this one came out in miniskirt with umbrella. now with a miniskirt you're supposed to wear these special sexless stockings, netted thick shit, or stocking panties with panty petticoat crap dangling sickly; but this one was dressed old-style — high heels, long nylon stockings, the mini way up around her butt, and she was built. christ, everybody looked, it was walking mad sex on the loose, my hand trembled on the keyring and I stared in the rain and she walked slowly toward me, smiling. I ran around the corner with the keyring. I wanna see that ass go by, I thought. but the ass turned the corner and walked past me, slowly, voluting, voluting, young, asking for it. a well-dressed guy ran up behind her. called her by name. "oh, I'm so glad to see you!" he said. he talked and talked and she smiled. "well, I hope you have a good time to-night!" she said. he was dropping her? the guy was sick. I got the key on the keyring and followed her into the grocery store. I watched her wobbling and wobbling right there in the market and men turned their heads and said, "Jesus, look at that!"

I walked up to the butcher counter and took a number. I needed meat. while I was waiting I saw her come back. then she leaned against the wall and stood there, 15 feet off, looking at *me* and smiling. I looked down in my hand. I was #92. there she was. she was looking at *me*. man of the world. something went out of me. maybe she's got a big pussy, I thought. she kept looking and smiling. she had a nice face, almost beautiful. but I've got to make the first post, 7:30 p.m. rent the 13th, child support the 14th, car payment the 15th, 4 pairs of shorts $5, wheel alignment, first post first post, #92, YOU'RE AFRAID OF HER, YOU DON'T KNOW WHAT TO DO, HOW TO ACT, MAN OF THE WORLD, YOU ARE AFRAID, YOU DON'T KNOW THE WORDS, BUT WHY DOES IT HAVE TO BE IN A BUTCHERSHOP? and it'll be trouble. she'll be insane, you know that. she'll want to move in. she'll snore at night, throw newspapers in the toilet, want to be fucked 8 times a week. god, it's too much, no no no no no, I've got to make that first post.

she read me. she read that I was chickenshit. suddenly she walked on past. 68 men stared and had dreams of glory. I passed. old. I was. on the dumpheap. she had wanted me. go play your horses, old man. go buy your meat, #92.

"#92," the butcher said and I got a pound of groundround, a small t-bone and a cube steak. wrap that around your dick, old man.

I walked out in the rain and back to my car, opened the trunk, threw the meat in and stood back against the wall, looking worldly, smoking a cigarette, waiting for them to run it up the rack, waiting for the first post, but I knew that I had failed, failed an easy one, failed a good one, a gift from the heavens on a shit rainy day, Los Angeles, a Friday going into evening, the cars still going by with wipers going going going, no faces behind the glass, and me, Bogart, me, the one who has lived, crouched up against that wall, asshole, rounded shoulders, the Benedictine monks laughing wildly as they drank their wine, all the monkeys scratching, the rabbis blessing pickles and weenies; the man of action — Bogart, leaning on a Biers-Sobuck wall, no fuck, no guts, it rained it rained it rained, I'll take Lumber King in the first and parlay it to Wee Herb; and a mechanic came and got it and ran it up the rack and I looked at the clock — 5:30, it was going to be close, but somehow it didn't matter so much anymore. I threw the cigarette out in front of me and stared at it. the red glow stared back. then the rain put it out and I walked around the corner looking for a bar.

NIGHT STREETS OF MADNESS

the kid and I were the last of a drunken party at my place, and we were sitting there when somebody outside began blowing a car horn, loud LOUD LOUD it was, oh sing loude, but then everything is axed through the head anyway. the world is done, so I just sat there with my drink, smoking a cigar, thinking of nothing — the poets were gone, the poets with their ladies were gone, it was fairly pleasant even with the horn going. a comparison. the poets had each accused each other of various treacheries, of bad writing, of having slipped; meanwhile, each of them claiming they deserved better recognition, that they wrote better than so and so and so forth. I told them all that they needed 2 years in the coal mines or the steel mills, but on they chattered, finky, precious, barbaric, and most of them rotten writers. now they were gone. the cigar was good. the kid sat there. I had just written a foreword to his second book of poems. or his first? well.

"listen," said the kid, "let's go out there and tell them to fuck-off. tell him to jam that horn up his ass."

the kid wasn't a bad writer, and he had the ability to laugh at himself, which is sometimes a sign of greatness, or at least a sign that you have a chance to end up being something else besides a stuffed literary turd. the world was full of stuffed literary turds talking about the time they met Pound at Spoleto or Edmund Wilson in Boston or Dali in his underwear or Lowell in his garden; sitting there in their tiny bathrobes, letting you have it, and NOW you were talking to THEM, ah, you see. ". . . the last time I saw Burroughs . . ." "Jimmy Baldwin, jesus, he was drunk, we had to trot him out on the stage and lean him on the mike . . ."

"let's go out there and tell them to jam that horn up their ass," said the kid, influenced by the Bukowski myth (I am really a coward), and the Hemingway thing and Humphrey B. and Eliot with his panties rolled. well. I puffed on my cigar. the horn went on. LOUDE SING KUKOOO.

"the horn's all right. never go out on the street after you've been drinking 5 or 6 or 8 or ten hours. they have cages ready for the likes of us. I don't think I could take another cage, not one more god damned cage of theirs. I build enough of my own."

"I'm going out to tell them to shove it," said the kid.

the kid was under the superman influence, Man and Superman. he liked huge men, tough and murderous, 6-4, 300 pounds, who wrote immortal poetry. the trouble was the big boys were all subnormal and it was the dainty little queers with the fingernail polish on who write the tough-boy poems. the only guy who fit the kid's hero-mold was big John Thomas and big John Thomas always acted as if the kid weren't there. the kid was Jewish and big John Thomas had the mainline to Adolph. I liked them both and I don't like very many people.

"listen," said the kid, "I am going to tell them to jam it."

oh my god, the kid was big but a little on the fat side, he hadn't missed too many meals, but he was easy inside, kind inside, scared and worried and a little crazy like the rest of us, none of us made it, finally, and I said, "kid, forget the horn. it doesn't sound like a man blowing anyhow. it sounds like a woman. a man will stop and start with a horn, make musical threats out of it. a woman just leans on it. the total sound, one big female neurosis."

"fuck it!" said the kid. he ran out the door.

what does this have to do with anything? I thought. what does it matter? people keep making moves that don't count. when you make a move, everything must be mathematically set. that's what Hem learned at the bullfights and put to work in his work. that's what I learn at the track and put to work in my life. good old Hem and Buk.

"hello, Hem? Buk calling."

"oh, *Buk,* so glad you called."

"thought I'd drop over for a drink."

"oh, I'd love it, kid, but you see, my god, you might say I'm kinda out of town right now."

"but why'd you do it, Ernie?"

"you've read the books. they claim I was crazy, imagining

161

things. in and out of the bughouse. they say I imagined the phone was tapped, that I imagined the C.I.A. was on my ass, that I was being tailed and watched. you know, I wasn't really political but I always fucked with the left. the Spanish war, all that crap."

"yeah, most of you literary guys lean left. it seems Romantic, but it can turn into a hell of a trap."

"I know. but really, I had this hell of a hangover, and I knew I had slipped, and when they believed in THE OLD MAN AND THE SEA, I knew that the world was rotten."

"I know. you went back to your early style. but it wasn't real."

"I know it wasn't real. and I got the PRIZE. and the tail on me. old age on me. sitting around drinking like an old fuck, telling stale stories to anybody who would listen. I had to blow my brains out."

"o.k., Ernie, see you later."

"all right, I know you will, Buk."

he hung up. and how.

I went outside to check on the kid.

it was an old woman in a new '69 car. she kept leaning on the horn. she didn't have any legs. any breasts. any brain. just a '69 car and indignation, great and total indignation. a car was blocking her driveway. she had her own home. I lived in one of the last slum courts on DeLongpre. someday the landlord would sell it for a tremendous sum and I would be bulldozed out. too bad. I threw parties that lasted until the sun came up, ran the typer day and night. a madman lived in the next court. everything was sweet. one block North and ten blocks West I could walk along a sidewalk that had footprints of STARS upon it. I don't know what the names mean. I don't hit the movies. don't have a t.v. when my radio stopped playing I threw it out the window. drunk. me, not the radio. there is a big hole in one of my windows. I forgot the screen was there. I had to open the screen and drop the radio out. later, whilst I was drunken barefoot my foot (left) picked up all the glass, and the doctor while slitting my foot open without benefit of a shot, probing for ballsy glass, asked me, "listen, do you ever walk around not quite knowing what you are doing?"

"most of the time, baby."

then he gave me a big cut that wasn't needed.

I gripped the sides of the table and said, "yes, Doctor."

then he became more kindly. why should doctors be better than I am? I don't understand it. the old medicine man gimmick.

so there I was out on the street, Charles Bukowski, friend of Hemingway, Ernie, I have never read DEATH IN THE AFTER-NOON. where do I get a copy?

the kid said to the crazy woman in the car, who was only demanding respectful and stupid property rights, "we'll move the car, we'll push it out of the way."

the kid was talking for me too. now that I had written his foreword, he owned me.

"look, kid, there's no place to push the car. and I really don't care. I'm going in for a drink." it was just beginning to rain. I have a most delicate skin, like an alligator, and soul to match. I walked off. shit, I'd had enough wars.

I walked off and then just as I about got to my front court hole, I heard screaming voices. I turned.

then we had this. a thin kid, insane, in white t-shirt screaming at the fat Jewish poet I had just written a foreword to poems for. what had the white t-shirt to do with it? the white t-shirt pushed against my semi-immortal poet. he pushed hard. the crazy old woman kept leaning against the car horn.

Bukowski, should you test your left hook again? you swing like the old barn door and only win one fight out of ten. when was the last fight you won, Bukowski? you should be wearing women's panties.

well, hell, with a record like yours, one more loss won't be any big shame.

I started to move forward to help the Jewish kid poet but I saw he had white t-shirt backing up. then out of the 20 million dollar highrise next to my slum hole, here came a young woman running. I watched the cheeks of her ass wobble in the fake Hollywood moonlight.

girl, I could show you something you will, would never forget — a solid 3 and one quarter inches of bobbling throbbing cock, oh my, but she never gave me a chance, she asshole-wobbling ran to her little 68 Fiaria or however you spell it, and got in, pussy dying for

163

my poetic soul, and she got in, started the thing, got it out of the driveway, almost ran me over, me Bukowski, BUKOWSKI, ummm, and ran the thing into the underground parking lot of the 20 million buck highrise. why hadn't she parked there to begin with? well.

the guy in the white t-shirt is still wobbling around insane, my Jewish poet has moved back to my side there in the Hollywood moonlight, which was like stinking dishwater spilling over us all, suicide is so difficult, maybe our luck will change, there's PENGUIN coming up, Norse-Bukowski-Lamantia . . . what?

now, now, the woman has her clearance for her driveway but she can't make it in. she doesn't even angle her car properly. she keeps backing up and ramming a white delivery truck in front of her. there go the taillights on first shot. she backs up. hits the gas. there goes half a back door. she backs up. hits the gas. there goes all the fender and half the left side, no the right side, that's it the right side. nothing adds. the driveway is clear.

Bukowski-Norse-Lamantia. Penguin books. it's a damn good thing for those other two guys that I am in there.

again chickenshit steel mashing against steel. and in between she's leaning on the horn. white t-shirt dangling in the moonlight, raving.

"what's going on?" I asked the kid.

"I dunno," he finally admitted.

"you'll make a good rabbi some day but you should understand all this."

the kid is studying to be a rabbi.

"I don't understand it," he said.

"I need a drink" I said. "if John Thomas were here he'd murder them all. but I ain't John Thomas."

I was just about to leave, the woman just kept on ramming the white pickup truck to pieces, I was just about to leave when an old man in a floppy brown overcoat and glasses, a real old guy, he was older than I, and that's old, he came out and confronted the kid in the white t-shirt. confronted? that's the right word ain't it?

anyhow, as they say, the old guy with glasses and floppy brown overcoat runs out with this big can of green paint, it must have been at least a gallon or 5 gallons, I don't know what it means, I have completely lost the plot or the meaning, if there ever was any in the first place, and the old man throws the paint on the insane kid in the white t-shirt circling around on DeLongpre ave. in the chickenshit Hollywood moonlight, and most of it misses him and some of it gets him, mostly where his heart used to be, a smash of green along the white, and it happens fast, like things happen fast, almost quicker than the eye or the pulse can add up, and that's why you get such divergent accounts of any action, riot or fist fight or anything, the eye and the soul can't keep up with the frustrating animal ACTION, but I saw the old man go down, fall, I think the first was a push, but I know that the second wasn't. the woman in the car stopped ramming and honking and just sat there screaming, screaming, one total pitch of scream that meant the same thing as her leaning on the honker, she was dead and finished forever in a '69 car and she couldn't fathom it, she was hooked and broken, thrown away, and some small touch inside of her still realized this – nobody ever finally loses their soul – they only piss away 99/100ths of it.

white t-shirt landed good on the old man on the second shot. broke his glasses. left him flopping and floundering in his old brown overcoat. the old man got up and the kid gave him another shot, knocked him down, hit him again as he got halfass up, the kid in the white t was having a good time of it.

the young poet said to me, "JESUS! LOOK WHAT HE'S DO-ING TO THE OLD MAN!"

"umm, very interesting," I said, wishing I had a drink or a smoke at least.

I walked off back toward my place. then I saw the squad car and moved a bit faster. the kid followed me in.

"why don't we go back out there and tell them what happened?"

"because nothing happened except that everybody has been driven insane and stupid by life. in this society there are only two things that count: don't be caught without money and don't get caught high on any kind of high."

"but he shouldn't have done that to the old man."

"that's what old men are for."

"but what about justice?"

"but that is justice: the young whipping the old, the living whipping the dead. don't you see?"

165

"but you say these things and *you're* old."

"I know, let's step inside."

I brought out some more beer and we sat there. through the walls you could hear the radio of the stupid squad car. 2 twentytwo year old kids with guns and clubs were going to be the immediate decision-makers upon 2,000 years of idiotic, homosexual, sadistic Christianity.

no wonder they felt good in their smooth and well-fed stretched black, most policemen being lower-middle class servants given a steak in the frying pan and a wife with halfway decent ass and legs, and a little quiet home in Shitland — they'd kill you to prove Los Angeles was right, we're taking you in, sir, so sorry, sir, but we've got to do this, sir.

2,000 years of Christianity and what do you end up with? squad-car radios trying to hold rotting shit together, and what else? tons of wars, little air raids, muggers in streets, knifings, so many insane that you just forget it, you just let them run the streets in policeman's uniforms or out of them.

so we went inside and the kid kept saying,

"hey, let's go out there and tell the police what happened?"

"no, kid, please. if you are drunk you are guilty no matter what happens."

"but they are right outside, let's go tell them."

"there's nothing to tell."

the kid looked at me as if I were some kind of chickenshit coward. I was. the longest he had ever been in jail was 7 hours under some kind of east L.A. campus protestation.

"kid, I think that the night is over."

I threw him a blanket for the couch and he went to sleep. I took 2 quarts of beer, opened both, set them on the headboard of my rented bed, took a big swallow, stretched out, waited on my death as Cummings must have done, Jeffers, the garbage man, the newspaper boy, the tout . . .

I finished off the beers.

the kid woke up about 9:30 a.m. I can't understand early risers. Micheline was another early riser. running around ringing doorbells, waking everybody up. they were nervous, trying to push down walls. I always figured a man was a damn fool if he got up before noon. Norse had the best idea — sit around in silk robe and pajamas and let the world go its way.

I let the kid out the door and off he went into the world. the green paint was dry on the street. Maeterlinck's bluebird was dead. Hirschman sat in a dark room with a bloody right nostril.

and I had written another FOREWORD to another book of somebody's poetry. how many more?

"hey, Bukowski, I've got this book of poems here. I thought you might read the poems and say something."

"say something? but I don't like poetry, man."

"that's all right. just say something."

the kid was gone. I had to take a shit. the toilet was clogged; the landlord gone for 3 days. I took the shit and put it in a brown paper bag. then I went outside and walked with the paperbag like a man going to work with his lunch. then when I got to the vacant lot I threw the bag. three forewords. 3 bags of shit. nobody would ever understand how Bukowski suffered.

I walked back toward my place, dreaming of supine women and everlasting fame. the former would be nicer. and I was running out of brown bags. I mean, paper bags. 10 a.m. there was the mailman. a letter from Beiles in Greece. he said it was raining there too.

fine, then, and inside I was alone again, and the madness of the night was the madness of the day. I arranged myself upon the bed, supine, staring upward and listened to the cocksucking rain.

PURPLE AS AN IRIS

One side of the ward was marked A-1, A-2, A-3, so forth and the men were kept on that side and the other side was marked B-1, B-2, B-3, and they kept the women over there. But then they decided it would be good therapy to let us mix now and then, and it was very good therapy — we fucked in the closets, out in the garden, behind the barn, everywhere. Many of the women were in there pretending to be crazy because their husbands had caught them doing the business with other men, but it was all a con — they asked to be committed, getting the old man's pity and then coming out and doing it all over again. Then going back in, coming out, so forth. But while the girls were in they had to have it and we did the best we could to help them. And, of course, the staff was so busy — doctors screwing nurses and orderlies screwing each other that they hardly knew what we were doing. That was all right.

I'd seen more crazy people outside — everywhere you looked: in dime stores, factories, post offices, pet shops, baseball games, political offices — than I ever saw in there. You sometimes wondered what they were in for. There was one guy, quite level, you could talk to him easily, Bobby his name was, he looked o.k.; in fact he looked a hell of a lot better than some of the shrinks who were trying to cure us. You couldn't talk to a shrink any length of time without feeling crazy yourself. The reason most shrinks become shrinks is because they are worried about their own minds. And examining your own mind is the worst thing a crazy man can do, all the theories to the contrary being bullshit. Every now and then some nut would ask something like this:

"Hey, where's Dr. Malov? Haven't seen him today. Is he on vacation? Or maybe he transferred out?"

"He's on vacation," another nut would answer, "and he transferred out."

"I don't understand."

"Butcher knife. Wrists and throat. He didn't leave a note."

"He was such a nice fellow."

"Oh, shit yes."

That's one thing I could never understand. I mean about the grapevine in places like that. The grapevine is never wrong. In factories, large institutions like that ... word either drips down that such and such has happened to so and so; and worse, days, weeks ahead of time you heard things that turned out to be true – Old Joe who had been there 20 years was going to get layed off or we were all going to get layed off, or anything like that, it was always true. Another thing about shrinks, getting back to shrinks, is that I could never figure out why they had to go the *hard* way when they had all those pills on hand. Not a brain in the whole lot of them.

Well, anyhow, getting back to it – the more advanced cases (advancing toward a seeming cure, I mean) were let out at 2 each afternoon on Mondays and Thursdays and were to return by 5:30 that evening or they lost privileges. The theory to this was that we could adjust to society slowly. You know, instead of just jumping out of the nut ward into the street. One look around could put you right back in. Looking at all those other nuts out there.

I was allowed my Monday and Thursday privileges, during which time I visited a doctor I had a little dirt on and stocked up on free dexies, bennies, meth, rainbows, librium and all the like. I sold these to the patients. Bobby ate them like candy and Bobby had a lot of money. In fact, most of them did. As I said, I often wondered why Bobby was in there. He was all right in almost all areas of behavior. He just had one little trick: every now and then he'd get up and put both of his hands in his pockets and lift his pants legs way up high and walk 8 or ten steps while giving out this dull little whistling sound from his lips. Some kind of tune that was in his head; not very musical, but some kind of tune, and always the same one. It only lasted a few seconds. That's all that was wrong with him. But he kept doing that, maybe 20 or 30 times a day. The first few times you saw it, you thought he was joking and thought, my god, what a droll and wonderful fellow. Then, later, you knew he *had* to do it.

O.k. Where was I? All right. They let the girls out at 2 p.m. too and then we had a better chance with them. It got hot fucking in those closets all the time. But we had to hustle fast because the cruisers were around. Guys with cars who knew the hospital schedule and they'd drive up with their cars and whisk our fine and helpless ladies away from us.

Before I got into the dope racket I didn't have much money and there was plenty of trouble. I had to take one of the best ones, Mary, into the ladies room of a Standard Service Station one time. We had quite some trouble finding a position — nobody wants to lay on the floor of a pisshouse — and it wasn't right standing — quite awkward — and then I remembered a trick I had once learned. In a train crapper passing through Utah. With a nice young Indian woman drunk on wine. — I told Mary to throw one leg up over the sink bowl. I worked a leg up over that bowl and stuck it in. It worked fine. Remember that one. You may need it sometime. You can even let hot water run on your balls for added sensation.

Anyhow, Mary came out of the ladies restroom first and then I walked out. The Standard Station attendant saw me.

"Hey, man, what were you doing in the ladies room?"

"Oh, good heavens, man!" I gave my wrist a delicate little twist. "You really *are* a little fart of a flirt, aren't you?" I wiggled off. He didn't seem to question me. That worried hell out of me for about two weeks, then I forgot about it . . .

I think I forgot about it. Anyhow, the dope moved well. Bobby swallowed anything. I even sold him a couple of birth control pills. He swallowed them.

"*Fine* stuff, man. Get me some more, will ya?"

But Pulon was the strangest of them all. He just sat in a chair by the window and never moved. He never went to the dining room. Nobody ever saw him eat. Weeks went by. He just sat in his chair. He really related to the far-out nuts — people who never spoke to anybody, not even the shrinks. They'd stand there and talk to Pulon. They'd speak back and forth, nodding, laughing, smoking. Outside of Pulon, I was best with relating to the far-out cases. The shrinks would ask us, "How do you guys break them down?"

Then we'd both stare back and not answer.

But Pulon could talk to people who hadn't spoken for 20

years. Get them to answer questions and tell him things. Pulon was very strange. He was one of those brilliant men who would go to their death without ever letting it out – which was why maybe it kept that way. Only a fathead has bags full of advice and answers to every question.

"Listen, Pulon," I said, "you never eat. I never see you eat food. How do you stay alive."

"Heeehehehehehehehe. Heeeheeeheeeheeehehehe . . ."

I volunteered for special jobs just to get out of the ward, just to get around the place. I was kind of like Bobby, only I didn't pull up my pants and whistle some off-tune version of Bizet's *Carmen*. I had this suicide complex and these heavy depressive fits and I couldn't stand crowds of people and, especially, I couldn't *bear* standing in a long line waiting for anything. And that's all society is becoming: long lines and waiting for something. I'd tried suicide by gas and it didn't work. But I had another problem. My problem was getting out of bed. I hated to get out of bed, ever. I used to tell people, "Man's two greatest inventions are the bed and the atomic bomb; the first keeps out out of it and the second gets you out of it." They thought I was crazy. Children's games, that's all people play: children's games – they go from the cunt to the grave without ever being touched by the horror of life.

Yes, I hated to get out of bed in the mornings. That meant starting life again and after you've been in bed all night you've built a special kind of privacy that is very difficult to surrender. I was always a loner. Forgive me, I guess I am off in the head, but I mean, except for a quickie piece of ass it wouldn't matter to me if all the people in the world died. Yes, I know it's not nice. But I'd be as contended as a snail; it was, after all, the people who had made me unhappy.

It was the same every morning:

"Bukowski, get up!"

"Waaaarf?"

"I said, 'Bukowski, get up!' "

"Yek?"

"Not 'YEK!' Up! Rise and shine, you freak!"

". . . arrr . . . go fuck your little sister . . ."

171

"I'll get Dr. Blasingham."

"Fuck him too."

And here would come Blasingham trotting up, disturbed, a little bit put-out, you know, he'd been finger-fucking one of the student nurses in his office who was dreaming of marriage and vacations on the French Rivi . . . with an old sub-normal who couldn't even get his pecker hard. Dr. Blasingham. Bloodsucker of county funds. A trickster and a shit. Why he hadn't been elected president of the United States I couldn't figure out. Maybe they had never seen him — he was so busy fingering and slobbering over nurse's panties . . .

"All right, Bukowski. UP!"

"There's nothing to do. There's absolutely nothing to do. Don't you see?"

"Up. Or you'll lose all privileges."

"Shit. That's like saying you'll lose your rubber when there's nothing to fuck."

"O.k., bastard . . . I, Dr. Blasingham, I am counting . . . Now, here we go . . . 'One . . . Two . . .' "

I leaped up. "Man is the victim of an environment which refuses to understand his soul."

"You lost your soul in kindergarten, Bukowski. Now wash up and get ready for breakfast." . . .

I was given the job of milking the cows, finally, and it got me up earlier than anybody. But it was kind of nice, pulling at those cows' tits. And I made an arrangement with Mary to meet me out in the barn on this morning. All that straw. It would be fine, fine. I was pulling the tits when Mary came around the side of a cow.

"Let's make it, Python."

She called me 'Python.' I had no idea why. Maybe she thinks I'm Pulon? I used to think. But what the hell good does thinking do a man? Only leads to trouble.

Anyway, we got up in the loft, undressed; both of us naked as sheared sheep, quivering, that clean hard straw sticking into us like icepicks. Hell, this was the stuff you read about in the old-time novels, by god, we were there!

I worked it in. It was great. I just got going good when it seemed as if the whole Italian army had burst into the barn —

"HEY! STOP! STOP! UNHAND THAT WOMAN!"

"DISMOUNT IMMEDIATELY!"

"GET YOUR PECKER OUT OF THERE!"

A bunch of male orderlies, fine fellows all, most of them homosexual, hell, I had nothing against them, yet — look: here they came climbing up the ladder —

"NOT ANOTHER STROKE, YOU BEAST!"

"IF YOU COME, IT'S OFF WITH YOUR BALLS!"

I speeded-up but it wasn't any use. There were 4 of them. They pulled me off and rolled me on my back.

"GOD O MIGHTY, LOOK AT THAT THING!"

"PURPLE AS AN IRIS AND HALF THE LENGTH OF A MAN'S ARM! PULSATING, GIGANTIC, UGLY!"

"SHOULD WE?"

"We might lose our jobs."

"It might well be worth it."

Just then Dr. Blasingham walked in. That solved everything.

"What's going on up there?" he asked.

"We have this man under our control, Dr."

"How about the woman?"

"The woman?"

"Yes, the woman."

"Oh . . . she's madder than hell."

"All right, get them into their clothes and into my office. One at a time. The woman first!"

They made me wait out there, outside of Blasingham's private God-ward. I sat between 2 orderlies on this hard bench, switching back and forth between a copy of the Atlantic Monthly and the Reader's Digest. It was torture, like dying of thirst in the desert and being asked which I'd prefer — to suck on a dry sponge or to have 9 or ten grains of sand thrown down my throat . . .

I guess Mary got quite a tongue-lashing from the good Dr.

Then they rather carried Mary out and pushed me in. Blasingham seemed quite stuffy about the whole thing. He told me that he had been watching me through field glasses for some days. I had been under suspicion for weeks. 2 unexplained pregnancies. I told the doctor that depriving a man of sex was not the healthiest way to help him recover his mind. He claimed that sexual energy could be

173

transferred up the spine and reconverted to other more gratifying uses. I told him that I believed this was possible if it were *voluntary* but that if it were *enforced,* the spine just didn't damn well *feel* like transferring energies for other more gratifying uses.

Well, it all ended up, I lost my privileges for two weeks. But someday before I cash in, I hope to make it in the straw. Breaking my stroke like that, they owe me one, at least.

EYES LIKE THE SKY

some time back Dorothy Healey came to see me. I had a hangover and a 5-day beard. I had forgotten about this until the other night over a quiet beer her name came up. I mentioned to the young man across the room that she had been by.

"why'd she come to see you?" he asked.

"I dunno."

"what'd she say?"

"I don't remember what she said. all I remember is she had on a pretty blue dress and her eyes were this beautiful glowing blue."

"you don't remember what she said?"

"not a thing."

"did you make her?"

"of course not. Dorothy must be very careful who she goes to bed with. think of the bad publicity if she unwittingly went to bed with an F.B.I. agent or the owner of a chain of shoe stores."

"I guess Jackie Kennedy's mates must be carefully selected too."

"sure. the Image. she'll probably never go to bed with Paul Krassner."

"I'd like to be there if she did."

"holding the towels?"

"holding the pieces," he said.

and Dorothy Healey's eyes had this beautiful glowing blue . . .

the comic strips have long ago gone serious and since they have they are truly more comic than ever. in a sense, the comic strip has taken over for the old time radio soap operas. both have in common the fact that they tend to project a serious, a very serious reality, and therein lies their humor — their reality is such plastic dimestore stuff that you have to laugh at it a bit if you are not having too much stomach trouble.

175

in the current Los Angeles Times (as this is being written) we are having the wind-up of a Hippie-Beatnik scene in Mary Worth. we have had here the campus rebel, bearded and in turtleneck sweater running off with the campus queen, a long-haired blonde girl with perfect figure (I almost got rocks looking at her). what the campus rebel stands for we are never quite sure except in a few short speeches which say very little. anyhow I will not bore you with the story line. it ends up with big bad poppa in necktie and expensive suit and baldheaded and eaglefaced giving out a few dictums of his own to the bearded one, then offering him a job with his outfit so that he can properly support his sexy daughter. the Hippie-Beatnik at first refuses and vanishes off the page and poppa and daughter are packing to leave him, to leave him there in his own idealistic slime, when the Hippie-Beatnik returns. "Joe! . . . What have you done?" says the sexy daughter. and Joe enters SMILING and BEARDLESS: "I thought it only fair for you to know what your husband really looked like, sweetheart . . . before it was too late!" then he turns to poppa: "Also, I figured that a beard would be more of a handicap than a help, Mr. Stevens . . . ON A REAL-ESTATE SALESMAN!" "Does this mean you've finally come to YOUR SENSES young man?" asks poppa. "It means that I'm willing to pay the price you put on your daughter, sir!" (ah, sex, ah love, ah FUCK!) "But," continues our x-hippie, "I still intend to fight INJUSTICE . . . wherever I find it!" well, that's good because our x-hip is going to find a lot of injustice in the real-estate business. then, as a parter poppa gives his line: "However, you're in for a big SURPRISE, Joe! . . . when you discover that we old mossbacks want a better world too! We just don't believe in BURNING the house down to get rid of the termites!"

but old mossbacks, you can't help thinking, just what ARE you doing? then you switch across the page to APARTMENT 3-G where a college professor is discussing with a very rich and beautiful girl her love for an idealistic and poor young doctor. this doctor has shown very nasty flairs of temperament — ripping tablecloth and dishes off of cafe tables, throwing egg sandwiches in the air, and, if I remember, beating up couple of boy friends. he gets angered because this beautiful rich lady keeps offering him money but meanwhile he has accepted a fancy new automobile, a lavishly decorated office uptown and other goodies. now if this doctor were a corner newsboy or a mailman he wouldn't get any of this stuff and I'd just like to see him go into some nightclub and rip dinner and wine and coffeecups and spoons and so forth onto the floor and then come back and sit down and not even apologize. I'd sure hate to have THIS doctor operate on my case of recurrent hemorrhoids.

so when you read your comic strips, laugh laugh laugh, and know that that is partly where we are.

a professor from a local university came by to see me yesterday. he didn't look like Dorothy Healey but his wife, a Peruvian poetess, did look pretty good. the object was that he was tired of the same insensible gatherings of so-called NEW POETRY. poetry is still the biggest snob-racket in the Arts with little poet groups battling for power. I do suppose that the biggest snob outfit ever invented was the old BLACK MOUNTAIN group. and Creeley is still feared in and out of the universities − feared and revered − more than any other poet. then we have the academics, who like Creeley, write very carefully. in essence, the generally accepted poetry today has a kind of glass outside to it, slick and sliding, and sunned down inside there is a joining of word to word in a rather metallic inhuman summation or semi-secret angle. this is a poetry for millionaires and fat men of leisure so it does get backing and it does survive because the secret is in that those who belong really belong and to hell with the rest. but the poetry is dull, very dull, so dull that the dullness is taken for hidden meaning − the meaning is hidden, all right, so well hidden that there isn't any meaning. but if YOU can't find it, you lack soul, sensitivity and so forth, so you BETTER FIND IT OR YOU DON'T BELONG. and if you don't find it, KEEP QUIET.

meanwhile, every 2 or 3 years, somebody in the academy, wanting to keep his place in the university structure (and if you think Vietnam is hell you ought to see what goes on between those so-called brains in battles of intrigue and power within their own little cellblocks) brings out the same old collection of glass and gutless poetry and labels it THE NEW POETRY or THE NEW NEW POETRY but it's still the same marked deck.

well, this prof was evidently a gambler. he said he was sick of the game and wanted to bring out some force, some new creativeness. he had his own thoughts but then asked me who I thought was writing the ACTUAL new poetry, who the boys were and what the stuff was. I couldn't answer him, truly. at first I mentioned a few names: Steve Richmond, Doug Blazek, Al Purdy, Brown Miller, Harold Norse, so forth, but then I realized that I knew most of these men personally, and if not personally then through correspondence. it gave me kind of a shit-twinge. if I tabbed these then it would be a kind of BLACK MOUNTAIN thing all over again — a grouping of another "in" type of thing. this is the way death begins. a kind of glorious personal death, but no good, anyhow.

so, say you throw these out; say you threw out the old glass-poetry boys, this leaves you what? a very energetic work, a very lively work of the young who are just beginning to write and appearing in little magazines put out by other very energetic and lively young. to these, sex is something new and life is fairly new and war too, and this is all right, it refreshes. they have not yet been "gotten to." but where is the follow-through? they give you one good line and then 14 bad ones. at times they even make you wish for the careful sparwork and constipation of a Creeley and they all sound alike. then you wish for a Jeffers, a man sitting behind a rock and carving the blood of his heart between the walls. they say don't trust a man over 30, and percentage-wise this is good formula — most men have sold out by then. so in a sense, HOW AM I GOING TO TRUST A MAN UNDER 30? he will probably sell-out. with Mary Worth picking her nose in the background.

well, it may be a matter of the times. so far as poetry goes (and this includes one Charles Bukowski) we simply, at this time, we simply do not HAVE the ramrods, the fearful innovators, the men, the gods, the big boys who could knock us out of beds or keep us going in the dark pit hell of the factories and the streets. the T. S. Eliots are gone; Auden has stopped; Pound is waiting to die; Jeffers left a hole never to be filled by any Grand Canyon Love-In; even old Frost had a certain spiritual grandeur; Cummings kept us from sleeping; Spender, " either this man's life dying" has stopped writing; D. Thomas was killed by American Whiskey, American admiration and American woman; even Sandburg, long since dimmed of talent and walking into American classrooms with his uncut white hair, bad guitar and addled eyes, even Sandburg has been kicked in the ass by death.

let's admit it: the giants are gone and there have not come up any giants to replace them. maybe it is this time. maybe it is this Vietnam time, this African time, this Arabian time. it could well be that the people want more than the poets are saying. it could well be that the people will be the final poets — with luck. god knows, I don't like the poets. I don't like to sit in the same room with them. yet it is hard to find what one does like. the streets seem lacking. the man who fills my gas tank at the corner gas station seems the most heinous and hateful of beasts. and when I see photos of my president or hear him speak, he seems like some big fattened clown, some dull and putty-like creature given my life, my chances, everybody else's to decide upon. and I do not understand it. and it is as with our president, so rides our poetry. it is almost that with our lack of soul that we have formed him, and therefore deserve him. Johnson is pretty safe from an assassin's bullet, not because of increased security precautions but because there is little or no pleasure in killing a dead man.

which gets us back to the professor and his question: who to put in a book of truly new poetry? I'd say nobody. forget the book. the odds are almost in. if you want to read some decent strong human stuff without fakery I'd say Al Purdy, the Canadian. but what's a Canadian, really? just somebody way out on the limb of some kind of tree, hardly there, screaming beautiful fire songs into his home-mixed wine. time, if we have it, will tell us about it, will tell us about him.

so professor, I am sorry I could not help you. it would have made some kind of rose in my buttonhole (EARTH ROSE?) we are at loss, and that includes the Creeleys, you, me, Johnson, Dorothy Healey, C. Clay, Powell, Hem's last shotgun, the grand sadness of my little daughter running across the floor toward me. everybody feels this godwigawful loss of soul and direction more and more, and we are trying to build more and more toward some type of Christ before Catastrophe, but no Gandhi or EARLY Castro has stepped forth. only Dorothy Healey with eyes like the sky. and she's a dirty communist.

so, the fix. Lowell turned down some kind of garden party invite from Johnson. this was good. this was a beginning. but unfortunately Robert Lowell writes well. too well. he is caught between a kind of glass-type poetry and a hard reality and does not know what to do — hence he mixes both and dies both ways. Lowell would like very well to be a human being but is deballed in his own poetic conceptions. Ginsberg, meanwhile turns gigantic extrovert hand-springs across our sight, realizing the gap and trying to fill it. at least, he knows what is wrong — he simply lacks the artistry to fulfill it.

so professor, thank you for calling. many strange people knock at my door. too many strange ones.

I don't know what's to become of us. we need a lot of luck. and mine's been bad lately. and the sun is getting nearer. and, Life, as ugly as it seems, does seem worth 3 or 4 more days. think we'll make it?

ONE FOR WALTER LOWENFELS

he shook the hangover and got out of bed and there they were
— woman and child — and he opened the door and in ran the kid and
there followed the woman. all the way from New Mexico. although
they'd made a stop first at Big Billy's, the lesbian. the kid threw
herself on the couch and they played the game of meeting each
other again. it was good to see the kid, it was good as hell to see the
kid.

"Tina's got an infected toe. I'm worried about it. I was kind of
in a daze for 2 days and when I came out of it she had this thing on
her toe."

"you ought to make her wear her shoes in those outhouses."

"THAT DOESN'T MATTER! THE WHOLE WORLD'S AN
OUTHOUSE!" she said.

she was a woman who seldom combed her hair, wore black in
protest of the war, wouldn't eat grapes because of the grape strike,
was a communist, wrote poetry, went to love-ins, made ashtrays out
of clay, smoked and drank coffee continually, collected various
checks from a mother and x-husbands, lived with various men and
loved to eat strawberry jam on toast. children were her weapons and
she had one after another in order to defend herself. although whatever could get a man in bed with *her* was beyond him, although he
had done it, evidently, and intoxication was a shitty excuse. but he
could never get *that* drunk anymore. basically she reminded him of a
religious fanatic turned inside-out — she could do no wrong, you see,
because she had these splendid ideas: anti-war, love, Karl Marx, all
that shit. she didn't believe in WORK either, but then, who did? the
last job she'd had was in World War II when she joined the WACS to
save the world from that beast who put people in ovens: A. Hitler.
but intellectually, that was the *good* war, you know. and now she
was putting *him* in the oven.

181

"christ, call my doctor."

she knew the number and the doctor: that's one thing she was good for. she got *that* done. then it was coffee and cigarettes and talk about the community living project down there.

"somebody pasted your poem MEN'S CRAPPER in the out-house. and there's an old drunk down there, Eli, 60, he's drunk all the time and he milks the goat."

she was trying to make it sound human to him, to trap him in with the flies and get his ass cut off from any chance of solitude or racetrack or the quiet beer, and then he'd have to sit around and watch the brain-damage cases hump her, and there wouldn't be the jealousy for him, just the simple pasty horrors and doldrums of mechanical people in a mechanical act, trying to tickle their cement souls back into life with a spurt of come.

"naw," he said, "I'd get on down there, look over a dusty hill and the droppings of chickens and go screaming out of my head. or find a way to kill myself."

"you'd like Eli. he's drunk all the time too."

he flipped the beercan into the paperbag. "I can find a 60-year-old drunk anywhere. if I can't, all I gotta do is wait 12 more years. if I can make it."

having lost that, she got at her coffee and cigarettes in a kind of hidden and yet, at the same time, a rather blank fury, and if you think that there isn't such a thing, well, you just haven't met Mrs. Pro-Love, Anti-War; Mrs. Poetry-writer, Mrs. sit-on-a-rug with a circle of friends and talk shit . . .

it was Wednesday and he went to WORK that night while she took the kid down to the local bookstore where the people read their stuff to each other. Los Angeles was vile with such places. poeple who couldn't write worth a cat's ass reading to each other and telling each other that they were good. it was kind of a spiritual jacking-off when there was nothing else left to do. ten people can suck each other's asses and tell each other what good writers they are but sometimes it's all hell finding the 11th and, of course, there's just no use sending to PLAYBOY, THE NEW YORKER, THE ATLANTIC, EVERGREEN, because they don't know *good* writing when they see it, right? "we read better stuff at our gatherings than all the big and little magazines combined . . ." a little scrub had said to him ten years ago.

well, fuck my dead mother's bones . . .

that night when he got in, 3:15 a.m., she had all the lights in the place on, the window shades all up and she was sleeping on the couch with her naked ass showing. he walked in, switched off most of the lights, pulled the shades, went in to see the kid. the girl had a lot of spark in her. the old woman hadn't killed her yet. 4 years of it. he looked at the kid sleeping, Tina, and she was a miracle, sleeping, living through the hell of it. it was hell for him too, but it was also simple and obstinate shit that he couldn't stand the woman. and it wasn't entirely the woman; there were few women he could bear, and there was plenty wrong with him too — they'd run the corkscrew through him good, real good; but the kid, why were the kids usually the ones who got it in the ass? two feet tall, no trade, no passport, no chance. we started killing them the minute they came out of the cunt. and kept it up, straight down through to the other hole. he leaned over and kissed her as she slept, but almost shamefully.

when he walked out she was awake. coffeewater going. cigarette going. he hit on a beer. what the fuck, everybody was mad.

"they liked my poem tonight," she said, "I read them my poem and they liked it. it's right there if you want to read it."

"listen, kid, they've beat my brains out on the job. I don't think I could give it a fair reading. tomorrow, o.k.?"

"and I'm so happy. I know I shouldn't be but I am. you know that poetry mag we put out of our group's readings?"

"yeh?"

"well, Walter Lowenfels got hold of a copy and he read it and he wrote asking who *I* was!"

"well, that's nice, really nice."

he was glad for her. anything to make her happy, to pull her out of the fucking snake pit.

"Lowenfels has good taste; of course, he tilts a little left but maybe I do too, it's hard to tell. but you've written some powerful shit, we both know that," he said.

she glowed in it and he felt glad for her. he wanted her to win. she needed to win. everybody did. what a cunt-smeared game.

"but you know your problem."

she looked up. "what?"

"the same 8 or 9 poems."

she packed the same 8 or 9 poems to each new poetry group she discovered, meanwhile looking for another man, another baby, another defense.

she didn't answer. then she said, "what are all those magazines in the big cardboard box?"

"my next book of poems. all I need is a title and a typist. the advance is all lined-up. all I have to do is to type up my own poems but I can't stand to type up my own poems. it's a waste of time and a going back over the same road. I can't stand it. that box has been sitting there 6 months."

"I need money. what'll you pay me?"

"20 or 30 bucks, but it's a terrible job, hard and boring."

"I'll do it."

"o.k.," he said, but he knew she'd never do it. she'd never done anything. 8 or 9 poems. well, like they say, if you write only one or two good poems in a lifetime, you're in.

into *what?*

clap pussy, he thought . . .

it was the kid's birthday, 2 or 3 weeks late, and a day or two later he drove around with Tina — the doctor had taken the nail off her toe and given her little bottles to drink every 4 hours — doing the chickenshit errands that eat a man up while he should be singing drunk — he got off 4 or 5 of them trying to keep the boat straight, then made the bakery, picked up the birthday cake, they had done it nicely, and they took the cake, Tina and he, in its pink box and made their way into the market for toilet paper, meat, bread, tomatoes, god knows what, icecream yes icecream, what kind icecream you want, Tina? while the Richard Nixon steel sky falls upon our heads, what kinda, huh, Tina?

when they got back the Walter Lowenfel poetess was in a snit, sniffling, cussing . . .

she'd decided to type the book of poems. but what? he'd given her a new typewriter ribbon.

"THAT FUCKING TYPEWRITER RIBBON DOESN'T WORK!"

she was very angry, sitting in her black anti-war dress. she looked ugly. she looked uglier.

"wait a moment," he said, "the cake and all that."

he took it into the kitchen and Tina followed.

thank christ for this beautiful child, he thought, which came out of this woman's body or I am afraid other than that I would have to murder this woman. thank god for my luck or even Richard Nixon. thank him, or even anything: the blue machines which never smile.

he and Tina went back into the typewriter room and he lifted the lid of the typer and he'd never seen anybody thread a ribbon like that. it was impossible to describe. what had happened was that she had gone to *another* poetry reading the next night and something had not come off so good; what it was, he could only guess: somebody she had wanted to fuck wouldn't fuck her or somebody she hadn't wanted to fuck had fucked her, or somebody had said something bad about her poetry or somebody after listening to her speak for a while had called her "neurotic"; whatever it was, it was a thing with those types, set off either internally or externally and they were either shining and full of phony love or they were crouched and leaping and terrible with hate.

she was off now and there was little he could do. he sat down and put the typewriter ribbon in the way it should be.

"AND THE 'S' STICKS TOO!" she screamed.

he didn't ask her what went wrong at the other poetry reading. no Walter Lowenfels' note at this one.

he and Tina went into the breakfastnook and he took out the cake, HAPPY BIRTHDAY TINA, and found the 4 candleholders and he worked the damned 4 candles into the holders and stuck them into the cake and then he heard the water running . . .

she was taking a bath.

"listen, don't you want to watch Tina blow out her candles? shit you came all the way from New Mexico. if you don't want to watch, tell us, and we'll go ahead."

"all right, I'll be out . . ."

"fine . . ."

here she came. and he lit the damned candles, four. fire. on the cake.

"Happy Birthday to you

185

Happy Birthday to you
Happy Birthday, dear, Tina . . ."

so on. and corny. but her face, Tina's, was like 10,000 films of happiness. he never saw anything like it. he had to put a steel bar around his belly and his lungs and his eyes to keep from crying.

"o.k., kid, blow 'em out. can you do it?"

Tina leaned forward and got the first 3, but the green candle held and he started to laugh. it was funny, it was really funny to him: "shit, you can't get the GREEN one! how come you can't get the GREEN one?"

she kept at it. then she got it. and they both laughed. he cut the cake and then they had the icecream with it. corny. but he liked her happiness. then mama got up.

"I have to take my bath."

"o.k." . . . .

she came out.

"the toilet's clogged."

he went on in. the toilet never clogged until she arrived. she threw in masses of grey hair, various cunt contrivances and bogs and clogs of toilet paper. he used to think that he *imagined* it all, but the moment of her arrival and the clogging of the toilet and the arrival of the ants and all *manner* of dark-death thoughts and gloom came with her — this very good person who hated war and hated hate and was for love.

he wanted to dig his hand in there and pull all that contrivance out but all she said was, "get me a saucepan!"

and Tina said, "what's a saucepan?"

and he said, "that's a word people like to say when they can't think of anything else to say. there is really and never has been anything like a saucepan."

"what'll we do?" asked Tina.

"I'll give her a pot," he said.

they brought her a pot and she fucked around the toilet bowl but nothing happened to all that terrible rubbery and heroic shit she had dumped into there. it just gurgled and farted back, like she was always farting.

"let me get the landlord," he said.

186

"BUT I WANT TO TAKE MY BATH!" she screamed.

"all right," he said, "you take your bath. we'll let the shitpot wait."

she went on in. and then she turned on the shower. she must have stood under that shower for 2 hours. something about the tinkling of that water upon her brain made her feel good and secure. he had to take Tina in once to peepee. she didn't even know they were there. *her* face and soul were turned to the heavens: anti-war, poetic, the mother, the sufferer. the non-eater of grapes, purer than distilled shit, his water and power bill mounting and dancing upon her mighty soul. But perhaps these were Communist Party tactics — to drive everybody crazy?

he finally joked her out of there and got the landlord. it was all right for her poetic soul to languish — Walter Lowenfels could have her — but he had to take a shit.

the landlord was o.k. with a few blips and blops of his famous red plunger the mind was cleared to the sea. the landlord left and he sat down and let go.

she was completely goofy when he came out so he suggested that she spend the rest of the day and night at the nearest bookstore or whorehouse or whatever it was and that he'd play around with Tina.

"fine. I'll be back with mother around noon tomorrow."

he and Tina packed her into the car and they drove her to the bookstore. immediately upon letting her out of the door, the hate on her face left, the hatred upon her *face* left, and walking toward the doorway, she was once again for PEACE, LOVE, POETRY, *all* things good.

he asked Tina to get in the front seat with him. she took one of his hands and he steered with the other.

"I said 'goodbye' to Mama. I love Mama."

"sure you do. and I'm sure Mama loves you too."

so there he drove, with her and him, both very serious, she 4, he a bit older, waiting on red lights, sitting next to each other. that's all there was.

it was plenty.

NOTES OF A POTENTIAL SUICIDE

I sit by the window as the garbage men drive up. they empty the garbage cans. I listen for mine. there it is: CRASK TINKLE CRASH BLUNK BLASH! one of the gentlemen looks at the other:
"man, they got one *powerful* drinker in there!"
I lift my bottle and wait for further developments in space flight.

***

somebody puts a book by Norman Mailer on me. it is called *Christians and Cannibals.* God, he just writes on and on. there's no force, no humor. I don't understand it. just a pushing out of the word, any word, anything. is this what happens to the famous? think how lucky we are!

***

2 come by. a Jew and a German.
"where we going?" I ask.
they don't answer. the German is driving. he breaks all laws of driving. he has the gas down to the floor. we are in the hills then and he's skimming along the edge of the road — there a 2 thousand foot drop.
it is not nice, I think, to die by another man's hand.
we make it to the observatory. how dull. they both seem happy with it. the Jew likes zoos but it is night and the zoo is closed. there are some people who must always go somewhere.
"let's go to a movie!"
"let's go boating!"
"let's get laid!"
"screw all that stuff," I always say, "just let me sit here."
so people no longer ask. they just get me in a car and then I can be surprised with whatever special dullness awaits.

so the German runs up to the building. there are notches between the blocks that run up the front of the building. the German starts climbing up the notches. then he's halfway up the building, hanging over the doorway. god, how dull, I think. I wait for him to either fall down or climb down.

a teacher comes by. he is with highschool students. they are all lined-up as they walk through the doorway. the teacher looks up and sees the German.

"is that one of mine?" he asks.

"no, that one's mine," I tell him.

they march in. the German climbs down. we walk into the building. it is the same as it was 30 years ago. the big swinging ball that hangs from a wire in the pit. everybody looks at the ball swinging.

god, I think, how dull.

then I follow the German and the Jew and they walk around and push buttons. things jiggle and move a bit. or there is an electric spark. ½ of the stuff is broken and pushing the buttons is futile. the German gets lost from us. I walk around with the Jew. he finds a machine that records tremors.

"Hey, Hank!" he hollers.

"yeh."

"come here! now look when I count 3, both of us will leap up into the air."

"all right."

he weighs 200, I weigh 225.

"one, two, three!"

we leap and land. the machine scribbles some lines.

"one, two, three!"

we leap.

"now once more! one —"

"to hell with it," I say, "let's go catch a drink!"

I walk away.

the German walks up. "let's get out of here," he suggests.

"sure," I say.

"some bitch repulsed me," the German says, "it's disgusting."

"don't worry," I say, "she probably has shitstains in her panties."

"but I like them that way."

"you like to sniff it?"

"of course."

"sorry, then, it's a bad evening for you."

the Jew runs up. "let's go to Schwab's drugstore!" he hollers.

"o, for christ's sake," I say.

we get back into the car and once again the German has got to show us how close he can carry us to death. then we are out of the hills.

all the people in Los Angeles are doing it: running ass-wild after something that is not there. it is basically a fear of facing one's self, it is basically a fear of being alone. my fear is of the crowd, the ass-wild running crowd; the people who read Norman Mailer and go to baseball games and cut and water their lawns and bend over the garden with a trowel.

the German drives toward Schwab's. he wants to sniff.

***

there is a symphony orchestra back east. the conductor makes it by playing what I might call the Beginner's Melodies. these extracts from music are what please almost any beginner in the classical music field. but if a man has any sensibilities at all he can't listen to these beginning pieces more than 4 or 5 times without becoming just a bit ill. but this particular orchestra lards it on week after week, and the audience is a middle-aged audience, and where they come from and what has retarded them, I have no idea. but after hearing these simplistic and basic and somewhat sugary pieces, they really believe they have heard something new and great and profound, and they leap from their seats and scream "BRAVO! BRAVO!" just like they've heard it's done. the conductor comes out and takes bow after bow and then asks the orchestra to stand. my only thought is, does this conductor *know* he is conning them or is he also retarded?

some of the pieces I would have to put in the grammar school of music and which this conductor likes to play are, Offenbach's *La Vie Parisienne*, Ravel's *Bolero*, Rossini's overture, *La Gazza ladra*, Tchaikovsky's *Nutcracker Suite* (may the devil save us!): Bizet's *Carmen* or portions thereof; Copland's *El Salon Mexico*, de Falla's *The Three-Cornered Hat Dance*, Elgar's *Pomp and Circumstance*

March, Gershwin's *Rhapsody in Blue* (may the devil save us twice over!); and there are many others which do not come to me at the moment . . .

but let this particular crowd come into contact with this basic sugar, they go harmlessly apeshit.

and driving home, you get a scene something like this. the old man about 52, owner of 3 furniture stores, feeling intelligent:

"by god, you've got to hand it to – – – –, there's a man who really knows his music! he can really make you *feel* it!"

wife:

"yes, I *always* feel so uplifted! by the way, should we eat at home or out!"

***

of course, there's no accounting for taste, or lack of it. one man's pussy is another man's handjob. I can't understand the popularity of Faulkner, baseball games, Bob Hope, Henry Miller, Shakespeare, Ibsen, the plays of Chekhov. G. B. Shaw makes me yawn all over. Tolstoy also. *War and Peace* is the biggest flop for me since Gogol's *Overcoat.* Mailer I have spoken of. Bob Dylan affects me as overacting while Donovan appears to have real style. I just don't understand. Boxing, professional football, basketball seem to move with force. the early Hemingway was good. Dos was a rough boy. Sherwood Anderson all the way. the early Saroyan. tennis and opera, you take it. new cars, to hell with them. stocking panties, ugg. rings, watches, ugg. very early Gorky. D. H. Lawrence, o.k. Celine, without a doubt. scrambled eggs, shit. Artaud when he gets hot. Ginsberg, sometimes. wrestling – what??? Jeffers, of course. on and on, you know. who's right? I am, of course. why, yes, of course.

***

when I was a boy I went to something that was called an Air Show. they had stunt fliers, air races, parachute jumps. one stunt flier, I recall, was very good. they'd put a hanky on a hook down close to the ground and he'd fly in very low in this old German fokker and pick up the hanky with a hook on one of his wings. then he'd do a barrel roll right down against the ground, almost. he had very good control of his plane. the air races were best – for kids, and maybe the others too — so many crashes. all the planes were built in different shapes, very strange-looking things. brightly colored. and they'd crash. crash after crash after crash. it was very exciting. my friend's name was Frank. he is now a superior court judge.

"hey, Hank!"

"yeah, Frank?"

"follow me."

we went under the stands.

"you can look up the women's dresses here," he said.

"yeah?"

"yeah, look!"

"geez!"

the stands were built of boards and you could see right up through them.

"hey, look at this one!"

"oh, boy!"

Frank went walking around.

"pssst! over here!"

I walked over. "yeah."

"look, look! you can see the pussy!"

"where? where?"

"look, look where I'm looking!"

we stood there and looked at that thing. we looked at it a long time.

then we walked out and watched the rest of the show.

the parachute jumpers were at it. they were trying to see how close they could come to a circle drawn on the ground. they didn't seem to come very close. then one guy jumped and his chute only opened part way. he had some wind in it so he wasn't dropping as fast as a man would without a chute, and you could watch him. he seemed to be kicking, and working his hands and arms out against the strings, trying to untangle the parachute. but he wasn't solving it.

"can't anybody help him?" I asked.

Frank didn't answer. he had a camera and was taking pictures. many of the people were taking pictures of the thing. some even had movie cameras.

the man was nearing the ground, still trying to untangle the strings. then he hit. when he hit you could see him bounce up from

192

the ground. the chute covered him. they canceled the rest of the jump. the Air Show was almost over.

it had been quite something. those crashes, the jumper and the pussy.

we rode our bicycles all the way home and talked about it.

it looked as if life were going to be quite a thing.

NOTES ON THE PEST

Pest, n. (Fr. peste, *from L.* pestis, *a plague, a pest (whence* pestilent, *pestiferous): same root as* perdo, *to destroy (PERDITION).) A plague, pestilence, or deadly epidemic disease; anything very noxious, mischievous, or destructive; a mischievous or destructive person.*

the pest, in a sense, is a very superior being to us: he knows where to find us and how — usually in the bath or in sexual intercourse or asleep. he is also very good at catching you in the crapper about halfway through a bowel-movement. if he is at the door you can scream, "Jesus, wait a minute, what the hell, wait a minute!" but the sound of the human voice in agony only encourages the pest — his beat, his ring becomes more excited. the pest usually beats and rings. you must let him in. and when he leaves — finally — you will be ill for a week. the pest not only pisses on your soul — he is also very good at leaving his yellow water on your toilet lid. he leaves hardly enough to see; you don't know it is there until you sit down and it is too late.

unlike you, the pest has hours of time to shoot through the head. and all his ideas are contrary to yours but he never knows this because he is continually talking and even when you get a chance to disagree, the pest does not hear. he really never hears your voice. it is just a vague area of break to him, then he continues his dialogue. and while the pest continues on you wonder how he ever got his dirty little snout into your soul. the pest is also very aware of your sleeping hours and he will phone you time after time while you are asleep and his first question will be, "did I awaken you?" or he will come upon your place and all the shades will be down but he will knock and ring anyhow, wildly, wildly in orgasm. if you do not answer he will shout out, "I know that you're in there! I can see your car outside!"

these destroyers, although they have no idea of your thought process, they do sense your dislike for them, yet in another way this only encourages them. also they realize that you are a certain type of person — that is, given a choice of hurting or being hurt, you will accept the latter. pests thrive on the best slices of humanity; they know where the good meat is.

the pest is always full of dry standard nonsense that he mistakes for self-wisdom. some of his favorite remarks are:

"there is no such thing as ALL bad. you say that *all* cops are bad. well they're not. I've met some good ones. there is such a thing as a good cop."

you never get a chance to explain to him that when a man puts that uniform on that he is the paid protector of things of the present time. he is here to see that things stay the way they are. if you like the way things are, then *all* cops are good cops. if you don't like the way things are, then all cops are bad cops. there is such as thing as ALL bad. but the pest is soaked in these addled and homespun philosophies and he will not let them go. the pest, being unable to think, attaches himself to people — grimly and finally and forever.

"we are not informed as to what is going on, we don't have the real answers. we must trust our leaders."

this one is so damned silly that I am not even going to comment on it. in fact, thinking it over, I am not going to list any more of the pest's comments for I am beginning to get ill.

so then. well, this pest need not be a person who knows you by name or location. the pest is everywhere, always, ready to attach his poisoned stinking deathray onto you. I remember one particular time when I was lucky with the horses. I was down at Del Mar driving a new car. each night after the races I would select a new motel, and after a shower and change of clothing I would get into the car and drive along the coast looking for a good place to eat. by a good place to eat, I meant a place not too crowded that served good food. it seems like a contrary thing. I mean, if the food is good the people should be there. but like many seeming truths, this truth is not necessarily so. sometimes the crowd flocks to places that serve absolute garbage. so each night it was my pilgrimage to search out a place that served good food but that was not filled with the madding crowd. it took some time. one night I drove for an hour and thirty minutes before locating my spot. I parked the car and went in. I ordered a New York cut, french fries, so forth, and sat there over my coffee until the food arrived. the whole diner was empty; it was a marvelous night. then just with the arrival of my New York cut, the door opened and in came the pest. of course, you guessed it. there were 32 stools in the place but he HAD TO take the stool next to mine and begin conversing with the waitress over his doughnut. he was a real flat fish. his dialogue knifed into my guts. dull rotting tripe, the stench of his soul swinging through the air wrecking everything. and he gave me just *enough* elbow in the plate. the pest is *very* good with just enough elbow in the plate. I got the New York cut down and then went out and got so drunk that I missed the first three races the next day.

the pest is anywhere you work, anywhere that you are employed. I am pest-meat. I once worked in a place where this man hadn't spoken to anybody for 15 years. on my second day there he spoke to me for 35 minutes. he was completely insane. one sentence would be on one subject, the other on another entirely unrelated. which is all right except the stuff was mottled dead humorless rankeled stink. they kept him because he was a good worker. "a good day's work for a good day's pay." there is at least one madman on every job, a pest, and they always find me. "every nut in the joint likes you," is a sentence that I have heard on job after job. it is not encouraging.

but perhaps it will help if we all realize that perhaps all of us have been pests at one time or another to somebody but we never knew it. shit, it's a horrible thought but most probably true and maybe it will help us bear up under the pest. basically, there is no 100 percent man. we are all run through with various madnesses and uglinesses that we ourselves are not aware of but that everybody else is aware of. how ya gonna keep us down on the farm?

yet, still you must admire the man who takes action against the pest. the pest shrivels against direct action and soon attaches himself elsewhere. I know a man, a kind of intellectual-poet type, a lively life-filled sort who has a large sign attached to his front door. I do not remember it directly but it goes something like this (and done in a beautifully-printed hand):

to whom it may concern: please phone me for appointments when you want to see me. I will not answer unsolicited knocks upon the door. I need time to do my work. I will not allow you to murder my work. please understand that what keeps me alive will make me a better person toward and for you when we finally meet under easy and unstrained conditions.

I admired this sign. I did not take it as a snobbery or an overevaluation of self. he was a good man in good sense and had enough humor and courage to state his natural rights. I first came upon the sign by accident, and after staring at it and hearing him in there I walked to my car and drove away. the beginning of understanding is the beginning of everything and it's time some of us began. for instance, I have nothing against Love-ins so long as I AM NOT FORCED TO ATTEND. I am not even against love, but we were speaking of pests, weren't we?

even I, prime pest-meat that I am, even I once made a move against a pest. I was, at the time, working 12 hours a night, god forgive me and god forgive god, but anyhow this very pesty pest could not resist phoning me every morning about 9 a.m. I got in about 7:30 and after a couple of beers I usually managed to go to sleep. he had it timed just right. and he gave me the same old stupid drab drivel. just knowing that he had awakened me and heard my voice charged him up. he coughed and mewed and hacked and sputtered. "listen," I finally said, "why in the hell do you keep waking me up at 9 a.m.? you know I work all night. 12 hours a night! why in the hell do you keep right on awakening me at 9 a.m.?"

"I thought," he said, "you might be going to the track. I wanted to get you before you went to the track."

"listen," I said, "first post is onefortyfive p.m. and how in the hell do you think I am going to play the horses when I work 12 hours a night? how in the hell do you think I can work all that in? I have to sleep, shit, bathe, eat, fuck, buy new shoelaces, all that stuff, don't you have any sense of reality? don't you realize that when I come in from the job that they've taken every damn thing out of me? don't you realize that there's nothing left? I can't make the racetrack. I'm too weak to even scratch my ass. why the hell do you keep phoning at 9 a.m. every morning?"

as they say, his voice was husky with emotion — "I want to get you before you go to the racetrack."

it was useless. I hung the phone up. then I got a large cardboard carton. then I took the phone and stuck it into the bottom of the large cardboard carton. then I stuffed the damn thing solidly with rags. I did it every morning when I arrived and I took the thing out when I awakened. the pest was dead. he came to see me one day.

"how come you don't answer your phone anymore?" he asked.

"I stuff the phone in a box of rags when I come home."

"but don't you realize that when you stuff that phone into a box of rags that, symbolically, you are stuffing *me* into a box of rags?"

I looked at him and said very slowly and quietly, "that's right."

it was never ever quite the same with us again. I heard from a friend of mine, an older man than I, very alive but not an artist (thank god) and he told me: "McClintock phones me 3 times a day. does he still phone you?"

"not any more."

the McClintocks are the joke of the town but the McClintocks never realize that they are the McClintocks. you can always tell a McClintock. each McClintock carries a little black book filled with phone numbers. and if you have a telephone, look out. the pest will strongarm your phone, first assuring you that all the calls are local (they aren't) and then he will begin (she will begin) unloading their never-ending poison spiel into the ear of the disgusted listener. these McClintock-pest types can talk for hours, and although you try not to listen, listening can't be helped and you feel a kind of humorous sympathy for the poor person at the other agony-end of the wire.

perhaps some day the world will be constructed, reconstructed, that the pest through the generosity of decent living and clear ways will no longer be the pest. there is the theory that the pest is created by things that should not be there. bad government, bad air, fucked-up sex, a mother with a wooden arm, a father who used to goose himself with brillo pads, so forth. whether the Utopian society will ever arrive we will never know. but right now we still have these screwed-up areas of humanity to deal with — the starvation hordes, the black the white and the red, the sleeping Bombs, the

love-ins, the hippies, the not-so hippies, Johnson, roaches in Albe-
querque, bad beer, the clap, chickenshit editorials, this this that that,
and the Pest. the pest is still here. I live today not tomorrow. my
Utopia means less pests NOW. and I'd sure like to hear your story. I
am sure that each of us bears one or 2 McClintocks. you could
probably make me laugh with your stories about the McClintock-
pest. god, which reminds me!!!!! I'VE NEVER HEARD A McCLIN-
TOCK LAUGH!!!

think of that.

think of any pest you have ever known and ask yourself have
they ever laughed? have you ever heard them laugh?

jesus, come to think of it, I don't laugh much myself. I can't
laugh except when I am by myself. I wonder if I have been writing
about myself? a pest pestered by pests. think of that. a whole pest
colony twisting and sinking fang and 69-ing. 69-ing?? let's light a
Chesterfield and forget the whole thing. see you in the morning.
stuffed in a box of rags and petting cobra tits.

hello. I didn't wake you up, did I?
umm, I didn't think so.

A BAD TRIP

did you ever consider that lsd and color tv arrived for our consumption about the same time? here comes all this explorative color pounding, and what do we do? we outlaw one and fuck up the other. t.v., of course, is useless in present hands; there's not much of a hell of an argument here. and I read where in a recent raid it was alleged that an agent caught a container of acid in the face, hurled by alleged manufacturer of a hallucinogenic drug. this is also a kind of a waste. there are some basic grounds for outlawing lsd, dmt, stp – it can take a man permanently out of his mind – but so can picking beets, or turning bolts for GM, or washing dishes or teaching English I at one of the local universities. if we outlawed everything that drove men mad, the whole social structure would drop out – marriage, the war, bus service, slaughterhouses, beekeeping, surgery, anything you can name. anything can drive men mad because society is built on false stilts. until we knock the whole bottom out and rebuild, the madhouses will remain overlooked. and cuts in mad-house budgets by our good governor are taken by me to indirectly imply that those driven mad by society are not fit to be supported and cured by society, especially in an inflationary and tax-mad age. such money could be better used to build roads or to be sprinkled ever-so-lightly upon the Negro to keep him from burning down our cities. and I have a splendid thought: why not assassinate the insane? think of the money we could save. even a madman eats too much and needs a place to sleep, and the bastards are disgusting – the way they scream and smear their shit on the walls, all that. all we'd need is a small medical board to make the decisions and a couple of good-looking nurses (male or female) to keep the psychiatrists' extracurricular sexual activities satisfied.

so let's get back, more or less, to lsd. as it is true that the less you get the more you chance – say beet-picking – it is also true that the more you get the more you chance. any explorative complexity — painting, writing poetry, robbing banks, being a dictator and so forth, takes you to that place where danger and miracle are rather like Siamese twins. you seldom go wire to wire, but while you're going the living is fairly interesting. it's good enough to sleep with another man's wife but someday you know you are going to be caught with your pants down. this only makes the act more pleasurable. our sins are manufactured in heaven to create our own hell, which we evidently need. get good enough at anything and you will create your own enemies. champions get the razzberry; the crowd aches to see them get knocked off in order to bring them down to their own bowl of shit. not many damn fools get assassinated; a winner can be brought down by a mail-order rifle (so the fable says) or by his own shotgun in a small town like Ketchum. or like Adolph and his whore as Berlin split its sides in the last page of their history.

lsd can flake you too because it is not an arena for loyal shipping clerks. granted, bad acid like bad whores can take you out. bathtub gin, bootleg liquor had its day too. the law creates its own disease in poisonous black markets. but, basically, most bad trips are caused by the individual being trained and poisoned beforehand by society itself. if a man is worried about rent, car payments, time-clocks, a college education for his child, a 12-dollar dinner for his girlfriend, the opinion of his neighbor, standing up for the flag or what is going to happen to Brenda Starr, an lsd tablet will most probably drive him mad because, in a sense, he is already insane and only borne along on social tides by the outward bars and dull hammers that render him insensible to any individualistic thinking. a trip calls for a man who has not yet been caged, who has not yet been fucked by the big Fear that makes all society go. unfortunately, most men overestimate their worthiness as basic and free individuals, and it is the mistake of the hippie generation not to trust anybody over 30. 30 doesn't mean a damn thing. most beings are captured and trained, totally, by the age of 7 or 8. many of the young LOOK free but this is only a chemical thing of body and energy and not a realistic thing of spirit. I have met free men in the strangest of places and at ALL ages — as janitors, car thieves, car washers, and some free women too — mostly as nurses or waitresses, and at ALL ages. the free soul is rare, but you know it when you see it — basically because you feel good, very good, when you are near or with them.

an lsd trip will show you things which no rules cover. it will show you things not in textbooks and things which you cannot protest to your city councilman about. grass only makes the present society more bearable; lsd is another society within itself. if you are socially orientated, you can probably mark lsd off as a "hallucinogenic drug," which is an easy way of getting off and forgetting the whole thing. but hallucination, the definition of it, depends upon which pole you are operating from. whatever is happening to you at the time it is happening does become the reality — it can be a movie, a dream, sexual intercourse, murder, being murdered or eating ice cream. only lies are imposed later; what happens, happens. hallucination is only a dictionary word and a social stilt. when a man is dying to him it is very real; to others, it is only bad luck or something to be disposed of. Forest Lawn takes care of everything. when the world begins to admit that ALL the parts fit the whole, then we may begin to have a chance. whatever a man sees is real. it was not brought there by an outside force, it was there before he was born. don't blame him because he sees it now, and don't blame him for going mad because the educational and spiritual forces of society were not wise enough to tell him that exploration never ends, and that we must all be little shits boxed in with our a, b, c's and nothing else. it is not lsd that causes the bad trip — it was your mother, your President, the little girl next door, the icecream man with dirty hands, a course in algebra or Spanish superimposed, it was the stench of a crapper in 1926, it was a man with a nose too long when you were told long noses were ugly; it was laxative, it was the Abraham Lincoln Brigade, it was tootsie rolls and Toots and Casper, it was the face of FDR, it was lemon drops, it was working in a factory for ten years and getting fired because you were five minutes late, it was that old bag who taught you American history in the 6th grade, it was your dog run over and nobody to properly draw you the map afterwards, it was a list 30 pages long and 3 miles tall.

a bad trip? this whole country, this whole world is on a bad trip, friend. but they'll arrest you for swallowing a tablet.

I'm still on the beer because basically, at 47, they've got a lot of hooks in me. I'd be a real damn fool to think that I've escaped all their nets. I think Jeffers said it pretty well when he said, more or less, look out for the traps, friend, there are plenty of them, they say even God got trapped when He once walked on Earth. of course, now some of us are not so sure it was god, but whoever he was, he had some fairly good tricks but it seemed he talked too much. anybody can talk too much. even Leary. or me.

it's a cold Saturday now and the sun's going down. what do you do with an evening? if I were Liza I'd comb my hair but I'm not Liza. well, I've got this old National Geographic and the pages shine like something's really happening. of course, it's not. all around in this building they are drunk. a whole honeycove of drunks for the end. the ladies walk by my window. I emit, I hiss a rather tired and gentle word like "shit," then tear this page from the machine. it's yours.

ANIMAL CRACKERS IN MY SOUP

I had come off a long drinking bout during which time I had lost my petty job, my room, and (perhaps) my mind. After sleeping the night in an alley I vomited in the sunlight, waited five minutes, then finished the remainder of the wine bottle that I found in my coat pocket. I began walking through the city, quite without purpose. When I was walking I felt as if I had some portion of the meaning of things. Of course, it was untrue. But standing in an alley hardly helped either.

I walked for some time, scarcely aware. I was vaguely considering the fascination of starving to death. I only wanted a place to lie down and wait. I didn't feel any rancor against society because I didn't belong in it. I had long ago adjusted to that fact.

Soon I was on the edge of town. The houses were spaced farther apart. There were fields and small farms. I was more sick than hungry. It was hot and I took off my coat and carried it over my arm. I began to get thirsty. There wasn't a sign of water anywhere. My face was bloodied from falling the night before, my hair was uncombed. Dying of thirst wasn't my idea of an easy death; I decided to ask for a glass of water. I passed the first house, which somehow looked unfriendly to me, and walked farther down the road to a very large, three-story, green house, hung about with vines and shrubbery and many trees. As I walked up on the front porch, I heard strange noises inside, and there seemed to be the smell of raw meat and urine and excreta. However, I felt a friendliness about the house; I rang the bell.

A woman of about thirty came to the door. She had long hair, a brownish red, quite long, and these brown eyes looked out at me. She was a handsome woman, dressed in tight blue jeans, boots, a pale pink shirt. Her face and eyes showed neither fear nor apprehension.

"Yes?" she said, almost smiling.

"I'm thirsty," I said. "Could I have a glass of water?"

"Come in," she said, and I followed her into the front room. "Sit down."

I sat down, lightly, upon an old chair. She went into the kitchen for the water. As I sat there, I heard something running down the hall toward the front room. It circled about the room in front of me, then stopped and looked at me. It was an orangutan. The thing leaped up and down in glee when it saw me. Then it ran toward me and leaped upon my lap. It put its face against mine. Its eyes looked into mine a moment, then its head pulled away. It grabbed my coat, leaped to the floor and ran down the hall with my coat, making strange sounds.

She came back with my glass of water, handed it to me.

"I'm Carol," she said.

"I'm Gordon," I said, "but then it hardly matters."

"Why doesn't it matter?"

"Well, I'm through. It's over. You know."

"What was it? Alcohol?" she asked.

"Alcohol," I said, then waved beyond the walls, "and them."

"I have trouble with 'them' too. I'm quite alone."

"You mean you live in this big house all alone?"

"Well, hardly." She laughed.

"Oh yeah, that big monkey stole my coat."

"Oh, that's Bilbo. He's cute. He's crazy."

"I'll need that coat for tonight. It gets cold."

"You'll be staying here tonight. You look like you need some rest."

"If I get some rest I might go on with the game."

"I think you should. It's a good game if you angle in on it right."

"I don't think so. And, besides, why should you help me?"

"I'm like Bilbo," she said. "I'm crazy. At least they thought I was. I was three months in a madhouse."

"No shit," I said.

"No shit," she said. "The first thing I'm going to do is fix you some soup."

"The county," she said later, "is trying to run me out. There's

205

a suit pending. Luckily, Daddy left me quite a bit of money. I can fight them. They call me Crazy Carol of the Liberated Zoo."

"I don't read the papers. Liberated Zoo?"

"Yes, I *love* animals. I have trouble with people. But, Jesus, I really *relate* to animals. Maybe I *am* nuts. I don't know."

"I think you're very nice."

"Really?"

"Really."

"People seem afraid of me. I'm glad you're not afraid of me."

Her brown eyes opened wider and wider. They were a dark brooding brown, and as we talked, some of the shield seemed to drop away.

"Listen," I said, "I'm sorry, but I have to go to the bathroom."

"Go down the hall, then turn in the first door on the left."

"Okay."

I walked down the hall, then turned left. The door was open. I stopped. Sitting on the shower rod above the bathtub was a parrot. And on the throw rug, a full-grown tiger stretched out. The parrot ignored me and the tiger gave me a bored and disinterested stare. I moved back to the front room quickly.

"Carol! My God, there's a *tiger* in the bathroom!"

"Oh, that's Dopey Joe. Dopey Joe won't hurt you."

"Well, I can't crap with a tiger looking at me."

"Oh, silly. Come on with me!"

I followed Carol down the hall. She walked into the bathroom and said to the tiger: "Come on, Dopey, you gotta move. The gentleman can't shit with your eyes on him. He thinks you wanta eat him."

The tiger just looked back at Carol with disinterest.

"Dopey, you bastard, I'm not telling you again! Now I'm giving you until *Three!* Here we go! Now: One . . . two . . . *three* . . . ."

The tiger didn't move.

"All right now, you *asked* for it!"

She took that tiger by the ear, and pulling at that ear, she raised the beast from his reclining position. The cat was snarling, spitting; I could see the fangs and tongue, but Carol seemed to ignore it. She led that tiger out of there by the ear, guided him down

206

the hall. Then she let go of the ear and said, "All right now, Dopey, you go to your room! You go right to your room!"

The tiger walked down the hall, turned in a half circle and lay down on the floor.

"*Dopey!*" she said. "Go to your room!"

The cat stared back, unmoving.

"That son of a bitch is getting impossible," she said. "I may have to take disciplinary action, but I hate to. I love him."

"You love him?"

"I love all my pets, of course. Listen, how about the parrot? Will the parrot bother you?"

"I guess I can bear up under the parrot," I said.

"Go ahead then, have a good crap."

She closed the door. The parrot kept looking at me. Then the parrot said, "Go ahead then, have a good crap." Then *he* did, right into the tub.

We talked some more that afternoon and evening and I got a couple of good meals down. I wasn't quite sure whether the whole thing was just a giant show of D.T.'s or if I had died or if I had gone mad and was having visions.

I don't know how many different types of animals Carol had there. And most of them were housebroken. It was a Liberated Zoo.

Then there was "shit and exercise time," as Carol called it. And she'd march them all out of there in groups of five or six and lead them to the yard. Fox, wolf, monkey, tiger, panther, snake — well, you've been to a zoo. She had almost everything. But the curious fact was that the animals didn't bother each other. Being well fed helped (her feed bill was tremendous — Pappa must have left plenty), but I got the idea that Carol's love for them put them into a rather gentle and almost humorous state of passivity — a transfixed state of love. The animals simply felt *good.*

"Look at them, Gordon. Really look at them. You can't help loving them. See how they *move.* Each one so different, each one so real, each one so much itself. They're not like humans. They're contained, they're unlost, never ugly. They have the gift, they have the same gift that they were born with . . ."

"Yes, I think I see what you mean . . ."

That night I was unable to sleep. I put on my clothing, except for shoes and stockings, and walked down the hall to the front room. I could look in without being seen. I stood there.

Carol was naked and spread upon the coffee table, her back on the table with just the lower parts of the thighs and the legs dangling over. Her whole body was excitingly white, as if it had never seen the sun, and her breasts were more vigorous than large — they seemed parts of their own, striving into the air, and the nipples were not the darker shade as were most women's but rather a bright pink-red, fire-like, only pinker, almost neon. Christ, the lady with the neon breasts! And her lips, the same color, were open in a dream state. Her head was hanging lightly back over the other edge of the coffee table, with this long red-brown hair dangling dangling, swinging slightly, curling a bit on the rug. And her whole body had this feeling of being *oiled* — there seemed no elbows or kneecaps, no points, no edges. Oiled *smooth,* she was. The only things that jarred out were the sharp-pointed breasts. And curled about her body was this long snake — I don't know what type. The tongue flicked and the snake's head moved back and forth to one side of Carol's head slowly, fluidly. Then raising, its neck bending, the snake looked at Carol's nose, her lips, her eyes — drinking at her face.

At moments, the snake's body would slide ever so slightly about Carol's body; it seemed a caress, that movement, and after the caress, the snake would contract slightly, squeezing her, coiling there about her body. Carol would gasp, pulsate, shiver; the snake would slide down by her ear, then rise, look at her nose, her lips, her eyes, and then repeat his movements. The snake's tongue flicked rapidly and Carol's cunt was open, the hairs begging, red and beautiful, in the lamplight.

I walked back to my room. A very fortunate snake, I felt; I had never seen such a body upon a woman. I had difficulty sleeping but finally managed.

The next morning when we had breakfast together I said to Carol, "You're *really* in love with your zoo, aren't you?"

"Yes, all of them, every last one of them," she said.

We finished breakfast, not saying much. Carol looked better than ever. She just radiated more and more. Her hair seemed alive; it seemed to leap about with her movements, and the light from the window shone through it, bringing out the red.

Her eyes were quite open, simmering, yet without fear, without doubt. Those eyes: she let everything in and everything out. She was animal, and human.

"Listen," I said, "If you can get my coat from that monkey, I'll be on my way."

"I don't want you to leave," she said.

"Do you want me to be part of your zoo?"

"Yes."

"But I'm a human, you know."

"But you're untouched. You're not like them. You're still floating inside; they're lost, hardened. You're lost but you haven't hardened. All you need to do is to be found."

"But I might be too old to be . . . loved like the rest of your zoo."

"I . . . don't know . . . I like you very much. Can't you stay? We might find you . . ."

Again the next night I couldn't sleep. I walked down the hall up to the beaded partition and looked in. This time Carol had a table in the center of the room. It was an oak table, almost black, with sturdy legs. Carol was spread upon the table, her buttocks just upon the edge, legs spread, with her toes just touching the floor. One hand covered her cunt, then moved away. As her hand moved away, her entire body seemed to blush a bright pink; the blood washed through, then washed away. The last of the pink hung for a moment just under the chin and about the throat, then it vanished and her cunt opened slightly.

The tiger walked about the table in slow circles. Then he circled faster and faster, the tail flicking. Carol gave this low moan. When she did this the tiger was directly in front of her legs. He stopped. Rose. He placed one paw on either side of Carol's head. The penis extended; it was gigantic. The penis poked at her cunt, seeking entrance. Carol put her hand upon the tiger's penis, attempting to guide it in. They both swiveled upon the edge of unbearable and heated agony. Then a portion of the penis entered. The tiger suddenly jerked his haunches; the remainder entered . . . Carol screamed. Then her hands reached up around the tiger's neck as he began working. I turned and walked to my room.

The next day we ate lunch in the yard with the animals. A

209

picnic lunch. I ate a mouthful of potato salad as a lynx walked by with a silver fox. I had entered a whole new totality of experience. The county had pressured Carol into erecting these high wire fences but the animals still had a wide area of wild land to roam in. We finished eating and Carol stretched out on the grass, looking up at the sky. My god, to be a young man again!

Carol looked at me: "Come on down here, old tiger!"

"Tiger?"

" 'Tyger Tyger, burning bright . . .' When you die, they'll know you, they'll see the stripes."

I stretched out beside Carol. She turned on her side, resting her head upon my arm. I faced her. The whole sky and earth ran through those eyes.

"You look like Randolph Scott mixed with Humphrey Bogart," she said.

I laughed. "You're funny," I said.

We kept looking at each other. I felt as if I could fall down inside her eyes.

Then my hand was on her lips, we were kissing, and I pulled her body into mine. My other hand ran through her hair. It was a kiss of love, a long kiss of love, yet I still got an erection; her body moved against mine, moved snake-like. An ostrich walked past. "Jesus," I said, "Jesus, Jesus . . ." We kissed again. Then she started saying, "You son of a bitch! Oh, you son of a bitch, what are you doing to me?" Carol took my hand and placed it inside her blue jeans. I felt the hairs of her cunt. They were slightly wet. I rubbed and fondled her there, then my finger entered. She kissed me wildly. "You son of a bitch! You son of a bitch!" Then she pulled away.

"Too fast! We must go slowly, slowly . . ."

We sat up and she took my hand and read my palm.

"Your life line . . ." she said. "You haven't been on earth long. See here. Look at your palm. See that line?"

"Yes."

"That's the life line. Now, see mine? I've been on earth many times before."

Carol was serious, and I believed her. You had to believe Carol. Carol was all there was to believe. The tiger watched us from twenty yards away. A breeze blew some of Carol's red-brown hair from her back over her shoulder. I couldn't bear it. I grabbed her and we kissed again. We fell backwards, then she broke off.

"Tiger, son of a bitch, I told you: go *slow!*"

We talked some more. Then she said, "You see — I don't know how to express it. I have many dreams about it. The world is tired. Some end is coming about. People have deadened into inconsequence — rock people. They are tired of themselves. They are praying for death and their prayers will be answered. I'm — I'm — well — I'm rather preparing a new creature to inhabit what is left of the earth. I feel that somewhere somebody else is preparing the new creature. Perhaps in several other places. These creatures will meet and breed and survive, you see? But they must contain the *best* of all the creatures, including man, in order to survive within the small particle of life which will remain . . . My dreams, my dreams . . . Do you think I'm mad?"

She looked at me and laughed. "Do you think I'm Crazy Carol?"

"I don't know," I said. "There's no way of telling."

Again that night I couldn't sleep and I walked down the hall toward the front room. I looked through the beads. Carol was alone spread upon the couch, a small lamp burning nearby. She was naked and appeared to be asleep. I parted the beads and entered the room, sat in a chair across from her. The light from the lamp fell upon the top half of her body; the rest was in shadow.

I disrobed and moved toward her. I sat upon the edge of the couch and looked at her. She opened her eyes. When Carol saw me she didn't seem surprised. But the brownness of her eyes, though clear and deep, seemed without intonation, without accent, as if I were not something she knew by name or manner, but something else — a force apart from myself. Yet there was acceptance.

In the lamplight her hair was as it was in the sunlight — the red showing through the brown. It was like fire inside; she was like fire inside. I bent and kissed her behind the ear. She inhaled and exhaled visibly. I slid down, my legs dropping off the couch, got at and tongued her breasts, went to the stomach, the bellybutton, back to the breasts, then slid down again, down lower where the hairs began and I began kissing there, bit lightly once, then went lower, jumped over, kissed down inside one leg, then the other. She moved, made a

211

small sound: "ah, ah . . ." And then I was down upon the opening, the lips, and I very slowly circled my tongue around the edge of the lips, then reversed the circle. I bit, plunged my tongue in twice, deep in, withdrew, circled again. It became wet there, the slight taste of salt. I circled again. The sound: "ah, ah, . . ." and the flower opened, I saw the little bud and with the tip of my tongue, as gently and easily as possible, I tickled and licked. Her legs kicked and as she tried to lock them about my head I rose upwards, licking upwards, stopping, rising upwards to the throat, biting, and my penis was then poking poking poking as she reached and placed me at the opening. As I slid in, my mouth found hers − and we were locked in two places − the mouth wet and cool, the flower wet and hot, an oven of heat down there, and I held my penis full and still in her body as she wiggled upon it, asking . . .

"You son of a bitch, you son of a bitch . . . move! Move it!"

I remained still as she floundered. I pressed my toes against the end of the couch and pressed further in, still without motion. Then I forced my penis to jump three times by itself while not moving my body. She answered with contractions. We did it again, and when I could bear it no longer, I withdrew it almost out, plunged it in − heat and smoothness − did it again, then held still as she wiggled upon the end of me as if I were a hook and she were the fish. I repeated this many times, and then, wildly lost, I thrust it in and out, feeling it growing, we climbed upward together as one − the perfect language − we climbed past everything, past history, past ourselves, past ego, past mercy and examination, past everything but the occult joy of savoring Being.

We climaxed together and I remained within her afterwards without my penis softening. As I kissed her, her lips were entirely softened and gave way under mine. Her mouth was loosened, surrendered to everything. We stayed in light and gentle embrace for a half-hour, then Carol rose. She went to the bathroom first. Then I followed. There were no tigers in there that night. Just the old Tyger who had burned bright.

Our relationship went on, sexual and spiritual, but meanwhile, I'll have to admit, Carol carried on with the animals too. The months went by in easy happiness. Then I noticed that Carol was pregnant. That was some drink of water I had stopped by for.

One day we drove to town for supplies. We locked the place as we had always done. There wasn't too much worry about burglary because of the panther and the tiger and the various other so-called dangerous animals walking about. The supplies for the animals were delivered each day but we had to go to town for our own. Carol was well known. Crazy Carol, and there were always people staring at her in the stores, and now at me too, her new pet, her new old pet.

We went to a movie first, which we didn't enjoy. When we came out, it was raining lightly. Carol bought a few maternity dresses and then we went to the market for the rest of our purchases. We drove back slowly, talking, enjoying each other. We were contented people. We only wanted what we had; we didn't need them and had long since stopped caring what they thought. But we would sense their hatred. We were outsiders. We lived with animals and the animals were a threat to their society — they thought. And we were a threat to their manner of living. We dressed in old clothing. I had an untrimmed beard; hair all over my head, and although I was fifty my hair was a bright red. Carol's hair came down to her butt. And we always found things to laugh about. Genuine laughter. They couldn't understand it. In the market Carol had said, "Hey, Poppa! Here comes the salt! Catch the salt, Poppa, you old bastard!"

She was standing way down the aisle with three people between us and she threw the salt over the people's heads. I caught it; both of us laughed. Then I looked at the salt.

"No, no, daughter, you whore! You tryin' to harden my arteries? We need *iodized!* Catch, my sweets, and be careful of the baby! That poor bastard is gonna get enough knocks later!"

Carol caught it and threw back the iodized. It was the look upon their faces . . . We were so undignified.

We had enjoyed our day. The movie had been bad but we had enjoyed our day. We made our own movies. Even the rain was good. We rolled down the windows and let it come in. As I drove up the driveway, Carol moaned. It was a moan of utter agony. She slumped and turned quite white.

"Carol! What is it? Are you all right?" I pulled her to me. "What is it? Tell me . . ."

"I'm all right. It's what they've done. I can sense it, I know it, o my God o my God — o my God, those rotten bastards, they've done it, they've done it, the horrible rotten swine."

"Done what?"

"Murder — the house — murder everywhere . . ."

"Wait here," I said.

The first thing I saw in the front room was Bilbo the orangutan. A bullet hole was in his left temple. His head lay in a puddle of blood. He was dead. Murdered. On his face was this grin. The grin read pain, and through the pain he had seemed to laugh as if he had seen Death and Death was something else — surprising, beyond his reason, and it had made him grin through the pain. Well, he knew more about that, now, than I did.

They had gotten Dopey the tiger in his favorite haunt — the bathroom. He had been shot many times as if the murderers had been frightened. There was much blood and some of it had hardened. He had his eyes closed but the mouth had frozen dead into a snarl, and the huge and beautiful fangs protruded. Even in death he was more majestic than a living man. In the bathtub was the parrot. One bullet. The parrot was down near the drain, its neck and head bent under its body, one wing under while the feathers of the other wing were spread wide, somehow, as if that wing had wanted to scream but couldn't.

I searched the rooms. Nothing was left alive. All murdered. The black bear. The coyote. The raccoon. All. The whole house was quiet. Nothing moved. There was nothing we could do. I had a large burial project on my hands. The animals had paid for their individuality — and ours.

I cleared the front room and the bedroom, cleaned up what blood I could and led Carol in. It had probably happened when we were in the movie. I held Carol on the couch. She didn't cry but trembled all over. I rubbed and caressed her, said things . . . Now and then a jolt would shake her body, she'd moan, "Ooooh, oooh . . . my God . . ." After a good two hours she began to cry. I stayed with her, held her. Soon she was asleep. I carried her to the bed, undressed her and covered her. Then I walked outside and looked at the backyard. Thank Christ, it was a large one. We were going from a Liberated Zoo to an animal graveyard overnight.

It took two days to bury them all. Carol played funeral marches on the record player and I dug and put the bodies in and covered them. It was unbearably sad. Carol marked the graves and we both drank wine and didn't speak. People came and watched, peering through the wire fence; adults, children, reporters and photographers from the newspaper. Near the end of the second day I filled the last grave and then Carol took my shovel and walked slowly toward the crowd at the fence. They backed away, mumbling and frightened. Carol threw the shovel against the fence. The crowd ducked and threw up their arms as if the shovel were coming through.

"All right, murderers," screamed Carol, "be *happy!*"

We walked into the house. There were fifty-five graves out there . . .

After several weeks I suggested to Carol that we might try another zoo, this time always leaving somebody to guard it.

"No," she said. "My dreams . . . my dreams have told me that the time has come. Everything is near the end. We've been just in time. We made it."

I didn't question her. I felt that she had been through enough. As the time for birth neared. Carol asked that I marry her. She said she didn't need marriage but since she had no next of kin she wanted me to inherit her estate. This was in case she died in childbirth and her dreams were wrong – about the end.

"Dreams can be wrong," she said, "though, so far, mine haven't been."

So we had a quiet marriage – in the graveyard. I picked up one of my old buddies from skid row to be witness and best man, and again the passersby stared. It was over quickly. I gave my buddy some money and some wine and drove him back to skid row.

On the way in, drinking from the bottle, he asked me, "Knocked her up, eh?"

"Well, I think so."

"You mean there were others?"

"Uh – yes."

"That's the way it is with these broads. You never know. Half the guys on the row have been put there by women."

"I thought it was drink."

"The women come first, then the drink follows."

"I see."

"You never know with them broads."

"Oh, I knew."

He gave me this look and then I let him out.

I waited downstairs at the hospital. How very odd the whole thing had been. I had walked from skid row to that house and all the things that had happened. The love and the agony. But for it all, the love had outdueled the agony. But it wasn't over. I tried to read the baseball boxscores, the race results. It hardly mattered. Then there were Carol's dreams; I believed in her but I was not so sure of her dreams. What were dreams? I didn't know. Then I saw Carol's doctor at the reception desk speaking to a nurse. I walked over to him.

"Oh, Mr. Jennings," he said, "your wife is all right. And the offspring is — is — male, nine pounds, five ounces."

"Thank you, doctor."

I took the elevator upstairs to the glass partition. There must have been a hundred babies in there crying. I could hear them through the glass. On and on it went. This birth thing. And this death thing. Each one had his turn. We entered alone and we left alone. And most of us lived lonely and frightened and incomplete lives. An incomparable sadness descended upon me. Seeing all that life that must die. Seeing all that life that would first turn to hate, to dementia, to neurosis, to stupidity, to fear, to murder, to nothing — nothing in life and nothing in death.

I told the nurse my name. She entered the glass room and found our child. As she held the child up, the nurse smiled. It was a tremendously forgiving smile. It had to be. I looked at the child — impossible, medically impossible: it was a tiger, a bear, a snake and a human. It was an elk, a coyote, a lynx and a human. It did not cry. Its eyes looked upon me and knew me, and I knew it. It was unbearable, Man and Superman, Superman and Superbeast. It was totally impossible and it looked upon me, the Father, one of the fathers, one of the many many fathers . . . and the edge of the sun gripped the hospital and the whole hospital began to shake, the babies roared, lights went on and off, a flash of purple crossed the glass partition in front of me. The nurses screamed. Three fluorescent light fixtures fell from their chains and down upon the babies. The nurse stood there holding my child and smiling as the first hydrogen bomb fell upon the city of San Francisco.

A POPULAR MAN

twice around I've had the flue, the flue, the flu, and the door
keeps banging, and there are always more people, and each person or
persons believes that they themselves have something special to offer
me, and bang bang bang goes the door, and it is always the same
thing, I say

"WAIT A MINUTE! WAIT A MINUTE!"

I get into some pants and let them in through the door. but I
am very tired, never get the sleep I should, haven't shit in 3 days,
precisely, you guessed it, I am going mad, and all those people have
their special energy, they all have points of goodness, I am a loner
but I am not that much of a crank, but it is always always –
something. I think of my mother's old saying in German, which is
not precise, but which went something like this: "emmer etvas!"
which means: always something. which a man never quite understands until he begins getting older. not that age is an advantage,
only that it brings the same scene again and again like a movie
madhouse.

it is a tough guy in soiled pants, just off the road, great self-
belief in his work, and not a bad writer at all, but I am wary of his
self-belief as he is wary of the fact that we do not kiss and lock arms
and assholes in midroom. he is entertaining. he is an actor. he ought
to be. he has lived more lives as one man than ten men have lived.
but his energy, in a sense, beautiful, is finally wearing on me. I don't
give a fuck about the poetic scene or that he phoned Norman Mailer
or knows Jimmy Baldwin, or the rest, or all the restly rest. and I see
that he does not quite understand me because I do not quite excite
to his preponderances. o.k. I still like him. he beats 999 out of a
thousand. but my German soul will not rest until I find the thou-
sandth. I am very quiet and listen but there is a huge boil of madness
underneath me that must be kept care of finally or I will do it

myself, someday, in an 8 dollar a week room just off Vermont Ave. so there. shit.

so he talks. and it's good. I laugh.

"15 grand. I got this 15 grand. my uncle dies. then she wants to get married. I am fatter than a pig. she's been feeding me good. 300 a week she's making, counselor's general's office, some god damn thing, now she wants to get married, quit her job. we go to Spain. all right, I'm working on a play, I've got this great idea for a play in my mind, so all right, I'm drinking, I'm fucking all the whores. then this guy in London he wants to see my play, he wants to put on my play, o.k., so I come back from London and what the fuck, here I find out my wife's been fucking the mayor of the town and my best friend, and I face her, I say, 'YOU LOUSY WHORE, YOU BEEN FUCKING MY BEST FRIEND AND THE MAYOR. I AM GOING TO KILL YOU NOW BECAUSE I WILL ONLY GET FIVE YEARS BECAUSE YOU ADULTURATED ME!' "

he paced up and down the room.

"then what happened," I asked.

"she said, 'go ahead and stab me, cocksucker!' "

"that's guts," I said.

"it was," he said, "I had this big butcherknife in my hand and I threw it on the floor. she had too much class on me. too much upper-middle class."

all right. so, all god's children — he left.

I went back to bed. I was merely dying. nobody was interested. I wasn't even interested. the chills came over me again. I couldn't put enough covers over me. I was still cold. and my mind too — all the human adventures of the mind seemed like con, like shit, it seemed as if the moment I were born I had been plopped in among the batch of con-men and if you didn't understand the con or play the side of the con you were dead, out. the con had it sewed, had it sewed for centuries, you couldn't bust the seams. he didn't want to bust the seams, he didn't want to conquer; he knew that Shakespeare was bad writing, that Creeley was fear; it didn't matter. all that he wanted was a small room, alone. alone.

he'd once told a friend he had once thought had some understanding of him, he'd once told his friend, "I have never been lonely."

218

and his friend had responded, "you're a god damned liar."

so, he went back to bed, sick, was there an hour, the doorbell rang again. he decided to ignore it. but the ringing and the pounding began with such violence that he felt it might be something of importance.

it was a young Jewish lad. quite a good poet. but what the hell?

"Hank?"

"Yeah?"

he pushed through the door, young, energized, believing in the poetic-hoax — all that shit: if a man is a good human being and a good good poet he will be rewarded somewhere this side of this side of hell. the kid just didn't know. the Gugg's were already set for those already comfortable and fat for sucking and lurking and teaching English I or II in the dull universities of the land. everything was fixed for failure. soul would never overcome con. only a century after death, and then they'd use that soul out of con to con you out of con. everything failed.

he came in. young, rabbinical student.

"ah, shit, it's awful," he said.

"what?" I asked.

"on the ride to the airport."

"yeh?"

"Ginsberg gets his ribs broken in the crash. nothing happens to Ferlinghetti, the biggest schmuck of them all. he's going off to Europe, to give these 5 to 7 dollar readings a night, and he doesn't even give himself a scratch. I was on stage with Ferlinghetti one night and he tries to upstage a man so bad, with tricks, that it's pitiful. they hissed him, finally, they caught on. Hirschman pulls a lot of that shit too."

"don't forget, Hirschman is hooked on Artaud. he figures if a man don't act crazy he ain't a genius. give him time. maybe."

"shit," says the kid, "you gave me 35 dollars to type up your next book of poems but there are too many. JESUS CHRIST, I didn't think there would be so MANY!"

"I thought I had given up writing poetry."

and when a Jew says Jesus Christ you know that he is in trouble. so he gave me 3 dollars and I gave him ten, and then we

219

both felt better. also he ate half a loaf of my french bread, a blessed pickle and left.

I got back in the sack and got ready to die, and for good or bad, good boys or bad boys, writing their rondos, flexing their two-bit poetic muscles, it does get tiresome, so many of them, so many of them trying to make it, so many of them hating each other and some on the top, of course, not deserving to be there, but many on the top deserving to be there, and so the whole thing a tear-down, a rip-down, up and down, "I met Jimmy at a party . . ."

well, let me swallow shit. so he got back into bed. and watched the spiders swallow the walls. this is where he belonged, always. he couldn't bear the crowd, the poets, the non-poets, the heroes, the non-heroes — he couldn't abide by any of them. he was doomed. his only problem in doom was to accept his doom as kindly as possible. he, I, wee, thee . . .

he made it back to bed, trembling, cold. death like the side of a fish, white-colored water of lisping. think of it. everybody dies. that's perfect except for me and one other person. fine. there are various formulas. various philosophers. I'm tired.

all right, the flue the flue, natural death of rustic frustration and not-caring, and so here we are, finally, spread in bed alone, sweating, staring at the cross, going mad in my *own* personal way, at least it was my own, those days, nobody bothering me, now it's always somebody at the door, I don't make $500 a year writing and they keep knocking at my door, they want to LOOK at me.

he, I, went to sleep again, sick, sweating, dying, really dying, just let them leave me alone, I don't give a damn if I am genius or idiot, let me sleep, let me have one more day my way, just 8 hours, the rest can be yours, and then the bell rang again.

you'd think he was Ezra Pound with Ginsberg trying to suck his dick —

and he said,

"wait a minute, let me put my pants on."

and all the lights were on, outside. like neon. or prostitute tickling hairs.

the guy was an English teacher from somewhere.

"Buk?"

"yaah. I'm sick man. flu. real contagious.

"are you having a tree this year?"

"I dunno. I'm dying right now. little girl in town. but I'm very sick now, contagious."

he stands back and hands me a six pack of beer, arm's length and then opens his latest book of poetry, autographs it to me. he leaves. I know that the poor devil can't write, never will, but that he is hooked on some lines that I once wrote somewhere that he never will.

but it isn't competition; great art is not competition at all, great art can be govt. or children or painters or cocksuckers or anything at all.

I said goodbye to the man and his 6 pack and then opened his book:

". . . spent the 1966-67 academic year on a Guggenheim Fellowship in studying and doing research at . . ."

he threw the book into the corner of the room, knowing that it would be no good. all the awards went to the already-fat who had the time and knowledge of where to get an application form for a motherfucking Gugg. he'd never seen one. you didn't see them while driving taxis or working as a hotel boy in Albuquerque. fuck.

he went back to sleep.

the phone rang.

they kept beating at his door.

that was it. he didn't care anymore. among all the sounds and sights, he didn't care. he hadn't slept for 3 days or 3 nights, hadn't shit for dinner, and now it was quiet. as close to death as you could without being an idiot. and being one close. it was great. soon they went away.

and across the christ of his rented ceiling came little cracks and he smiled as the 200 year old plaster came down onto his mouth, he breathed it in, and then choked to death.

FLOWER HORSE

I stayed up all night with John the Beard. we discussed Creeley — him for, me against, and I was drunk on arrival and brought some beer with me. we discussed this and that, me, him, just general talk, and the night went. around 6 a.m. I got into the car, it started, and I rolled down out of the hills and ran it down Sunset. I made it in, found another beer, drank that, managed to undress, get into bed. I awakened at noon, sick, leaped up, into clothing, brushed teeth, combed hair. looked at sick face lolling in glass, quickly turned, the walls spinning, got out door and made it to car, headed south for Hollywood Park. harness.

I put a ten on the 8 to 5 favorite and turned to walk out and see the race. a tall young kid in a dark suit ran toward the window trying to get in on the last minute action. the bastard must have been 7 feet tall. I tried to get out of the way but his shoulder caught me right in the face. it almost knocked me out. I turned, "you rotten crazy son of a bitch, WATCH YOURSELF!" I screamed. he was too intent on the betting, he couldn't hear. I walked up to the ramp and watched the 8 to 5 come in. then I walked out of the clubhouse and into the grandstand portion and got a cup of hot coffee, no cream. the whole track looked like a psychedelic wavering.

5.60 times 5. 18 bucks profit, first race. I didn't want to be at the track. I didn't want to be anywhere. sometimes a man must fight so hard for life that he doesn't have time to live it. I went back to the clubhouse, destroyed the coffee, sat down so I wouldn't faint. sick, sick.

with a minute left I slid back into line. a little Japanese guy turned to me, put his face into my face. "who do you like?" he didn't even have a program. he tried to peer at my program. these guys can bet ten or 20 bucks at a race but they are too cheap to buy a 40 cent program which also contains the past form of the horses. "I don't like anybody," I rather snarled at him. I think I got through to him. he turned around and tried to read the man's program who stood ahead of him. he peered around the man's side, tried to look over his shoulder.

I made my bet and went out to see the running, Jerry Perkins ran like the 14 year old gelding he was. Charley Short looked like he was asleep in the bike. maybe he'd been up all night too. with the horse. they ran in Night Freight at 18 to one and I tore up my tickets. the day before they had run in a 15 to one shot and followed it with a 60 to one. they were trying to send me to skid row. my clothes and shoes looked like ragman Sam. a gambler will blow it on anything but clothes − booze is all right, food, pussy, but no clothes. as long as you aren't naked and have the green they'll let you bet.

the boys were looking at something in a very short miniskirt. I mean it was SHORT! and she was young and cool. I checked it out. too much. a night in bed would cost me 100. she said she worked as a cocktail waitress somewhere. I moved out with my raggedy clothes and she went up to the bar and bought her own drink.

I had another coffee. I was telling John the Beard the night before that Man usually pays 100 times the worth of a pussy in one way or another. I don't. the others do. Miniskirt's pussy was worth about 8 dollars. she was only charging about 13 times the worth. nice gal.

I moved into line for the next play. the board read zero. the race was about off. the fat boy in front of me looked asleep. he didn't look like he wanted to bet. "call 'em and move," I said. he looked like he was stuck in the window. he turned slowly and I armed him good, elbow and side working into him, shoved him from the window. if he said a damned thing I was going to swing. the hangover had me jumpy. I got 20 win on Scottish Dream. a good horse but I was afraid Crane couldn't drive it. he hadn't shown me a good ride all meet. so, all right − he was due. they ran an 18 to one shot past him in the stretch. he hung on for second. old Clarence Hansen could still nurse them in.

skid row looked closer all the time. I looked at the people. what were they doing there? why weren't they working? how did they make it? there were a few rich ones at the bar. they weren't worried but they had that special dead look of the rich which comes when the struggle goes out of them and there is nothing to replace it — no interest, just being rich. poor devils. yeh. ha, hahaha, ha.

I kept drinking water. I was dry, dry. sick and dry. and hung out. for the taking. cornered again. what tiresome sport.

a well dressed Spanish type who smelled of murder and incest walked up to me. he smelled like a clogged sewer pipe.

"lemme have a dollar," he said.

I said it very quietly: "go to hell."

he turned and walked up to the next one. "lemme have a dollar," he said. his answer came. he'd hit on New York Dutch. "lemme have ten, you jackoff," Dutch told him.

other people walked around, gypped out of the Dream. broke, angry, worried. slugged, mutilated, tricked, taken, gouged, nailed, fucked. they'd be back for more if they managed to get some money. me? I was going to start picking pockets or pimping or something.

the next race was no better. I was second again, Jean Daily outfinishing me on Pepper Tone. I began to feel more and more that all my years' experience with racing — the studying for hours at night — was all an illusion. hell, they were just animals and you turned them loose and something happened. I'd be better off at my place listening to something very corny — Carmen in English — and waiting for the landlord to kick me out.

in the 5th race I was second again wtih Bobbijack, Stormy Scott N beating me. Stormy was an even-money underlay on a morning line of 5/2, mostly because of having the leading rider, Farrington, and having closed 11 lengths in his last stretch run.

2nd. again in the 6th. with Shotgun, a good price at 8 to one and they went with him but Pepper Streak had too much. I tore up my ten dollar win ticket.

I finished 3rd in the 7th and was 50 bucks down.

in the 8th I had to choose between Creedy Cash and Red Wave. I got sucked in on the late action on Red Wave, so naturally Creedy Cash won at 8/5 for O'Brien. which was no big surprise — Creedy already having won 10 out of 19 that year.

I had gone heavy on Red Wave and was 90 bucks down.

I went to the men's room to take a leak, they were all circling
in there, ready to kill, snatch wallet. a hoary beaten-looking crew.
soon they'd all be walking out, the whole thing over. what a way to
go — broken families, lost jobs, lost businesses. madness. but it paid
taxes to the good state of California, babe. 7 or 8 percent out of
each dollar. some of that built roads. hired Patrolmen to menace
you. build madhouses. fed and paid Ronald.

one more shot. I went for an 11-year-old gelding, Fitment, a
horse that broke in its last race, finished 13 lengths out against 6500
claimers and now was running against a couple of 12,500 claimers
and one 8000. I had to be crazy, and to take only 9 to 2 on it too. I
bet 10 win on Urrall at 6 to one as a saver and put 40 win on
Fitment. that put me $140 in the hole. 47 years old and still playing
around in Never-Never Land. taken like the rawest of country hicks.

I went out to watch the race. Fitment went 2 wide around the
first curve, but was running easily. don't break, sweetheart, don't
break. at least give me a little run, a little tiny run. no need for the
gods to always shit on the same man: me. let everybody have their
turn. good for their fortitude.

it was getting dark and the horses ran on through the smog.
Fitment ran into the lead down the backstretch. his stride was easy.
but Meadow Hutch the 8/5 favorite circled around and dropped
back in front of Fitment. they ran that way around the last curve
and then Fitment pulled out, ran up to Meadow Hutch, hooked him
and left him there. well, we'd chopped up the 8/5 favorite, now only
6 other horses to beat. shit, shit, they won't let me have it, I
thought. something will come out of the pack. a wake-up. the gods
won't let me have it. I'll go back to my room and lay in the dark,
lights out, staring at the ceiling, wondering what it was all about.

Fitment held 2 lengths in the stretch and I waited. it seemed a
long stretch. god, it WAS long! LONG!

it won't happen. I can't hold it. look how dark it is.

140 bucks down. sick. old. stupid. unlucky. warts on the soul.

the young girls are sleeping with giants of body and intellect.
the young girls laugh at me as I walk down the street.

Fitment. Fitment.

he held the 2 lengths. he rolled. they stretched it to 2 and 1/2.
nothing got close. beautiful. a symphony. even the smog smiled. I

saw him go over the line and then I walked over and drank some more water. when I got back they had put the price up. $11.80 for 2. I had 40 win. I took my pen and figured it. return: $236. minus my 140 down. I had made 96 dollars profit.

Fitment. love. baby. love. flower horse.

the ten dollar line was long. I went to the men's room, threw water on my face. my stride had bounce in it again. I went out and pulled out the tickets.

I could only find THREE tickets on Fitment! I had lost one somewhere!

amateur! stupid! oxhead! I was sick. one ten buck ticket was worth $59. I traced my steps. picking up tickets. no number 4's. somebody had gotten my ticket.

I stood in line, looking through my wallet. what an asshole! then I found the other ticket. it had slipped behind a crevice in my wallet. that had never happened before. what an asshole wallet!

I picked up my $236. I saw Miniskirt looking at me. oh, no no no NO!! I hustled down the escalator, bought a newspaper, dodged through the parking lot drivers, made it to the car.

I lit a cigar. well, I thought, let's not deny it: genius just can't be held down. with that thought I started my '57 Plymouth. I drove with great care and courtesy. I hummed the Peter Ilyich Tchaikovsky Concerto in D major, for violin and orchestra. I had invented a word passage that covered the major theme, the major melody: "Once more, we will be free again. oh, once more, we will be free again, free again, free again . . ."

I drove out among the angry losers. their unpaid for and highly-insured cars were all they had left. they dared each other at mutilation and murder, zooming and slashing, not giving the inch. I made it to the exit at Century. my car stalled right at the turnout, blocking 45 cars behind me. I flipped the gas pedal rapidly with my foot, winked at the traffic cop, then hit the starter. it caught up and I moved out, drove on through the smog. Los Angeles wasn't really a bad place: a good hustler could always make it.

THE BIG POT GAME

the other night I found myself at a gathering — usually an unpleasant thing for me. basically I am a loner, an old sot who prefers to drink alone, maybe only hoping for a little Mahler or Stravinsky on the radio. but there I was with the maddening crowd. I won't give the reason, for that's another story, maybe longer, maybe more confusing, but standing alone, drinking my wine, listening to the Doors or the Beatles or the Airplane mixed in with all the voices going, I realized I needed a cigarette. I was out. I usually am. so I saw these 2 young men nearby, arms dangling and swinging; bodies loose, goosey; necks bent; fingers of hands loose — all told, they were like rubber, shredded rubber stretching and pulling and coming apart.

I walked over: "hey, one of you fellows got a cigarette?"

this really started the rubber to jumping. I stood there watching, they turned it on, flipping and flapping.

"we don't smoke, man! MAN, we don't ... s m o o k. cigarettes."

"no, man, we don't smoke, like that, no, man."

flipflop. flipflap. rubber.

"we goin' to M-a-li-booo, man! yeah, we're goin' to M a l l l - i - bOOOO! man, we're goin' to M-a-ly-boooooo!"

"yeah, man!"

"yeah, man!"

"yeah!"

flipflap. or, flapflap.

they simply couldn't tell me that they didn't have a cigarette. they had to give me their pitch, their religion: cigarettes were for cubes. they were going to Malibu, to some seeming loose and easy shack in Malibu and burn a bit of grass. they remind me, in a sense, of old ladies standing on a corner selling "The Watchtower." the whole LSD, STP, marijuana, heroin, hashish, prescription cough medicine crowd suffers from the "Watchtower" itch: you gotta be with us, man, or you're out, you're dead. this pitch is a continual and seeming MUST with those who use the stuff. it's no wonder they keep getting busted − they can't use the stuff quietly for their pleasure; they have to make it KNOWN that they are members. further, they tend to tie it in with Art, Sex, the Drop-out scene. their Acid God, Leary, tells them: "drop out. follow me." then he rents an auditorium here in town and charges them 5 dollars a head to hear him speak. then Ginsberg arrives at Leary's side. then Ginsberg proclaims Bob Dylan a great poet. self-advertisement of the potty-chair headline-makers. America.

but let that go, for that too is another story. this thing has a lot of arms and not much head, the way I tell it, and the way it is. but back to the "in" boys, the potheads. their language. groovy, man. like it is. the scene. cool. in. out. square. swinging. making it. baby. daddy. so forth and so on. I'd heard these same phrases − or whatever you call them − when I was 12 years old in 1932, to hear the same things 25 years later doesn't do much to endear you with the user, especially when he considers them hip. much of the word-age came originally from the users of harder stuff, the spoon and needle set, and also the old Negro jazzband boys. the terminology among the real "in" has changed now but the so-called hip-boys like the duo I asked the cigarette from − these are still talking 1932.

and that pot creates art, si, it's doubtful, and how. DeQuincy wrote some fair stuff, and "The Opium Eater" was nicely written, tho in parts, dull enough. and it is the nature of most artists to try almost anything. they are explorative, desperate, suicidal. but the pot comes AFTER the Art is already there, after the artist is already there. the pot does not produce the Art. but it often becomes the playground of the established artist, a kind of celebration of being, these pot parties, and also some damn good material for the artist of people caught with their spiritual pants down, or if not down, then perhaps not so guarded.

in the 1830's Gautier's pot parties and sex-orgy parties were the talk of Paris. that Gautier wrote poetry on the side was also known. now his parties are better remembered.

jumping out on another arm of this thing: I would hate to get busted for use and/or possession of grass. it would be like being charged with rape for smelling a pair of panties on somebody's clothesline. grass is simply not that good. much of the effect is caused by a pre-mental state of believing one is going to get high. if a drugless, same-smelling artifice could be substituted, most of the users would feel the same effects: "hey, baby, this is GOOD stuff, real fine!"

for me, I can get more out of a couple of tall cans of beer. I stay clean not because of the law but because the stuff bores me and has little effect. but I will grant that the effects between alcohol and mary are different. it is possible to get high on grass and hardly sense it; with the booze you generally pretty much know that you are there. me, I'm of the old school: I like to know that I am there. but if another man wants grass or acid or the needle I have no objection. it's his way and whatever way is best for him is best for him. that's all.

there are enough social commentators with low-level brain-power now. why should I add my high-level snarl? we've all heard the old women who say, "oh, I think it's just AWFUL what these young people do to themselves, all that dope and stuff! I think it's terrible!" and then you look at the old gal: no eyes, no teeth, no brain, no soul, no ass, no mouth, no color, no flux, no humor, nothing, just a stick, and you wonder what her tea and cookies and church and home on the corner have done for HER. and the old men sometimes get quite violent about what some of the young are doing – "hell, I worked HARD all my life!" (they think this is a virtue, but it only proves a man is a damn fool.) "these people want every-thing for NOTHING! sitting around wrecking their bodies with dope, hoping to live off the fat of the land!"

then you look at HIM:

amen.

he's only jealous. he's been tricked. fucked-out of his good years. he'd really like to have a ball too. if he could do it over. but he can't. so now he wants them to suffer like he did.

and generally, that's about it. the potheads make too much about their damned pot and the public makes too much about their using their damned pot. and the police are busy and the potheads get busted and holler crucifixion, and liquor is legal until you drink too

229

much of it and are caught on the street and then you're jailed. give the human race anything and they'll scrabble and scratch and pewk all over it. if you legalize pot the u.s. will be a little more comfortable, but not much better. as long as the courts and the jails and the lawyers and the laws are there, they are going to be used.

to ask them to legalize pot is something like asking them to put butter on the handcuffs before they place them on you, something else is hurting you — that's why you need pot or whiskey, or whips and rubber suits, or screaming music turned so fucking loud you can't think. or madhouses or mechanical cunts or 162 baseball games a season. or vietnam or israel or the fear of spiders. your love washing her yellow false teeth in the sink before you screw.

there are basic answers and there are ticklers. we are still playing with the ticklers because we are not yet men enough or real enough to say what we need. for some centuries we thought it might be Christianity. after throwing the Christians to the lions we let them throw us to the dogs. we found Communism might be a little better for the average man's belly but did little for his soul. now we play with drugs, thinking it will open doors. the East has been on the stuff longer than gunpowder. they find they suffer less, die more. to pot or not to pot. "we goin' to M-a-li-booo, man! yeah, we're goin' to Malllll-i-bOOOOO!"

pardon me while I roll a bit of Bull Durham.

wanta drag?

THE BLANKET

I have not been sleeping well lately but this is not what I am getting at exactly. It is when I seem to go to sleep that it happens. I say "seem to go to sleep" because it is just that. More and more of late I appear to be alseep, I sense I am asleep and yet in my dream I dream of my room, I dream that I am sleeping and everything is just where I left it when I went to bed. The newspaper on the floor, an empty beer bottle on the dresser, my one goldfish circling slowly at the bottom of his bowl, all the intimate things that are as much a part of me as my hair. And many times when I am NOT asleep, in my bed, looking at the walls, drowsing, waiting to sleep, I often wonder: am I still awake or am I already asleep, dreaming of my room?

Things have been going bad lately. Deaths; horses running poorly; toothache; bleeding, other unmentionable things. I often get the feeling, well, how can it get worse? And then I think, well, you still have a room. You are not out in the street. There was a time when I did not mind the streets. Now I can not bear them. I can stand very little any more. I have been pin-pricked, lanced, yes even bombed ... so often, I simply want no more; I cannot stand up under it all.

Now here's the thing. When I go to sleep and dream I am in my room or whether it is actually happening and I am awake, I do not know, only things begin to happen. I notice that the closet door is open just a bit and I am sure it was not open a moment ago. Then I see that the opening in the closet door and the fan (it has been hot and I have the fan on the floor) are lined up in a direct point that ends at my head. With a sudden whirl I rage away from the pillow, and I say "rage" because I usually curse some most vile thing at "those" or "it" that is trying to remove me. Now I can hear you saying, "The lad is insane," and indeed, I might be. But somehow I

231

do not feel it is so. Although this is a very weak point in my favor, if a point at all. When I am out among people I am uncomfortable. They speak and have enthusiasms that are not a part of me. And yet it is when I am with them that I feel strongest. I get this idea: if they can exist on just these fragments of things, then I can exist too. But it is when I am alone and all comparisons must fall upon a comparison of myself against the walls, against breathing, against history, against my end, that the odd things begin to happen. I am evidently a weak man. I have tried to go to the bible, to the philosophers, to the poets, but for me, somehow, they have missed the point. They are talking about something else entirely. So long ago I stopped reading. I found some small help in drinking, gambling and sex, and in this way I was much like any man in the community, the city, the nation; the only difference being that I did not care to "succeed," I did not want a family, a home, a respectable job and so forth. So there I was: neither an intellectual, an artist; nor did I have the saving roots of the common man. I hung like something labeled in between, and I guess, yes, that is the beginning of insanity.

And how vulgar I am! I reach in my anus and scratch. I have hemorrhoids, piles. It is better than sexual intercourse. I scratch until I bleed, until pain forces me to stop. Monkeys, apes, do this. Have you seen them in the zoos with their red bleeding asses?

But let me get on. Although if you would care for a bit of an oddity I tell you of the murder. These Dreams of the Room, let me call them, began some years ago. One of the first was in Philadelphia. I seldom worked then either and perhaps it was worrying about the rent. I was not drinking any more than a little wine and some beer, and sex and gambling had not yet come upon me with full force. Although I was living with a lady of the streets at that time, and it seemed odd to me that she wanted more sex or "love" as she called it when I did it, after indulging with 2 or 3 or more men that day and night, and although I was as well-traveled and well-jailed as any Knight of the Road, there was something about sticking it in there after all THAT ... it turned against me and I had a rough time. "Sweetie," she'd say, "ya got to understand I LOVE you. With them it's nothing. You just don't KNOW a woman. A woman can let you in and you think you're there but you're not even in there. You, I let in." All the talk didn't help much. It only made the walls closer.

And one night, say I was dreaming, say I wasn't, I awakened and she was in bed with me (or I dreamt I awakened), and I looked around and here were all these little tiny men, 30 or 40 of them wiring us both down in the bed, a kind of silver wire, and around and around us they went, under the bed, over the bed, with the wire. My lady must have sensed my nervousness. I saw her eyes open and she looked at me. "Be quiet!" I said. "Don't move! They are trying to electrocute us!" "WHO'S TRYING TO ELECTROCUTE US?" "God damn it, I told you to be QUIET! Be still now!" I let them work a while longer, pretending to be asleep. Then with all my strength I surged upward, breaking the wire, surprising them. I swung on one and missed. I don't know where they went but I got rid of them. "I just saved us from death," I told my lady. "Kiss me, daddy," she said.

Anyway, getting back to now. I have been getting up in the morning with these welts on my body. Blue marks. There is a particular blanket I have been watching. I think this blanket is closing in on me while I sleep. I awaken and sometimes it is up around my throat and I can hardly breathe. It is always the same blanket. But I have been ignoring it. I open a beer, split the Racing Form with my thumb, look out the window for rain and try to forget everything. I just want to live comfortably without trouble. I am tired. I do not want to imagine things or make up things.

And yet again that night the blanket bothers me. It moves like a snake. It takes various forms. It will not stay flat and wide across the bed. And the night after that. I kick it to the floor by the couch. Then I see it move. Ever so quickly I see this blanket move when my head seems turned away. I get up and turn on all the lights and get the newspaper and read, I read anything, the stock market, the latest styles in fashion, how to cook a squab, how to get rid of crab grass; letters to the editor, political columns, help wanted, the obituaries, etc. During this time the blanket does not move and I drink 3 or 4 bottles of beer, maybe more, and then it is daylight sometimes, and then it is easy to sleep.

The other night it happened. Or it began in the afternoon. Having had very little sleep I went to bed about 4 p.m. in the afternoon and when I awakened or dreamed of my room again it was dark and the blanket was up around my throat and it had decided that this was THE time! All pretense was over! It was after me, and it was strong, or rather I seemed rather weak, as if in a dream, and it took all I had to keep it from finally closing off my air, but it hung about me still, this blanket, making quick strong lunges, trying to find me off guard. I could feel the sweat coming down my forehead. Who would ever believe such a thing? Who would ever believe such a damn thing? A blanket coming to life and trying to murder one? Nothing is believed until it happens the FIRST time – like the atom bomb or the Russians sending a man into space or God coming down to earth and then being nailed to a cross by that which He created. Who is to believe all the things that are coming? The last snuff of fire? The 8 or 10 men and women in some space ship, the New Ark, to another planet to plant the weary seed of man all over again? And who was the man or woman to believe that this blanket was trying to strangle me? No one, not by a damn sight! And this made it worse, somehow. Although I had little sensitivity toward what the masses thought of me, I did, somehow want them to realize the blanket. Odd? Why was that? And odd, I had often thought of suicide, but now that a blanket wanted to help me, I fought against it.

I finally wrung the thing off and threw it to the floor and turned on the lights. That would end it! LIGHT, LIGHT, LIGHT!

But no, I saw it still twitch or move an inch or 2 there under the light. I sat down and watched it carefully. It moved again. A good foot this time. I got up and began to get dressed, walking wide around the blanket to find shoes, stockings, etc. Then dressed, I didn't know what to do. The blanket was still now. Perhaps a walk in the night air. Yes. I would talk to the newsboys on the corner. Although that was bad too. All the newsboys in the neighborhood were intellectuals: they read G. B. Shaw and O. Spengler and Hegel. And they weren't newsboys: they were 60 or 80 or 1000 years old. Shit. I slammed the door and walked out.

Then when I got to the top of the stairway something made me turn and look down the hall. You are right: the blanket was following me, moving in snake-movements, folds and shadows at the front of it making head, mouth, eyes. Let me say that as soon as you begin to believe that a horror is a horror, then it finally becomes LESS horror. For a moment I thought of my blanket like an old dog that didn't want to be alone without me, it had to follow. But then I got the thought that this dog, this blanket, was out to kill, and then I quickly moved down the steps.

Yes, yes, it came after me! It moved as quickly as it wanted over and down the stairs. Soundless. Determined.

I lived on the third floor. Down it followed. To the second. To the first. My first thought was to run outside but it was very dark outside, a quiet and empty neighborhood far from the large avenues. The best idea was to get next to some people to test the reality of the situation. It took at LEAST 2 votes to make reality real. Artists who have worked years ahead of their time have found that out, and people of dementia and so-called hallucination have found it out too. If you are the only one to see a vision they either call you a Saint or a madman.

I knocked on the door of apartment 102. Mick's wife came to the door. "Hello, Hank," she said, "come on in."

Mick was in bed. He was all puffed up, his ankles twice their size, his belly larger than a pregnant woman. He had been a heavy drinker and his liver had given out. He was full of water. He was waiting on an empty bed in the Veteran's hospital.

"Hi, Hank," he said, "did you bring some beer?"

"Now, Mick," said his old lady, "you know what the doctor said: no more, not even beer."

"What's the blanket for, kid?" he asked me.

I looked down. The blanket had leaped up over my arm to gain an unnoticed entrance.

"Well," I said, "I have too many. Thought you could use one."

I tossed the thing over on the couch.

"You didn't bring a beer?"

"No, Mick."

"I sure could use a beer."

"Mick," said his old lady.

"Well, it's hard to cut it cold after all these years."

"Well, maybe one," said his old lady. "I'll run down to the store."

"That's o.k.," I said, "I'll get some out of my refrigerator."

I got up and walked toward the door, watching the blanket. It did not move. It sat there looking at me from the couch.

"Be right back," I said, and closed the door.

I guess, I thought, it's my mind. I carried the blanket with me and imagined it was following me. I should mix more with people. My world is too narrow.

I went upstairs and put 3 or 4 bottles of beer in a paper sack and then started down. I was about at the 2nd floor when I heard some screaming, a curse, and then a gunshot. I ran down the remaining steps and into 102. Mick was standing there all puffed up holding a .32 magnum with just a little smoke trailing up from it. The blanket was on the couch where I had left it.

"Mick, you're crazy!" his old lady was saying.

"That's right," he said, "the minute you went into the kitchen that blanket, so help me, that blanket leaped for the door. It was trying to turn the knob, trying to get out but it couldn't get a grip. After I recovered from the first shock I got out of bed and moved toward it and when I got close it leaped from the knob, it leaped for my throat and tried to strangle me!"

"Mick's been sick," said his old lady, "been taking shots. He sees things. He used to see things when he was drinking. He'll be all right once they get him to the hospital."

"God damn it!" he screamed standing there all puffed up in his nightshirt, "I tell you the thing tried to kill me and lucky the old magnum was loaded and I ran to the closet and got it and when it came at me again I shot it. It crawled away. It crawled back to the couch and there it is now. You can see the hole where I put the bullet through it. That's no imagination!"

There was a knock on the door. It was the manager. "Too much noise in here," he said. "No television or radio or loud noise after 10 p.m.," he said.

Then he went away.

I walked over to the blanket. Sure there was a hole in it. The blanket seemed very still. Where is the vital place in a living blanket?

"Jesus, let's have a beer," said Mick, "I don't care if I die or not."

His old lady opened 3 bottles and Mick and I lit up a couple of Pall Malls.

"Hey, kid," he said, "take that blanket with you when you leave."

"I don't need it, Mick," I said, "you keep it."

He took a big drink of beer. "Take that God damned thing out of here!"

"Well, it's DEAD, isn't it?" I asked him.

"How the hell do I know?"

"Do you mean to say you believe this nonsense about the blanket, Hank?"

"Yes, mam."

She threw back her head and laughed. "Boy, a couple of crazy bastards, if I ever saw any." Then, she added, "You drink too, don't you, Hank?"

"Yes, mam."

"Heavy?"

"Sometimes."

"All I say is take that god damned blanket OUT of HERE!"

I took a big drink of beer and wished it were vodka. "O.k., pal," I said, "if you don't want the blanket, I'll take it."

I folded it into squares and put it over my arm.

"Good night, folks."

"Good night, Hank, and thanks for the beer."

I moved up the stairway and the blanket was very still. Maybe the bullet had done it. I walked into my place and threw it in a chair. Then I sat a while looking at it. Then I got an idea.

I got the dishpan and put some newspaper in it. Then I got a paring knife. I put the dishpan on the floor. Then I sat in the chair. I put the blanket on my lap. And I held the knife. But it was hard to cut into the blanket. I kept sitting there in the chair, the night wind of the rotten city of Los Angeles coming in on the back of my neck, and it was hard to cut. How did I know? Maybe that blanket was some woman who had once loved me, finding a way to get back to me through that blanket. I thought of 2 women. Then I thought of one woman. Then I got up and walked into the kitchen and I opened the vodka bottle. The doctor said any more hard stuff and I was dead. But I had been practicing on him. A thimbleful one night. 2 the next, etc. This time I poured a glassful. It was not the dying that mattered, it was the sadness, the wonder. The few good people crying in the night. The few good people. Maybe the blanket had been this woman either trying to kill me to get me into death with

her, or trying to love as a blanket and not knowing how . . . or trying
to kill Mick because he had disturbed her when she tried to follow
me at the door? Madness? Sure. What isn't madness? Isn't Life
madness? We are all wound-up like toys . . . a few winds of the
spring, it runs down, and that's it . . . and we walk around and
presume things, make plans, elect governors, mow lawns . . . Madness, surely, what ISN'T madness?

I drank the glass of vodka straight down and lit a cigarette.
Then I picked up the blanket for the last-time and THEN I CUT! I
cut and cut and cut, I cut the thing into all the little pieces that were
left of anything . . . and put the pieces into the dishpan and then I
put the dishpan near the window and turned on the fan to blow the
smoke out, and while the flame was starting I went into the kitchen
and poured another vodka. When I came out it was going red and
good, like any old Boston witch, like any Hiroshima, like any love,
like any love at all, and I did not feel well, I did not feel well at all. I
drank the second glass of vodka down and felt almost nothing. I
walked into the kitchen for another one, carrying the paring knife
with me. I threw the knife on the sink and unscrewed the cap from
the bottle. I looked again at the paring knife on the sink. Upon its
side was a distinct smear of blood.

I looked at my hands. I searched my hands for cuts. The hands
of Christ were beautiful hands. I looked at my hands. There was not
a scratch. There was not a nick. There was not even a scar.

I felt the tears coming down my cheeks, crawling like heavy
senseless things without legs. I was mad. I must truly be mad.